SPQR X

A POINT OF LAW

SPQR

Senatus Populusque Romanus

The Senate and the People of Rome

Also by
JOHN MADDOX ROBERTS

SPQR X

A
POINT
OF LAW

JOHN MADDOX ROBERTS

THOMAS DUNNE BOOKS
ST. MARTIN'S MINOTAUR
NEW YORK

THOMAS DUNNE BOOKS.

An imprint of St. Martin's Press.

SPQR X: A POINT OF LAW. Copyright © 2006 by John Maddox Roberts.
All rights reserved. Printed in the United States of America.
No part of this book may be used or reproduced in any manner
whatsoever without written permission except in the case of brief
quotations embodied in critical articles or reviews.
For information, address St. Martin's Press,
175 Fifth Avenue, New York, N.Y. 10010.

Library of Congress Cataloging-in-Publication Data

Roberts, John Maddox.
    SPQR X : a point of law / John Maddox Roberts.—1st. ed.
        p. cm.
        ISBN-13: 978-0-312-33725-4   6/06
        ISBN-10: 0-312-33725-6   B 9 T
                                          23.95
    1. Metellus, Decius Caecilius (Fictitious character)—Fiction. 2. Rome—
History—Republic, 265–30 B.C.—Fiction. 3. Private investigators—Rome—
Fiction. I. Title.   Fic
                        R
PS3568.O23874S678 2006
813'.54—dc22   2006040166

First Edition: May 2006

10   9   8   7   6   5   4   3   2   1

For John Vanover Jr.,

our own Prometheus: fighter, survivor,

and a great brother-in-law

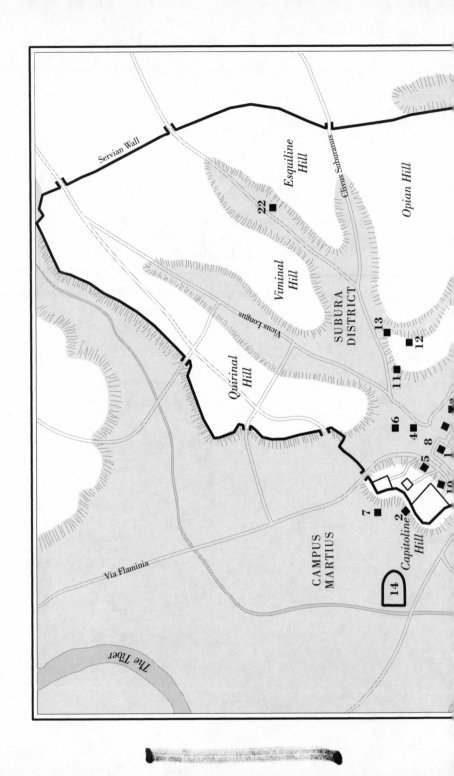

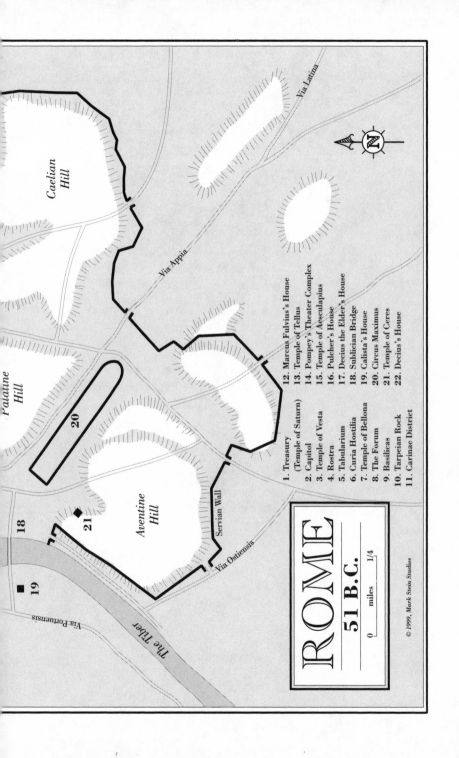

ROME
51 B.C.

0   miles   1/4

© 1999, Mark Stein Studios

1. Treasury (Temple of Saturn)
2. Capitol
3. Temple of Vesta
4. Rostra
5. Tabularium
6. Curia Hostilia
7. Temple of Bellona
8. The Forum
9. Basilicas
10. Tarpeian Rock
11. Carinae District
12. Marcus Fulvius's House
13. Temple of Tellus
14. Pompey's Theater Complex
15. Temple of Aesculapius
16. Pulcher's House
17. Decius the Elder's House
18. Sublician Bridge
19. Calista's House
20. Circus Maximus
21. Temple of Ceres
22. Decius's House

Caelian Hill

Palatine Hill

Aventine Hill

Via Latina

Via Appia

Via Ostiensis

Servian Wall

Via Portuensis

The Tiber

N

DRAMATIS PERSONAE

Roman names* can be confusing because of frequent duplication, even multiplication. In 63 B.C. there were no fewer than five very prominent men of the Caecilian family, all named Quintus Caecilius Metellus. Most Romans went by nicknames, and prominent men usually had cognomens bestowed in honor, so those Metelli are all remembered by their cognomens: Celer (dead at this point in the SPQR series), Nepos, Creticus, Pius, and the wonderfully named Quintus Caecilius Metellus Pius Scipio Nasica, Scipio for short.

To add to the confusion, we know many Romans from the shortened forms of their names used in the Middle Ages and Renaissance. Thus Pompeius became "Pompey," Marcus Antonius became "Marc Antony," Livius became "Livy," Plinius became "Pliny," Sallustius be-

---

*Look in the Glossary under "Families and Names" for more information on prenomens, nomens, cognomens, etc.

came "Sallust," and so forth. Shakespeare did much to fix these names in everyone's minds.

Names could also change with changes of status. Thus Caius Octavius was adopted in Caesar's will and became Caius Julius Caesar Octavianus popularly remembered as "Octavian" (Shakespeare again). Eventually he became the first emperor, and the Senate bestowed upon him the honorific "Augustus," the name by which he is best known.

Following are the more prominent characters featured in *SPQR X*.

Pawns in the Conspiracy Against the Ruling Classes in Republican Rome

The Metelli and Their Allies

Decius Caecilius Metellus the Younger. Decius the Younger is the focal point of the conspirators' plot, despite his reputation as an upright citizen given to ferreting out crime and corruption wherever he finds it. He is first accused of extortion by Marcus Fulvius, a nobody as far as the great families know, and is afterward accused by Publius Manilius, a Tribune of the People, of murdering Marcus Fulvius.

Decius Caecilius Metellus the Elder, father of Decius the Younger. He is one of the great Metelli and has held every office including the censorship. He gathers the Metelli men and their allies together to help defend Decius against the charges being brought against him.

Quintus Caecilius Metellus Creticus. He is growing old and stout but is still a voice among the Metelli. A war in Crete got him the cognomen "Creticus." He stood up to Pompey when others were afraid to, and so he enjoys a high reputation.

Quintus Caecilius Metellus Nepos. He is the only member of the family to champion Pompey but is still high in family councils.

Quintus Caecilius Metellus Pius Scipio Nasica, adopted son of

Quintus Caecilius Metellus Pius. Scipio is a pontifex and Caecilian by adoption but a Metellus on his mother's side.

Hermes, Decius's freedman. He does most of his scut work and acts as Decius's bodyguard.

Julia, Decius's wife, Julius Caesar's niece. She is well-educated (better than Decius) and a great help to Decius in solving the crimes he ferrets out. Here she helps Callista decipher the code the conspirators use to communicate with each other.

Quintius Hortensius Hortalus. He is a friend of Decius's father and ardent in his defense of Decius.

Marcus Porcius Cato. Decius dislikes him personally but welcomes his support.

Callista, an Egyptian mathematician. She (with Julia's aid) helps Decius by breaking the code the conspirators use to communicate with one another.

Asklepiodes, a Greek physician and foremost expert on wounds made by weapons. He examines Marcus Fulvius's wounds and pronounces that he was held from behind while others attacked him from the front, an important point in Decius's defense.

Claudius Marcellus, oldest member of the College of Augurs and a friend of the Metelli. He is apparently not a part of his relatives' conspiratorial dealings and may or may not know about the conspiracy.

Known Conspirators and Their Cabal

The Fulvias

Fulvia, a descendant of the noblest families, formerly married to Clodius, currently engaged to Curio. Clodius was killed by Milo's thugs. Fulvia was suspected of poisoning others. Though one of the great beauties of Rome she has the worst reputation as a slut, but she is politically astute and usually in on any nefarious goings on in Rome.

Marcus Fulvius, Fulvia's brother. While he is an unknown upstart in Rome, he has financial backing in Baiae and in Rome. He accuses Decius the Younger of extortion while on Cyprus. He is found murdered on the basilica steps when Decius shows up for his trial at the extortion court.

Manius Fulvius, another brother of Fulvia's. He is a duumvir of Baiae and is probably also backing Marcus Fulvius.

The Claudia Marcelli* (Old Sullans who are rabidly anti-Caesar)

Marcus Claudius Marcellus. He has an old sword scar on his face and is this year's consul.

Caius Claudius Marcellus, cousin to Marcus Claudius Marcellus, the current consul, and brother to Marcus Claudius Marcellus, most likely next year's consul, married to Octavia, great-niece of Caesar. He stands firmly with the *optimates*. He owns the building that Marcus Fulvius lived in and where the conspirators met.

Marcus Claudius Marcellus, brother to Caius. He is probably a candidate for the following year's consulship.

Octavia, married to Caius Claudius Marcellus. She cut her ties with the Julian family when she married, perceives Caesar as a potential tyrant, as do her husband and his brother, and denies even knowing the young Octavius. She believes the Fulvias are connected to the Claudia Pulchri family and considers the tribunes to be "jumped up peasants."

The Claudia Pulcri

Publius Clodius Pulcher (born Claudius). He was born a patrician and changed his name from Claudius to Clodius, and so became a member of the plebeian class in order to run for Tribune of the People.

*Decius believes the Marcelli men murdered Marcus Fulvius.

Clodia, sister of Publius and Appius. She changed her name when her brother Publius did. She is considered one of the most scandalous women of her time and is believed to have poisoned her husband, Metellus Celer, and maybe others as well.

Appius Claudius Pulcher, brother of Publius Clodius. He is standing for censor, and plans to expel many from the Senate if elected, among them Caius Sallustius (who appears to be no more than a harmless gossip but may be more dangerous than he looks).

The Manilii

Publius Manilius (Publius Manilius Scrofa), a Tribune of the People. He is prosecuting Decius for the murder of Marcus Fulvius. He is also one of the conspirators.

Sextus Manilius, a close friend of Fulvia's and a regular duumvir of Baiae. He is probably also backing Marcus Fulvius.

Other Characters Who May Be Involved

Caius Scribonius Curio. He is standing for Tribune of the People and is an enemy of the *optimates.* He is also engaged to Fulvia.

Marcus Brutus, a pontifex. He considers Caesar all too arrogant.

SPQR X

A
POINT
OF LAW

SPQR

Senatus Populusque Romanus

The Senate and the People of Rome

1

ROME AT ELECTION TIME! CAN THERE be any prospect more pleasant? Is it possible for any place to be more wonderful? For any activity to be more agreeable? Certainly not for me, and not that year. I was just back from Cyprus after a successful, mildly glorious, and none-too-bloody campaign to suppress a recent outburst of piracy. I had found their base, destroyed their fleet, and, best of all, captured a good part of their loot. The captives I had returned to their homes and had restored a part of the loot to the people from whom it had been stolen.

Luckily for me, a great deal of the loot had been impossible to trace, so it belonged to me. I had split up some of it with my men, made a handsome donation to the Treasury, and with the rest had cleared my considerable debts. I now had reached the proper age and had accumulated the requisite military experience to stand for the office of praetor. Perhaps best of all, I was a Caecilia Metella, and the men of my family expected automatic election to the higher offices by right of birth.

To top it all off, the weather was beautiful. It seemed that all the gods of Rome were on my side. As usual, the gods were about to play one of their infamous jokes on me.

The morning it all began I was at the Porticus Metelli on the Campus Martius, across from the Circus Flaminius, presiding over the consecration of my monument. This *porticus,* a handsome rectangle of colonnades surrounding a fine courtyard, had been erected by my family for the convenience of the people and to our own glory, and we paid for its upkeep. Some of my pirate loot had bought it a new roof. A monument in the Forum might have been more prestigious, but by that time the Forum was already so cluttered with monuments that one more would not have been noticeable. Besides, mine was not very large.

But in those days the City was spilling outside its old walls and the formerly rustic Campus Martius, the assembly place and drill ground for the legions of old, was now a prosperous suburb, growing full of expensive businesses and fine houses. And my monument wasn't just a statue, it was a naval trophy: a pillar studded with the bronze rams of the ships I had captured.

Actually, the pirate ships had had small, unimpressive rams, since pirates usually tried to board rather than sink ships, and mostly they raided shore villages so their ships had to be able to beach and escape quickly: not an easy task when you have a large ram sticking out in front. So I had had big, fearsome-looking rams cast, one for each pirate ship. Atop the pillar was a statue of Neptune, raising his trident in victory. A little grandiose for a campaign against scummy pirates, but that year all the real military glory was Caesar's so I took what I could get.

I was dressed in my *toga candida,* specially whitened with fuller's earth, to announce my candidacy for the praetorship. This surprised nobody. My friends and clients applauded as the trophy was unveiled and priests of Bellona and Neptune pronounced the consecration. They were both relatives of mine and glad to help out. Quintus Hortensius Hortalus, my father's old friend, now grown old and portly, took the auguries and pronounced them favorable in his incomparable voice.

Many of Rome's dignitaries were there. Pompey was there to offer his congratulations, as was the tiresome Cato. I would have liked to have Cicero in attendance, but he and his brother were off in Syria putting down a Parthian incursion. My wife, Julia, and many of her relations attended, providing perhaps an excessively large Caesarian contingent. Far too many people already considered me to be one of Caesar's flunkies. My good friend Titus Milo could not attend as he was in exile for killing Clodius and had not long to live, although I could not know that at the time.

Still, the morning was glorious, the monument was fine, my future was bright. At last I would hold an office of real power instead of one with endless responsibilities and duties and costing a fortune to support. I would have imperium and would be attended by lictors. With luck, when I left office I would be given a province to govern, one that was at peace, where I could get rich in relative safety. Most politicians wanted a province at war where they could win glory and loot, but I knew that any such position would put me in competition with Caesar and Pompey. I knew far too much of both men to want any part of that.

My father, ailing and leaning on a cane, had managed to attend. He swore he'd live to see me elected consul, but I feared he would never make it that long. Indeed, it depressed me to look at the knot of my senior kinsmen who accompanied him. All the great Metelli were dead or too elderly for political significance. Dalmaticus and Numidicus had died with my grandfather's generation, the generation of Marius. My father's generation had included Metellus Celer, now dead; Creticus, there that day but also growing old and very stout; Metellus Scipio, a pontifex, a Caecilian by adoption; and Nepos, closer to me in age but Pompey's man, and Pompey was a has-been if only his supporters would realize it. They had all been Sulla's supporters, and Sulla had been dead for more than twenty-five years. The Metelli of my own generation were still numerous, but they were political nonentities. I included myself in this category.

Also beside me was my freedman Hermes, still uncomfortable in his citizen's toga, a garment to which he had been entitled for only a few months. Of course, for official purposes his name was Decius Caecilius Metellus, but that was for his tombstone. He elected to keep his slave name, even though it was Greek. Well, it was a god's name after all, and many citizens of my generation went by Greek nicknames, some of which were quite indecent and for which there were no Latin equivalents.

With the dedication ceremony done, we all trooped to the Forum, past the temples of Apollo and Bellona, through the Carmentalis Gate in the old wall, around the base of the Capitol, and into the northwestern end of the great assembly place. It was even more thronged than usual, with the elections coming up and everyone who counted for anything in from the country. It was the season for parties and politics, for intrigue, bribery, and coercion.

At this time most of the Senate had split into two factions: pro-Caesarian and anti-Caesarian. Caesar was overwhelmingly popular with the plebs at Rome and hated violently by a large part of the aristocratic faction. As usual, such polarization led to strange juxtapositions. Men who, a few years previously, had reserved their greatest scorn for Pompey, now courted him as the only viable rival to Caesar. Theirs was a short-sighted policy, but desperate men will grasp at anything that promises respite from the thing they fear. I tried to keep my distance from all such factions, but my family connections made that difficult. One of the year's consuls, Marcus Claudius Marcellus, was among the most rabid of the anti-Caesarians and had not attended my little unveiling ceremony. The other consul, Sulpicius Rufus, congratulated me ostentatiously. Such were the times.

Doing the usual round of meeting and greeting, we made a leisurely progress toward the foot of the Capitol, near the old meeting place of the comitia, where all the year's candidates were accustomed to congregate, stand around, preen, and generally proclaim their willingness to serve Senate and People. Here our friends and well-wishers would drop by, take our hands, and trumpet loudly to anyone who would listen what splendid fellows we all were. It was one of our less dignified customs and a constant source of amazement to foreigners, but we'd always done it that way and that was a good enough reason to continue.

As a candidate for an office with imperium, it was my first order of business to greet the candidates I was supporting for the junior offices in order to take each by the hand and tell everyone what a splendid fellow he was.

First to get my hand was Lucius Antonius, standing for quaestor that year. Accompanying him was his brother Caius, who was himself serving as quaestor and would be standing down with the upcoming election. These were the brothers of the famous Marcus Antonius, who was serving with Caesar in Gaul. I had always gotten on well with these brothers, who were bad men but good company.

"Best of luck, Lucius!" I exclaimed, clapping him on the shoulder and raising a cloud of chalk dust. There was always a temptation to overdo it with the chalk when standing for office.

"And to you, Decius," the younger brother said, his eyes slightly unfocused and his voice a bit unsteady. At the wine already, I thought. Typical Antonian.

"I suppose you have your purple-bordered toga already ordered," Caius said, referring to my aforementioned certainty of election.

"As luck would have it, there was some Tyrian dye among the items I acquired in Cyprus," I said. No harm in reminding everybody who'd missed my monument dedication of my latest distinction. "Julia wove me a new toga and dyed the border herself. It's on the drying rack right now. A very handsome garment, I might add." Well, my wife had supervised her women while they did the actual weaving, and, of course she had called in a professional dyer to do the border. That pur-

5

ple dye is the most expensive substance in the world, even more dear than saffron or silk.

"Some people have all the luck," said Lucius. "By the time our brother gets through with Gaul there won't be any gold, wine, or good-looking women left to steal."

"It'll be another ten years before there's more pirate loot to pick up," Caius said tipsily. "If Pompey conquers Parthia, there'll be nothing left for the rest of us."

"I suppose there'll always be India," I said, not really serious. I had no ambitions to be a conqueror so I didn't take the problem as seriously as those two dedicated thieves.

"Too far," Caius said. "You have to march for a year just to get there. Now Egypt—"

"Forget it," I said. "The Senate will never let even an Antonius take Egypt." This was a statement fraught with great portent, had I but known it.

"Yes, just getting elected quaestor is problem enough for now," Caius said. "And, Decius, don't worry about Fulvius. You know how to handle people like him."

"Yes," said Lucius, "the man is nothing. Don't let him distract you from the election."

"What? Fulvius?" But they were already turning away to return the greetings of the latest batch of well-wishers.

I walked away wondering at this enigmatic advice. Which Fulvius did they mean? There were ten or twelve senators of that name known to me, and any number of *equites*. Which of them had it in for me?

I took up my place with the other candidates for the praetorship. After an hour of loud hailing and greeting, I was approached by one of my least favorite Romans, Sallustius Crispus. The year before he had been Tribune of the People, and in that powerful office had established himself as Caesar's champion. Upon the death of Clodius, he had tried to fill those vacated sandals. Since he considered me Caesar's man, too, he acted as if we were great friends.

Sullustius fancied himself a historian, and for twelve years he had tried to weasel from me everything I knew about the sorry Catiline business. He was an insinuating, sleazy wretch with overlarge ambitions. Actually, I suppose he was a typical Roman politician of the day and no worse than many others I knew. I just couldn't help disliking him.

One thing was for certain: with his love of gossip, Sallustius would know who this Fulvius might be and what sort of grievance he had.

"Fine day for politicking, eh, Decius Caecilius? I'd have been at your monument dedication, but I was seeing my brother off." His younger brother, surnamed Canini for some reason I never learned, had been another of the year's quaestors.

"Where is he bound?" I asked, waving heartily to a band of my Subura neighbors who were there to support me and others of our district standing for office that year.

"Syria. He's to be proquaestor for Bibulus."

"He'll be safe, then. Bibulus is a cautious man. He's doing as little fighting as possible and leaving what there is to his legates." Bibulus had been careful to arrive late to take up administration of his province. Young Cassius Longinus, a mere proquaestor who had survived the debacle at Carrhae, had been successfully driving the Parthians back until he arrived. The boy deserved a triumph for it; but with the tiny forces at his command he had been unable to score a decisive victory, and he was considered too young and too low-ranking for such an honor. So little praise for so much accomplishment may well account for his later hostility toward Caesar—but I get ahead of myself.

"Just as well," Sallustius was saying. "The talents of my family lie in the literary field, not the military." I would have said neither, but I didn't.

"A little while ago I was told to ignore somebody named Fulvius. Who is he and why should I ignore him?"

"You haven't heard?" he said gleefully. Sallustius loved to be the bearer of bad news. "This morning one Marcus Fulvius denounced you before the extortion court for corruption and plundering in Cyprus and adjacent waters."

"What!" At my shout heads turned so violently that you could hear vertebrae popping all over the Forum.

"Calm yourself, Decius." He smiled. "The man's just an aspiring politician out to make a name for himself. Prosecuting a successful man for corruption is how it's usually done. It's how Cicero made his reputation, you know."

"Yes, but Verres really *did* plunder Sicily with legendary thoroughness. I did nothing of the sort in Cyprus!"

"What difference does that make?" he asked, honestly puzzled. "You should be glad it's an accusation of extortion and plunder. It might've been for screwing a Vestal Virgin, and think how undignified the trial would've been then."

"I'm to take it that his accusation contained more than just a lot of noise and wind?"

"He says he has a number of witnesses to back him up."

"Cyprians? He'll be laughed out of Rome if he hauls a pack of half-Greek mongrels before a Roman jury."

"He claims he has Roman citizens ready to swear before the gods what a bad boy you were."

"Damn!" I had offended a number of Romans during my stay on Cyprus. Most were businessmen and financiers, who were profiting handsomely from the pirates' activities. "Who is this man and where is he from?" I suspected Sallustius would know, and he didn't disappoint me.

"He's from Baiae, been here in Rome for the last few months, making connections and learning politics from high-placed friends. I don't doubt he's had some expert advice as to how to go about it."

"I've spent so much time away from Rome these past few years it's hard to keep track of everyone. Baiae, you say?" I tried to make some sort of connection. Then it dawned on me. "Is this man Clodius's brother-in-law?"

He grinned his ugly grin. "He's Fulvia's brother."

Fulvia, the widow of my old enemy, had quite possibly the worst reputation of any woman in Rome.

"But since Clodius was killed, she's taken up with Marcus Antonius, and he bears me no ill-will. It doesn't make sense."

"You're just a convenient target, Decius. You're just back from overseas with a little glory and a lot of money, and you're standing for praetor. Why assume that it's personal?"

"You're probably right. I'll just handle him the usual way." Since a serving magistrate couldn't be prosecuted, my best tactic would be to stall until after the elections. By the time I stepped down, this pest would have found somebody else to plague.

"Like most ambitious men," Sallustius said, "he's poor. He may be amenable to a bribe to drop the charges. Would you like me to sound him out?" How like Sallustius. If I'd shown a liking for his sister, he'd have offered to act as pimp.

"No, I'll avoid the trouble if I can, but I refuse to buy my way out of a charge of which I'm innocent."

"I don't see why not. Innocence rarely exempts a man from the consequences of a false accusation. Counterattack is usually the way to go. Don't tell me you've spent all your money already?"

"Thank you for the news and advice, Sallustius. I'll deal with this my way."

I looked around until I spotted Hermes, near Vulcan's altar, talking me up to a little group of voters. One of the rules was that a candidate could not canvass for votes personally. Instead, our clients and freedmen did it for us. I caught his eye and beckoned.

"You don't want a drink already, do you?" he asked as he joined me. "It's going to be a long day." This insolence was the result of his years as my personal slave. Also, he knew me all too well.

"It's about to get longer, wretch. Go get my father and any other men of the family who may be standing around and my highest-placed supporters. There's going to be trouble."

He grinned. "An attack?" Hermes was an inveterate brawler.

"Not the kind you enjoy. A political offensive from an unexpected quarter."

"Oh," he said, downcast. "I'll find them."

My mind seethed even as I smiled and shook hands with well-wishers. How serious was this man's support? How would I counter his charges? How much support could I get behind me? How long could I stall? I was going to need legal advice. For this I would automatically have gone to Cicero, but a sea lay between us that year.

Father limped toward me, his face as grim as a thundercloud. Hortensius Hortalus was with him, as were Metellus Scipio and Creticus and even Cato. Much as I disliked Cato, I was ready to welcome anyone's support.

"We've already heard," Father said, before I could speak. "How did a worm like Marcus Fulvius set this up without us knowing of it?"

"Because we've paid him no notice at all, I don't doubt," Hortalus rumbled.

"Whose court was it?" I asked.

"Juventius," Cato said. He meant Marcus Juventius Laterensis, once a close friend of Clodius.

"Wonderful," I said. "Even dead, Clodius can cause me trouble."

"Time is on your side," Cato said. "With the election coming up, the court will be sitting for only four more days."

"If Juventius is willing to move fast," I pointed out, "four days is plenty of time to prosecute me." I didn't have to point out that a guilty verdict could prevent me from taking my place among the candidates on election day. Even if I were to be voted in anyway, I could be prevented from assuming office on the new year.

"We have to get your backside planted on that curule chair before the bugger can haul you before a court," said the eminently practical Creticus.

"Tonight," Hortalus said, "I'll go outside the walls and take the auguries. Perhaps I'll see a sign that the courts can't meet for the next few days."

"You're known as my father's closest friend," I said. "You'll be denounced before the Senate for falsifying auguries, even if you see a thunderbolt strike a night-soaring eagle."

"I'll take Claudius Marcellus with me. Nobody will question his auguries." He did not refer to the Claudius Marcellus who was one of that year's consuls, nor to the Claudius Marcellus who was to be one of the next year's consuls, nor yet to the Claudius Marcellus who was consul the year after that, but rather to yet a fourth Claudius Marcellus, who was the oldest member of the College of Augurs and trusted the way we always trust men who are too old to do much harm.

I looked out over the Forum crowd. No uproar yet. I didn't really expect one. Scurrilous accusations against candidates were among the more common entertainments of any election. Strolling entertainers and vendors were everywhere, doing a great business as always when the voters thronged the City. I wished that I could consult with Julia, whose political acumen exceeded even that of my own family. But she had gone back home. In any case, it would have been a scandal beyond redemption had I been seen discussing politics with my wife right out in public.

"Here he comes!" It was the excited voice of Sallustius. He was still standing close by, eager to pick up gossip from the Metellan faction.

I followed his pointing finger and saw a commotion within the crowd. In the sea of scalps I detected a motion heading our way, the way a shark's fin cuts the water. As it got closer, the motion resolved itself into a little knot of men striding along purposefully in our direction. In their lead was a tall, light-haired man who had the look of a Forum warrior—the sort who does all of his fighting in the courts. I recognized some of the men behind him as old followers of Clodius. The others were strangers to me.

11

"Decius Caecilius Metellus!" the man cried as he reached us.

"That's me," Father said. "What do you want?"

For an instant the man was nonplussed. His timing had been upset. "Not you! I meant your son." He leveled a skinny finger toward me.

"Then why didn't you say so, you whey-faced buffoon? Until I croak, he's Decius the Younger." Our faction whooped and clapped. People began to pack the already crowded area, sensing a good show.

"He's talking to your whelp, you bald-headed old fart!" shouted one of the man's flunkies.

Father squinted in the man's direction. "Who's that? Oh, I remember you. I had your mother flogged from the City for whoring and spreading disease." Of course, he had no idea who the man was, but he would never let a trifling detail like that stop him.

I was maintaining a dignified silence, which the light-haired man duly noted.

"Can't you speak Decius Caecilius Metellus the *Younger*? I accuse you of bribery, corruption, oppression of Roman citizens, and collusion with enemies of Rome during your naval operations on Cyprus!"

"And you would be—?" I inquired.

"I am Marcus Fulvius." He drew himself to his full height, adopting an orator's pose.

My mouth dropped open. "Not *the* Marcus Fulvius? The Marcus Fulvius who is renowned in Baiae for public fornication with goats? The Marcus Fulvius who took on an entire auxilia cohort of Libyan perverts until the oil supply ran out? To think Rome has been graced with such a celebrity." Now the whole Forum was laughing. The man's face reddened, but he held his ground. He was about to shout something when Cato stepped forward, seized his hand, and turned it palmside up.

"Here's a hand that never held a sword," he said with withering scorn, and nobody could pour on the scorn more witheringly than Marcus Porcius Cato. "Listen to me, you small-town nobody. Go put in some time with the legions, distinguish yourself in arms before you dare come to Rome and accuse a veteran of Gaul and Iberia, the crusher of pirates and exposer of a score of traitors."

This was making a bit much of my military and court record, but the words were deadly earnest and nobody was laughing now. I doubt that it was affection for me speaking. Cato despised men who came from out of town to make their reputations in Rome.

"Any Roman citizen may bring suit against any other in public court," Fulvius said. "As you know well, Marcus Porcius."

Hortensius Hortalus came forward. "That is very true. In fact, it was my impression that you made this very accusation this morning in the extortion court of Marcus Juventius Laterensis. Wherefore do you now, Marcus Fulvius, repeat these charges here in the ancient and sacred gathering place of the comitia, thus bringing disturbance to the grave deliberations of the citizens of Rome as they partake in the most venerable of our Republican institutions, the choosing among candidates for the highest offices?"

This speech would sound stilted and awkward in my mouth, but it was always a joy to hear Hortalus speak. The sonorous vowels of his old-fashioned Latin flowed over the crowd like honey.

Fulvius yanked his hand away from Cato. "I speak forth boldly because I want Rome to know it is a degenerate criminal who demands that the citizens grant him imperium. This man"—Once again he extended the skinny, slightly dirty-nailed finger toward my face, this time shaking with ill-bridled wrath—"laid hands on crucial naval stores, public property, citizens! And sold them for his own profit! He set his slaves to break into the houses of honest Roman citizens, to beat and torture them until they bought their lives with gold! He took great bribes from foreign merchants who trafficked with the very pirates he was sent to suppress. *This* is the man who wants to preside over a court that will try Roman citizens. *This* is the man who would go forth to govern a propraetorian province and command legions, no doubt to plunder our provincials and betray our allies!"

13

"Wasn't there something about collusion with enemies of Rome?" I asked.

"Beyond all this," he said, scarcely pausing for breath, "he consorted with the notorious slut Princess Cleopatra, daughter of the degenerate Ptolemy the Flute Player, that disgusting tyrant of Egypt."

At this time not one Roman in a thousand had ever heard of Cleopatra, who was barely seventeen years old. But her father, Ptolemy, was a worldwide joke.

"King Ptolemy," said Metellus Scipio, "has been recognized by the Senate of Rome as the lawful king of Egypt and has been accorded the status of Friend and Ally of the Roman People. Not only do you bring frivolous charges against a blameless servant of the Senate and People, but you slander the daughter of an allied prince. I've a mind to haul you into court for it."

"Everyone knows old Ptolemy bribed half the Senate to get that title!" shouted one of Fulvius's toadies. It was perfectly true, but hardly to the point.

I held up a hand for silence, and in a few seconds the hubbub calmed. "Marcus Fulvius, you bring serious charges against me, and your slanders are worthless. Bring out your witnesses."

"You will see them in court."

"Then why are you yammering at me here?" Of course, I knew perfectly well. The man was an unknown, a nobody. He wanted all of Rome to know his name, and by nightfall it surely would.

"I am here," Fulvius announced grandly, "to invite every citizen of Rome to witness my prosecution of the mighty Caecilius Metellus, whose loathsome guilt I shall prove through the testimony of Roman citizens wronged. The gods of Rome themselves will call for his exile!" This brought cries of admiration for his eloquence, at which he preened.

Hortalus spoke again. "You've learned rhetoric from a good master, Fulvius. That last turn of phrase was from Junius Billienus's prosecution of Minucius, one hundred and sixty-five years ago"—

Hortalus's knowledge of the law was truly comprehensive, admired by Cicero himself, but he paused for effect and let fall a telling addendum—"in the consulship of Paullus and Varro."

Half unconsciously, everyone there made some gesture to ward off evil, making apotropaic hand signs, fishing out phallic amulets, or reciting protective cantrips. Those lucky enough to be standing near an altar or statue of a god kissed their hands and pressed them to the sacred object. This we always do when that ill-starred year is mentioned, for it was in the consulship of Paullus and Varro that Hannibal met the greatest Roman army ever assembled and annihilated it at Cannae.

At that point a pair of lictors, their fasces shouldered, pushed their way through the crowd and stopped in front of me.

"Decius Caecilius Metellus the Younger," said one of them, "you are summoned to appear before the court of the praetor Marcus Juventius Laterensis at dawn tomorrow." They looked a bit uncomfortable carrying out this commonplace duty. If I should be elected praetor they might be assigned to me, and they feared I would remember them with disfavor.

"Why wait?" I said. "Let's go see him now." I left my spot and began to walk toward the basilica with my whole crowd behind me. I couldn't accomplish anything at court until my trial began, but I didn't want to give Fulvius anymore free publicity at my expense.

One of Fulvius's men, an ugly, scar-faced thug, pushed toward me. "Hey! You can't—" He got that far when Hermes stepped up to him and punched him in the face. The boy could hit as hard as any professional boxer, and the man went down like a sacrificial ox. My father clouted another over the head with his cane, and the rest fell back before us.

Had something like this occurred just a few years before, there would have been real bloodshed, but Pompey had finally set the city in order, expelled the gangs that had made elections so uproarious, and restored a little of our dignity. In consequence, everybody was bored and ready for a fight.

It was a very short walk to the basilica where Juventius had his court. The lictors had to hold the mob back while we stormed in, interrupting some case he was hearing. Juventius looked up, his face furious.

"I will hear your case tomorrow! Get out of my court!" He was a hard-faced man of no real distinction. Like most, he had done no more than put in the requisite civil and military time and had spent enough on his games as aedile, and so he got his year in the curule chair. Of course, some would say the same of me.

"Tomorrow!" I yelled. "This malicious wretch has had who knows how many months to put his plot together, to rehearse his perjurious witnesses, to bribe and suborn the testimony he needs to prove his false accusations, and I have until *tomorrow* to prepare my case! Citizens!" I smote my breast dramatically and almost choked on my own cloud of chalk dust. "Is this justice?" I was shouting loud enough to be heard outside and sounds of a gratifying agreement came back to me.

"Lictors!" Juventius shouted. "Throw these trespassers out!" Since his lictors were outside trying to hold the crowd back, they were in something of a quandary.

"What's all this unseemliness?" The voice was not terribly loud, but all disorder quieted instantly. Pompey entered the basilica, preceded by his twelve lictors. Technically, he was proconsul for Nearer and Farther Spain, but he also had an extraordinary oversight of the grain supply, so he remained in Italy to keep everyone from starving while his legates attended to both Spanish provinces. It was an unheard-of arrangement for a proconsul with full imperium to remain in Italy; but in this, as in everything else, Pompey was a law unto himself.

"Proconsul," Juventius said, "I've summoned Metellus the Younger to appear before me tomorrow, and he has shown up instead today, interrupting court business."

"You gave him short enough notice. Why should he do less for you?" Then he turned to me. "Decius, you've been provoked, but I'll not have disorder in Roman courts. Go home and get your defense ready. I'm sure you'll have a good one."

"Naturally," I said to him. "I have hundreds of witnesses to my activities, and they're all on Cyprus! If I were, at great expense, to dispatch a fast cutter I could bring a few dozen here in about a month. At least I could if it were the sailing season, which it isn't."

"You'd better think of something," Pompey advised, "because if your case is carried over into the next year, you can't be elected praetor."

He turned around, strode to the entrance, and bellowed, "This matter is to be settled tomorrow! I want you all to go about your business. There are to be no unlawful assemblies or disorderly demonstrations."

Meekly, the whole crowd did his bidding. Pompey was acting as if he were sovereign of the City. Since the City was well-supplied with his veterans in those days, he might as well have been.

"We'll meet at my house this evening," Father said. "Summon our highest-ranking supporters. We have some serious planning to do."

2

By the time I got home, Julia already knew most of the story. Her network of slaves, tradesmen, and the women of her social circle rivaled the espionage organization of any Eastern potentate. She met me in our atrium that afternoon with a harried expression and a formidable degree of preparation. She clapped her hands, and the household slaves bustled to do her bidding. A slave took my candidate's toga as another toweled the chalk from my neck and arms.

"Come along," Julia said. "We have a lot to discuss and not much time." I followed her into the dining room where more slaves were already setting the table for us. I flopped onto a couch and somebody took my sandals.

"Eat," Julia commanded. "You're going to have a long night of plotting ahead of you at your father's house."

"You already know about that?" I reached for the wine, and she slapped my hand. I grabbed a roll instead.

"How should I not?" She mixed the wine with water. Far too much water. "They'll want to organize a legal defense for you. Tell them they are wasting their time."

"Why should I do that? Even perjured testimony has to be answered and countered. I don't see how the man can hope to make his charges stick."

Julia rolled her eyes. "Isn't it obvious? He has no intention of bringing in a conviction! He just wants to keep you out of the election!"

"But why? He can't hope to make his reputation on an abortive trial resulting in an acquittal."

"That's the question we have to answer." She shoved a cup of the weak mixture into my hand. I dipped my bread into balsam-steeped oil and chewed.

"If he doesn't benefit directly from my exclusion from office, then who does? That's always Cicero's question, isn't it? 'Who benefits?'"

"There is another question to ask: Are you the real target of this attack?"

"What do you mean?" I downed a couple of oysters and went after a roast chicken.

"His words, as reported to me, were that he would bring down 'the great Caecilius Metellus.' *You* are not the most distinguished of your family. He may be attacking the family through you."

"If we were known Pompeians or Caesarians that would make sense, but we aren't. The family supported Sulla and has gone its own way since his death."

"There are those who may find that intolerable," Julia said obscurely.

"How well do you know Fulvia? He's her brother."

"I've scarcely seen her these past few years, except when we both attended noblewomen's ceremonies the Bona Dea festival and the rites of Ceres and so forth. When she was married to Clodius, she was tight with that circle, naturally. Now it looks as if she'll marry Marcus Antonius, and Antonius has thrown in his lot with Caesar. So I can't imagine that she's put her brother up to this, evil bitch though she may be."

"Do you think she's all that bad?"

"Clodia's a Vestal by comparison." The notorious Clodia had retired to virtual seclusion since her brother's death, thus robbing Rome of its favorite focus for scandal. As always, I grew uneasy when my wife mentioned Clodia. I had a checkered and somewhat unsavory past with that woman.

"Then who? The major factions should be trying to court the Metelli, not to alienate them." I attacked an unoffending but delicious rabbit, tore off its leg and dipped it in *garum*.

Julia thought about it for a while, then she seemed to get off the subject. "Who do you think your family will support? They can't stay neutral forever. Sooner or later they'll have to declare for Caesar or Pompey."

"Not necessarily," I said. "For one thing, a year from now, Caesar or Pompey or both could be dead. Gaul is not a healthy place, as I can attest from experience. One stray arrow, one determined assassin, an unexpected German offensive—any number of things could spell an abrupt end for Caesar. For that matter, an ague or a disgruntled officer could do it. Recall if you will that half the Senate cooperated to send him to Gaul in hopes that he'd die there.

"As for Pompey, he's at the age when men drop dead suddenly of natural causes. He's put on weight and doesn't get around like he used to."

"You aren't answering me." Julia was as relentless as any lawyer.

"It depends on who frightens them the most. They've spent decades scared of Pompey and his soldiers, and they've opposed him most of the time. Now they're getting apprehensive of Caesar. He has an unprecedentedly large and happy army, and for several years he's been virtual king of Gaul and Illyricum. When the time comes, they'll take sides against the one who gives them the biggest scare. They'll back the weaker man."

"When will they decide who frightens them most?"

"It depends on how Caesar and Pompey act. They'll try to keep things peaceful as long as they can. If Pompey keeps his veterans in the south, and if Caesar lays down his imperium when his term expires, comes back to Rome and takes his place in the Senate, then my family will try to keep the peace and stay in the good graces of both of them."

"Do you think that will happen?"

"I think it's unlikely. Caesar has shown his contempt for the Senate too clearly. If he tries to do what Sertorius did and set himself up as an independent king, there will be civil war and Pompey will lead the campaign against him. If Pompey takes it into his head to call up his soldiers and capture southern Italy, my family will go to Caesar and beg him to crush Pompey."

"And if Caesar returns to Rome but doesn't lay down his imperium? If he brings his soldiers with him and camps outside the walls of Rome?"

"Then my family will side with Pompey. They always back the weaker man, the one they think they can control. I hope it doesn't come to any of these ends, because then it will make no difference whom we back. It will mean the end of the Republic."

"Perhaps it's time," Julia said.

"Never! If there is another civil war, whoever wins, Caesar or Pompey or another man, he will make himself dictator. And unlike Sulla, this one will not retire and restore the Republic. It will be monarchy, just like in the Orient. That would be unworthy of Rome."

"We're getting away from the subject," Julia said. She would never say it, but the idea of her uncle as monarch didn't bother her a bit. "I am going to look into this man Fulvius and his past. Someone is behind him and when we know who it is, we'll know how to fight him."

"Much as I detest Sallustius," I told her, "I am almost ready to take his advice and offer the bastard a bribe to back off."

"Whoever is behind him will have thought of that," she said. "He's been offered something better than money."

"Better than money," I pointed out, "there is only honor and public office, which he is unlikely to attain if he follows this course."

"Men value different things," she said. "Not everyone is a Roman of great family."

"This is quite true," I agreed. "We need to find out who this man is. We haven't a great deal of time to do it in."

She glanced at the slant of sunlight pouring through the triclinium door. "It's not late yet. I think I'll go pay Fulvia a call. She is still at the house of Clodius, I believe. She is so snubbed by women of quality that she'll be eager to talk."

"You be careful around that woman," I told her. "Take along some of my clients, the ex-legionaries and brawlers."

"A Caesar needs no bodyguard," she said contemptuously. Julia always saw her status as Caesar's niece as a sort of invisible armor protecting her wherever she went. I saw it more as an archer's mark painted between her shoulder blades.

I ARRIVED AT MY FATHER'S HOUSE just as the sun was setting. Hermes was with me, and I had stopped by the houses of a few friends, men of high rank and good reputation, whose support I could count upon. There was already a goodly crowd outside the gate, servants, clients, and supporters of the important men already gathered within.

As I approached the gate a large litter arrived. It was Hortalus, who had grown too old, stout, and infirm to walk great distances. He was already dressed in his striped augur's robe and carried the *lituus:* the crook-topped staff of that sacred office. With him was the eminent Appius Claudius Pulcher, a very distinguished soldier and administrator. He was standing for censor and was sure to be elected. This man was the elder brother of Clodius; but he was a man of entirely different character, and I had never had any but cordial relations with him.

Inside, a sizable chunk of Rome's senatorial power was assembled. I qualify this because the real power was elsewhere, fighting Gauls and Parthians.

"Here's Hortensius," Metellus Scipio said, as we came in. "That was a good stab you got in today about the unspeakable year. Was it true?"

"Oh, yes," Hortalus said. "I never lie about legal precedents. I wish that sort of opening came my way more often in court."

"I've been wondering about that," I said. "Aside from the fact that Fulvius steals the words of better men, where was he likely to have learned them?"

"Aulus Sulpicius Galba is the great scholar of the jurisprudence of that era," said Hortalus. "He used to make all his students memorize the orations of Billienus."

"Used to?" I said.

"He retired from Roman practice at least twenty years ago. We rarely see him here now. Last I heard he was teaching law in Baiae and has been elected duumvir of the town."

"If I could be the most important man in Baiae," I said, "I wouldn't be in Rome either. Well, that much makes sense. Fulvius is from Baiae, so he must have studied law there under Galba."

"Nobody here knows much about Fulvius," Father said. "He's been in the City only a few months at most."

"Appius," said Creticus, who held a huge goblet of wine, "not to dredge up any family scandals, but do you know anything about him? He is a relative of yours by marriage."

"I never heard of him before today," Appius Claudius said. "I had little to do with my brother his last few years and even less with his wife. This brother of hers never approached me for patronage and wouldn't have got it if he had."

I took a cup from a passing slave. The wine was, mercifully, not as heavily watered as Julia served it.

"Marcus Cato can't be here tonight," Scipio said, "but he's agreed to begin tomorrow's proceedings with an oration concerning conditions on Cyprus. He saw to the Roman annexation of the island, and he briefed Decius before he went out there. We've yet to locate any citizens who were there during Decius's activities against the pirates, and we're unlikely to anytime soon. We have, however, a great many important men ready to testify to his splendid character."

"He'll have more, swearing what an utter, degenerate criminal and pervert I am," I pointed out.

"What's more, his witnesses will be more believable," Creticus said, raising a general laugh at my expense.

"Your aedileship was the most popular since Caesar's," Scipio pointed out. "The plebeians will be solidly behind you."

"Yes," I agreed, "but virtually all my fines and prosecutions were leveled against crooked contractors, dishonest entrepreneurs, violators of the business and building codes, all of them *equites*. Guess who will be on the jury."

"*Equites*, of course," Father replied. "In Sulla's day, a senator was tried before his peers." I could have pointed out the injustice of that policy, but at that moment I was entirely in agreement with the bloody old butcher.

"Perhaps," I said, "we're approaching this from the wrong direction." I sketched the possibility Julia had raised. Of course, I pretended that it had been my idea.

"I don't believe that his odd phrasing escaped any of us who were there," Hortalus said. " 'The mighty Caecilius Metellus' indeed! I, too, am inclined to think that this represents an attack on the whole gens Caecilia."

"I agree," Father said. "Has anyone any better idea?" None had. "Very well. The fact remains that the form this attack has taken is a personal one against my son. As such we must address it, and we have three days to clear this matter up so that we can get Decius the younger elected praetor."

"Now," Creticus said, "we need to discuss the various under-handed ways we can counter this exceedingly underhanded offensive. Scipio, will Pompey intervene for us?"

Scipio's daughter, widow of Publius Crassus who had died at Carrhae, had married Pompey, a man somewhat older than her father. The old boy was quite besotted with her, and when his father-in-law was prosecuted Pompey called the jury together at his own house and asked personally for an acquittal. Scipio was immediately cleared of all charges and carried from the Forum on the shoulders of the men who were to have tried him.

"That won't work twice," Scipio said. "He earned enough resent-ment last time. To do it again, for a member of the same family, could turn the whole Senate against him."

"How about a bribe?" Father asked. He saw my mouth open and pointed a bony finger at my face. "None of your delicate scruples now, Son. This is politics at its dirtiest, and bribing the fellow may turn out to be the easiest, simplest, and, in the long run, cheapest way to go. How much of your pirate loot remains?"

"Very little. After the monument and the new roof of the portico, clearing my debts, and my donation to the Treasury, there's barely enough remaining to support my state as praetor." The praetorship wasn't as costly an office as the aedileship, but my expenses would still be heavy: compensation for my clients, who would attend me every court day; regular gifts for my lictors; and the lavish entertaining ex-pected of an office holder.

"You shouldn't have given so much to the Treasury," Creticus said.

"We could all lend you a few talents to buy the man off," Scipio suggested.

"He won't be bought if it's the family he's after," I pointed out. Once again I presented Julia's suspicions as my own.

"So who can afford to outspend us?" Scipio asked. "Or place him in high office? The only likely suspects are Caesar and Pompey, and it makes little sense for either of them to do this."

"There are other men of ambition," said Appius Claudius. "Desperate men who can't climb by constitutional means are apt to employ desperate tactics."

"You mean like Catilina?" I said. "Some frustrated, would-be dictator currying favor among the malcontents and the dispossessed?"

"I am thinking more of the exiles," he answered. "Gabinius would dearly love to come back to Rome and resume his career. You had a run-in with him on Cyprus, did you not?"

"Yes, early on," I told him, "but we patched it up."

"You are not his lifelong friend though," Father said, "and no man is your friend where great ambition is concerned. I think we should consider Gabinius as a possibility. What about Curio?"

"The man's a pauper!" Hortalus protested.

"So was Caesar until a few years ago," Creticus said. "Curio's standing for Tribune of the People, he has a slate of proposed legislation that's as ambitious as anything since the brothers Gracchi—"

"And," Scipio put in, "he's suddenly presenting himself as the enemy of the *optimates*. Just a month ago he was solidly in our camp."

I could see that my family had been discussing Curio quite a bit already. I barely knew Caius Scribonius Curio, who was a wellborn, high-living young man of little accomplishment, although he was said to be extremely intelligent and a fine speaker.

"If he's elected tribune," Father said, "he'll be in a strong position to push Fulvius's career. Let's consider him a possibility."

It went on like this for some time, one name after another being brought forth for consideration. There were a lot of names to consider, too. A family as politically important as mine had as many enemies as friends. And not everyone at the gathering possessed as logical a brain as mine. Some names were raised simply because the raiser disliked the man, or he was known for some especially unusual vice, or he practiced a suspect religion. Someone even brought up the name of Vatinius, an eccentric senator who was fond of wearing a black toga even when he wasn't in mourning. It was some sort of Pythagorean practice. Otherwise, the man was harmless.

By midnight we had run through just about all the legal and political possibilities except for assassination. I think that was omitted only because the problem wasn't quite that serious. I could always stand for election again the next year, annoying though that might be.

"Well," Hortalus said, lurching to his feet, "I'm off. I am going to the house of Claudius Marcellus, where we shall watch the skies from his excellent garden. All of you take my advice and get some sleep. We really can't formulate our defense until we know more about this upstart, Flavius. This time tomorrow we will know all we need to about that man."

"Let me accompany you," I said. "The streets are black, and the night is moonless. My men brought plenty of torches, and they're all veterans."

"A good idea," Father said. "When you've seen our friend to his destination, get some rest and we'll all meet at dawn on the basilica steps."

Outside, I got Hermes and my men arranged, some in front of Hortalus's litter, some behind. Just because the great gangs had been broken up did not mean that the streets of Rome were perfectly safe, especially on a moonless night. My men were armed, discreetly, with weapons beneath their cloaks. So was I.

"Come join us in the litter, Decius," Hortalus said, as he and Appius Claudius got in. "There's room for three."

Nothing loath, I climbed in. At that time it was considered rather effeminate for a man of military age to use a litter. They were supposed to be conveyances for wellborn women, the sick, and the elderly. But I wasn't about to stumble around in Rome's filthy, benighted streets if something better was offered. The bearers groaned at the extra weight when they hoisted us.

"Are you going to the house of Claudius Marcellus, too?" I asked Appius Claudius. I knew the two Claudian families were related, but distantly.

"No," he said, "I've been staying as a guest at Quintus's country villa. Tonight I'll go on to my own house."

Hortensius Hortalus had spent most of his time in recent years in his splendid country houses, where he had been developing fish ponds with his friend Marcus Phillipus. The two wrote long books on the subject.

"With country estates like yours," I said to Hortalus, "I wonder that you bother coming to the City at all."

"I'm an old Forum politician," he said. "I just can't stand to miss an election. Especially not when the issues being debated in the Senate are so crucial to the state. I am long past my days of highest influence, but I flatter myself that my voice is still listened to."

"Rome ignores your wisdom at her peril," said Appius.

"Which issues concern you so?" I asked.

"Why the growing insolence of Caesar, of course! Forgive me, Decius, but you've been away from the City too long. Did you know that Caesar this year petitioned to stand for consul while *keeping* his army and his provinces? Unheard of! Might as well crown the bugger king and be done with it."

"Caesar has been courting that man Curio we just spoke of," Appius put in. "I think he's trying to bribe every man standing for next year's tribuneship: Pansa and Caelius that I know of, probably the others. But he'll win over Curio for certain."

"How do you know?" I asked.

"The usual. The man's terrifically debt-ridden, and Caesar will pay off his debts. Has it occurred to anyone that the root of most of our political disorder is not the generals who go out and accumulate loot but the young, wellborn wastrels who accumulate debt instead? There is nothing more dangerous to the public good than a senator or young man of senatorial family made desperate by crushing debt. They can be bought by any politician with a heavy purse."

"That is very true," Hortalus said, nodding.

"Next year, if I succeed in being elected censor—"

"The censorship is yours for the asking, Appius Claudius," I assured him.

"Hear, hear," Hortalus affirmed.

"I thank you both. Anyway, I intend to use that office to purge the Senate of its worst elements, starting with all those disgraceful debtors."

"I hope," Hortalus said, "that you get a colleague who will cooperate with you. My own censorship was ideal because I had the elder Decius as colleague. But poor Crassus could do nothing because his colleague kept overruling every decision he made. He had to quit before even finishing the census or performing the lustrum."

"Who is most likely to win the other censorship?" I asked. "As Quintus Hortensius has observed, I've been out of touch."

"I am hoping for the elder Cassius," Appius said, "but it's more likely to be Calpurnius Piso. If so, I can work with him. He's one of those who tries not to declare for Caesar or Pompey, but they're a vanishing breed. It's a disgrace that Romans of rank have to be seen as supporters of one would-be tyrant or the other, but one must face the situation realistically."

By this time we were near the house of Marcellus. I got out of the litter, took my leave of the two men, and proceeded to walk the short distance to my own home with Hermes and the rest of my men. They had spent the evening loitering around Father's house, doubtless talking politics like the rest of Rome.

"Did you get anything accomplished?" Hermes wanted to know.

"Just a lot of talk," I told him. Around us the others held torches aloft and peered into dark alleys, their faces truculent, hands resting on hilts.

"Same here. The mood in the city's strange since we got back. The quiet is unnatural. Everybody is waiting for something to happen. People are seeing omens everywhere. I just heard about a two-headed calf born near Arpinum, and a hawk killed one of Juno's geese this morning."

"At least it wasn't a snake," I said. "When a snake gets into the temple and swallows a goose egg, the city's on edge for days waiting for disaster. People need something to take their minds off all this peace and quiet. Now would be a good time for some games. It's been almost two months since the Plebeian Games and the next official celebrations won't be until spring. Hasn't anybody important died? A good *munera* would be just the thing."

"Valerius Flaccus is just back from Cilicia. He was at the *ludus* yesterday arranging for his father's funeral games, but that won't be until March." Hermes trained with weapons at the Statilian school on most mornings when he had no duties to perform for me, like that day's canvassing for votes.

"What a time for Rome's wealthy and bereaved to turn stingy." One by one my men left us to return to their own homes, accepting my thanks for their support and promising to be at my home before dawn to accompany me to the basilica. By the time we reached home, only Hermes and the torch boy were with me.

Once inside I sent Hermes off to his bed and sought my own. Julia was already asleep. I threw off my clothes and lay down beside her, pleasantly tired and only slightly annoyed by the day's proceedings. It was still good to be back in Rome, and anything was better than being in Gaul.

IN THE MORNING THE SLAVES BROUGHT water for me to splash on my face, and within a few minutes I was sitting in the triclinium being shaved, having my hair dressed, and eating breakfast all at once. I was almost awake. Julia came in to supervise my grooming.

"Did you find out anything yesterday?" I asked her.

"Some odd things, but you don't have time to hear about it if you're going to be in the Forum at sunrise. Come home for lunch and I'll tell you about it then."

"All right. In the meantime, make a few morning calls, gossip with your friends, and see what you can learn about the candidates for the tribuneships, particularly Scribonius Curio."

"Curio?" she said, but I was already out the door.

OUTSIDE THE MORNING AIR WAS COOL, but not truly cold. This was because we were still using the old calendar, which Caesar, as *Pontifex Maximus*, had allowed to get lamentably out of synchronization with the true season. Thus, while we were still some days prior to the Ides of December, the true date was closer to late October in the new calendar. Caesar's calendar (actually the work of Sosigenes, the wonderful Alexandrian astronomer) makes more sense, but it lacks the variety and unpredictability of our old one.

By the time we reached the Forum, the sky was getting gray over the crest of the Esquiline. We passed by the Curia Hostilia, the old Senate House, which was still streaked with black and was near-ruinous. In the riots following the death of Clodius, it had been severely damaged by fire, and, as yet, nobody had undertaken its restoration.

Past the great portico of the Temple of Saturn, where I had spent a miserable year as treasury quaestor, we came to the Basilica Opimia, which was the only one where courts were sitting that year. The Basilica Porcia had been damaged by the same fire that almost destroyed the Curia, the huge Basilica Aemilia was undergoing lavish restorations, and the Basilica Sempronia was devoted solely to business purposes due to the shortage of basilica space.

We trudged up the steps, passing a drunk who had staggered his way homeward as far as the Basilica Opimia, then wrapped himself in his cloak and passed out on the steps. Well, I had awakened in many strange parts of Rome myself in past years.

My father, naturally, was already there. "Slept late enough, did you?"

"We still beat the crowd to the Forum," I answered.

Gradually the light grew, and the crowd duly arrived: my own supporters and a miscellaneous pack of idlers, country people just arrived to take part in the elections, vendors, mountebanks, beggars, and senators.

Juventius came trudging up the steps in his purple-bordered toga, preceded by his lictors.

"I see the Metellans are here in force," he said, as he reached the top. "Where are Fulvius and his people?"

"Waiting to make a grand entrance, no doubt," I said. "Now what—"

"This man is dead!" someone shouted. I looked down the steps to see a little group of people gawping at an inert form on the steps. It seemed that the drunk was actually a corpse. Now that the sun's rays were slanting into the Forum, I could see that the dark cloak in which he was wrapped was actually a heavily bloodstained toga.

"Here's a fine omen," Juventius said, annoyed. "We may have to meet outdoors if the building has to be purified."

"It looks like he died on the steps," I pointed out. "It isn't as if he died inside."

"If this were a temple," Father mused, "a purification would be necessary if one drop of blood struck any stone of the building. I'm not sure if that holds true for a basilica though. We may have to consult with a pontifex. Where is Scipio?"

"It's all a great bother anyway you look at it," Juventius said. He turned to one of his lictors. "Let's have a look at him."

The lictor went down the steps and carefully raised a flap of the toga with the butt end of his fasces.

"Does anyone here know this man?" Juventius demanded of the crowd in general. We all went closer to see.

"I think we all know him," I said, feeling a bit queasy, not at the sight, which was a common one, but at its implications. "I've only seen him once, and that briefly, but I believe this is Marcus Fulvius."

3

"LOOKS LIKE THE TRIAL'S OFF," SAID someone, sounding disappointed. Probably, I thought, one of the jury, who had been hoping one of us would offer him a bribe. We went back to the top of the steps to talk this matter over.

Word spread through the Forum with bewildering speed and within seconds the whole mob had flocked to the western end, at the foot of the Capitoline, to get a look at the body and at us.

"This could get ugly," Juventius said.

"Why?" I asked him. "The man is—was—all but unknown. It's not like he was Tribune of the People or a gang leader like Clodius."

"You know how it works," Juventius said. "He was a nobody. He dared to challenge one of the great families. He ended up dead. How do you think they're going to interpret it?"

"The man was an impertinent scoundrel who must have had plenty of enemies," Father said. "Anyone could have killed him."

"Would just anyone," Juventius replied hotly, "have killed him and left his body on the steps of *this* basilica on the morning his case was to be heard in *my* court?"

"Lower your voice," I advised him. "You're encouraging a bad mood here yourself."

"Oh, I am? I do hope you had plenty of witnesses as to your whereabouts last night, young Decius Caecilius, because you now face charges a good deal more serious than skinning some pack of provincials and tax-gouging *publicani*."

"Are you calling me a suspect in this man's murder?" I shouted, forgetting my own advice. Among other things, I hated being called "Young Decius," even when my father was there.

"Uh-oh," Hermes said, touching my arm and pointing to the southeast. A pack of determined men were pushing their way through the crowd. In their forefront was a man with a swollen nose and two blackened eyes. He was the one Hermes had punched the previous day. They shoved everyone out of their way until they stood over the body of Fulvius. At the bloody sight, they cried out in dismay.

"We met this morning at the house of Marcus Fulvius," said the black-eyed man, his voice slightly distorted by his swollen nasal passages. "We waited for him to come out so we could accompany him to court. When he did not come out by gray dawn, we made search for him. He was nowhere to be found. We came to the Forum expecting to find him here, and when we reached the Temple of the Public Lares, at the north end of the Forum, we heard that someone lay murdered in the basilica.

"Now," he roared, playing to the mob, "we find our friend Marcus Fulvius lying here, drenched in his own blood, and his *murderer*"— he jammed a dirty finger toward my breast as if he were throwing a javelin—"standing over him!"

Hermes was about to give him a broken jaw to go with the rest, but I restrained him.

"I am innocent of this man's blood," I proclaimed, "and I can produce witnesses, among them the most distinguished men in Rome, to attest to my whereabouts last night!" But not, I reminded myself, for the early hours of this morning. It was not my job to point these things out to my accusers.

"Is this justice?" howled another man, this one a red-haired lout. "Are we to allow these *nobles,* these *Caecilians* to murder good Roman men? Does their high birth give them leave to shed blood on the very steps of the basilica?" There were mutters from the crowd, along with cries of "Never!" and "Down with them!" from here and there. But it was too early, the crowd still too somnolent and surprised for riot conditions.

"Lictors," Juventius said impatiently, "arrest those troublemakers."

"Don't do that," I cautioned. "It's what they want."

"That sounds odd coming from you," he said. "These men are howling for your blood."

"This is a well-rehearsed gang. Anyone can see that. They were primed for this long before they got to the Forum."

"Will you answer us?" yelled the black-eyed man.

"Who are you to make demands of a praetor?" Juventius yelled back.

More people were forcing their way forward. The people made way for one of them, and he mounted the steps. He wore no insignia of office, but he was treated with unmistakable respect. He stepped up to the body and studied it for a moment. He was a very young man with good bearing and a tough-looking, pugnacious face. I didn't recognize him, but such youth coupled with such respect from the people meant one thing: a Tribune of the People.

Others were gathering on the steps behind me. Cato had arrived and Appius Claudius. I beckoned Cato to me. "Who is this boy?" I asked him.

He studied the youth for a moment. "Publius Manilius. Not a

supporter of Caesar and no friend of Pompey either. He's one to watch."

At that moment the young man we were discussing was watching me. Fulvius's crowd were speaking urgently into his ears, which I almost expected to curl up and wither under the assault of all that garlic. At last he waved them off and came up the steps toward us.

"Marcus Fulvius," he proclaimed in a fine, resonant voice, "has been murdered on the day he was to appear in court to denounce Decius Caecilius Metellus the Younger before the court of the praetor Marcus Juventius Laterensis. Murder has been committed, and no one had a greater reason to see Fulvius dead than you, Metellus."

"I had every reason to show him for a fool and his witnesses as perjurers, no more than that. I never heard of him before yesterday. I need to know a man better than that to want to kill him."

"I will convoke the Plebeian Assembly to discuss this matter," Manilius said. "Until our decision has been reached, the election for praetors will not be held!" At this a huge shout went up.

"You can't do that!" Cato said, when the crowd had quieted.

"You've been a tribune, Cato," Manilius shot back. "And you know that I can. I will not allow a man under suspicion of murdering a citizen to be elected to high office, immune from prosecution for a full year and holding imperium to boot."

"I have a question," I said.

"What is it?" Manilius asked.

I pointed at the knot of Fulvius's men. "Where are the witnesses against me? Fulvius said he would bring before the court these citizens I supposedly oppressed and robbed on Cyprus. Where are they?"

"You stand accused of a far more serious charge, Metellus," the tribune said. "You would do well to concentrate on defending yourself against this charge, not the one you will not now be tried on."

"I still want an answer! You!" I pointed at the red-haired flunky. "What has happened to these witnesses?"

"They—they were staying in the house of Fulvius. We were to bring them all here to the court, but we found his house deserted. You must have done away with all of them!" He spoke too fast, his eyes darting about. He had not rehearsed this. Nobody had prepared him for the question.

Manilius raised a hand. "I enjoin silence! I am calling a *contio* of the Plebeian Assembly to meet this afternoon, and there I will entertain motions for a trial of Decius Caecilius Metellus the Younger on the charge of the murder of Marcus Fulvius. For now I bid you all disperse!"

Slowly the big knot of people began breaking up into smaller and smaller knots, until people were distributed almost evenly in all parts of the Forum, back to the usual market-day business of the election season. It was an almost magical process and one that never ceased to amaze me, how a nearly riotous mob can revert to a peaceful gathering of citizens in a moment. I was especially glad to see it happen this time.

Fulvius's little band still stood around the body, apparently at a loss what to do with it.

"I want to examine that body," I said. "Maybe the way he was killed can tell us something."

"No one touch that body until the *Libitinarii* get here," Juventius ordered. "You lot leave now. I will see that Fulvius is delivered to whatever family he may have in the City. Go now."

"Do as the praetor says," Manilius told them. "We will discuss this at the meeting, where our decisions will have legal authority. What we say here is just idle noise."

Reluctantly they obeyed him. Then Manilius himself left, probably to round up his fellow tribunes.

"Damned tribuneship," Father groused. "It gives too much power to men too young and inexperienced. That boy is acting like a consul, and he hasn't a lictor to his name."

I shrugged. "He handled the situation well enough. We might

have had a riot. That's what those men wanted, but they didn't dare dispute with a Tribune of the People, whatever their hostility to the Senate."

"So there's to be no trial," Appius said, "but no election either! If their plan is to keep you from office, they're succeeding so far."

"But," I pointed out, "if he'd let the praetorship elections go on, he could have demanded that I be taken off the ballot because I'm charged with murder. This way I have a chance to clear myself and still be present for the election. In the meantime the Centuriate Assembly can amuse itself electing next year's consuls and censors. It will just mean a longer election season. What Roman ever complains about a prolonged holiday?"

"But *can* you clear yourself?" Juventius asked.

"Easily," I told him. "I'm innocent and the gods love me. Now if you will excuse me, I want a look at this body."

The *Libitinarii* had arrived on the scene, dressed in their bizarre, Etruscan outfits, carrying their stretcher and accompanied by their priest. The priest went through his purification ritual, then the masked undertakers tugged the bloody toga off, then peeled away the sticky tunic, exposing the mortal remains of the late Marcus Fulvius.

There had been a tremendous effusion of blood, and it was easy to see why. He had been stabbed enough times to kill Achilles. I was no expert like my friend Asklepiodes, but even I could see that more than one weapon had been involved and that meant more than one assailant. There were stab wounds from a narrow-bladed dagger, others from a broad-bladed dagger or sword, yet others that looked like slashes, or rather wide rents, like a clumsy job of butchering. Some of the wounds gaped wide enough that I could see they were not especially deep. Loops of viscera bulged through cuts in his belly, but none of the gashes was large enough to eviscerate the man.

There was a large cut slanting from just behind his left ear to the joining of the collarbones. This wound alone would have been sufficient to kill him. None of the others I could see would have been immediately fatal. There were no wounds visible on his limbs or head.

"Turn him over," I told the undertakers. They rolled him over. There were no wounds on his back.

"That poor bastard died hard." I looked up to see Sallustius, who was never far from the center of excitement in Rome.

"Any man who's served in the legions knows how to kill a man better than that," Cato said. "A quick stab in the right place is all it takes. He must have been set upon by common cutthroats."

I looked at the tunic, which was almost stiff with blood. It was a dark one, made of coarse cloth. The almost equally bloody toga was little better, made of raw, undyed wool, a dingy brown color.

I stood. "He wasn't on his way to court dressed like this," I noted. "And look how nearly dry this blood is. He must have died hours ago. I want this body taken to the Temple of Venus Libitina before it's turned over to his family so that Asklepiodes can examine it."

"You have no authority to order such a thing," Juventius reminded me. "But I'll order it so. If your prosecutor wants an explanation, it's because the end of the year is near and you have little time to formulate your defense, so I am allowing you extraordinary privileges to clear yourself." He left it unsaid that I now owed him a big political favor.

I took Hermes by the shoulder. "Go get Asklepiodes. Tell him to meet with me and the unfortunate Marcus Fulvius at the temple immediately."

"I'm off." And so he was.

"What do you expect to learn from the Greek?" Father wanted to know.

"I have some fairly strong suspicions, and I'd like to have them confirmed by an expert. I'll explain when I am more certain of the facts."

They all took on the look they got when I spoke of my methods of ferreting out the facts of a case. I had won many prosecutions my way, but it never convinced them. They thought the proper way to win a case was to get prominent people to swear to your innocence and the vileness of your opponent. Then you bribed the jury.

A litter made its way across the Forum and stopped at the basilica. Hortensius Hortalus emerged, accompanied by the aged Claudius Marcellus. Still augur-robed and leaning on his *lituus*, he trudged up the steps to where we stood.

"What's all this?" he asked, looking down at the body. His friends filled him in on the morning's doings while I examined the steps. I hoped to find signs of whether the body had been dragged or carried to the basilica, but the crowd had gathered too quickly. If there had been bloodstains, they were now on the bottoms of a thousand pairs of sandals. I was, however, certain that the murder had not been committed on the spot where the body was found. There would have been a small river of blood running down the steps, more than could have been obliterated by a legion tramping through.

"Did you perceive any omens?" I asked Hortalus.

"Not a thing," he admitted. "It was too cloudy to see the stars, no birds flew in the night, and we heard no thunder from any direction. Of course, since there's to be no trial, omens were scarcely called for. Marcus Fulvius was no prince, so comets and bloody rains are hardly to be expected."

"It would have been convenient," Cato said, "if you'd seen something to stop this convening of the Plebeian Assembly."

"Actually," Father put in, "some good legal advice is what is called for now."

Hortalus turned to me. "Decius, I think you should find out whatever you can to blacken the reputation of Marcus Fulvius. Treason would be nice."

I managed to shake my way free of Sallustius and the others and made my way to the Temple of Venus in her aspect as death goddess. It had recently been handsomely restored by Caesar. Although his family traced their descent from Venus Genetrix, Caesar had been generous to any temple of Venus in need of refurbishing.

Asklepiodes arrived shortly after I did, carried on a fine litter by a team of matched Nubians. Hermes and two of the physician's Egyptian slaves followed. He had grown quite wealthy over the years, and, unlike most of his profession, he did it through sound medical practice not by selling quack cures. He was the only physician to whom I entrusted my lacerations.

"Greetings, Decius Caecilius!" he said, alighting from his conveyance. "Rejoice! So lately returned to Rome; so soon involved in a murder!"

"Not just involved. Accused."

"And not for the first time. Let's have a look at the departed."

The body had been laid out on a bier and washed. With the blood off him Marcus Fulvius looked, if anything, even more ghastly. There is something especially grotesque about a body that has had all the blood drained from it. He was white as a cauliflower, except for the relatively colorful bulges of viscera. Even the gaping wounds were pale pink instead of scarlet. Adding to the strangeness of the scene was the contrast between the ravaged body and the untouched head and limbs.

Asklepiodes made a gesture and the Egyptians came forward. One carried, by a strap over his shoulder, a box elaborately decorated with mother-of-pearl and lapis lazuli. This man opened the box and the other, at Asklepiodes' murmured instructions, removed surgical instruments and began to probe at the wounds. In his own surgery, Asklepiodes might have wielded the instruments himself, but he would never allow the priests of the temple to see a haughty physician using his hands like a common surgeon. As each wound was spread wider he leaned over, examined it, and made wise sounds. Finally, he stepped back.

"Well?" I said.

"No doubt about it, this man is dead."

"It is good to be in the presence of genius. What else?"

"Someone was being—how shall I put this?—rather delicate about this murder. We have the marks of at least three different blades, any one of which would have been quite sufficient to cause death, but they were used to deal wounds that were grievous, some of them fatal over a matter of hours or days, yet not causing immediate death."

"Cato noted the inefficiency of the blows," I said, "and he is not a particularly observant man."

"The cut to the great vessel of the neck"—Asklepiodes pointed to the wound below the left ear—"would have been fatal within seconds, yet I believe it was dealt last, as if the man were being too leisurely about dying. All these stabs to the abdomen for instance. A single stab here," he pointed to the apex of the rib arch just below the sternum, "angled slightly upward, would have pierced the heart and brought about immediate death. I have the distinct impression that these men did not *want* their victim to die quickly."

"You mentioned three weapons."

"At least three, possibly more."

"Can you describe them?"

"There were two types: one narrow-bladed, the other broad. I see wounds produced by at least one of these narrow blades. The dagger was no more than an inch wide, its cross-section of a flattened diamond shape. There were at least two broad-bladed daggers used: both were in excess of two inches wide, one made of rather thin steel with a thickened midrib for rigidity. The other was of stouter metal without the midrib. Instead it had three parallel grooves to add strength and rigidity to the blade, as well as to lighten it and confer better balance." As physician to the gladiators of the Statilian *ludus*, his knowledge of edged weapons was comprehensive.

"Like a soldier's *pugio?*" I asked.

"*Pugios* have such blades."

"And all the weapons were double-edged? These cuts look like they were made by a *sica*." I referred to the curved, single-edged knife favored by street thugs.

"These were not delivered as cuts. The wounds are very asymmetrical. In each case the blade was stabbed in, then dragged from right to left as it was withdrawn. This is characteristic of a right-handed assailant. The gash thus opened is wide, but not very deep. A typical *sica* cut is symmetrical and deepest in the center."

"So we are looking at a minimum of three murderers?" I asked.

"At least three knife wielders and possibly more. But there were others involved."

"How so?"

"You notice that there are no wounds to the hands and arms?"

"I wondered at that."

"Any man, seeing hostile blades attacking his body, will try to ward them off instinctively. For this many weapons to have landed on his torso, he should have received many cuts on his arms and hands."

"He was held."

"Held from behind, hence no wounds in the back."

"Is it possible he was bound?" I asked.

"A man being killed struggles hard against bindings. It leaves deep ligature marks on the wrists, and this man has none. I believe that, had the body not bled out so thoroughly, we should see bruises on the shoulders and arms, where at least two strong men held him fast while he was stabbed."

Hermes spoke up. "Might he have been asleep? If he was lying on his back there'd be no wounds there, and by the time he woke up he might have been too weak to defend himself."

"No," Asklepiodes said, "these blows were not delivered downward. The angle of entry would be quite different."

"Besides," I said, "he was stabbed through his tunic." I looked around and found a temple slave. "Bring us the dead man's garments." He trotted off and in a few minutes I told the physician about the strange events of the last two days.

A few minutes later the slave brought the bloody toga and tunic. He even had the dead man's sandals. "We were about to burn them," the slave said.

"I am going to keep these as evidence." At my request Asklepiodes' slaves spread the clothes on the floor. There were numerous rents in the tunic, but the toga, though stained, was whole.

"It looks like he wasn't wearing the toga when he was killed. The murderers must have wrapped him up in it to carry him to the Forum and leave his body where we were sure to find it."

"Why was he wearing such shabby clothes?" Hermes wanted to know.

"I am wondering that, too. He was of good birth, although he'd won no distinction in Rome. Yesterday, when he berated me in the Forum, his clothes were of good quality. He would have worn his best coming to appear in court today. Hermes, I want you to take these home with you. They might prove significant later on."

"Carry these rags?" he exclaimed with horror. "They're unclean!"

"You're ready enough to shed other peoples' blood. I don't see why you should object to getting a little of it on you. It's all but dry, anyway."

"I'm not going to touch this stuff," he said stubbornly. "I don't care how many purifications the priest performs."

"I hate superstition," I said. "All right, there should be a sack around here someplace. Get a temple slave to bag this up for you first." He went off in search of one.

"Sometimes I regret giving that boy his freedom," I said to Asklepiodes. "Now he thinks he's too good to run errands."

"He's grown into a fine-looking young man though. I've missed seeing him practice at the school in recent months."

"He should be glad I never sent him to the mines."

"I trust your lady, Julia, is well? Is she still bothered by her family complaint?" By this he meant the famous difficulty the Caesars had with conception and pregnancy. Since our marriage Julia had conceived three times and miscarried by the fourth month in all three cases.

"Still. I try to comfort her, tell her that this is her heritage and there is no disgrace in it, but she feels humiliated nonetheless."

He shook his head. "I do hope she is not going to unscrupulous physicians and wise women to cure the problem. They are all frauds, and their remedies are sometimes dangerous."

"I warn her not to, but I fear she does it anyway."

"I know of no treatment for infertility other than maintaining her health through a good diet and moderate living. Beyond that, one can only sacrifice to the gods of fertility and hope for their favor."

"I thank you for your concern, old friend."

At that moment Hermes returned with a bag and a slave. With the gory clothes bundled up, we took our leave of Asklepiodes and left the temple.

Julia was ready when I got back home. "What's this about you being involved in a murder?" she said, even as the door swung open. She caught sight of Hermes behind me. "And what's in that bag?"

"Just some bloody clothes," he said. "What the murdered man was wearing."

"You will not bring any such thing into this house!"

"Oh, come now, my dear," I said reasonably, "I've bled all over this house and no harm has come of it."

"*Your* blood attracts nothing but flies," she answered. "A murdered man's garments can attract his vengeful spirit, and that man wasn't well-disposed toward you when he was alive!"

I turned to Hermes. "Go stash that bag with the tavern keeper down the street. He won't ask questions." Most of my neighbors were under obligation to me. "And don't hang around drinking either. We have a lot still to do today." I went on inside.

Julia had laid out baked fish, sliced melon, and bread. Between bites I told her of the morning's doings. She didn't pale much when I described the condition of the body. She'd seen worse.

"So it wasn't just one man out for a reputation," she said. "I didn't think so. But now there seems to be a whole crowd involved. A conspiracy. I think it's to be expected if it's a move against your family."

"Possibly against the great families in general," I pointed out.

She raised a hand to her brow. "Let's try to limit this. If it's a prelude to class war, it's too big for us."

"Do you know anything about this tribune, Manilius?" Julia had spent far more time in Rome than I in recent years.

"Just another young climber. Do you think he's involved?"

"He was on the scene awfully fast, and of all the tribunes, he's the only one I've heard of who has declared neither for Caesar nor Pompey."

"That *is* odd. Will you attend this *contio* he's called?"

"My presence might be seen as disruptive. Besides, I want to use whatever time I have left free to investigate. If he gets a decision to go to trial before the whole assembly, he may call for my arrest." Usually, that meant that I would be confined to the house of one of the praetors until trial. I could always flee the City; but that would be an admission of guilt and I would just be tried in absentia, found guilty, and exiled.

I pushed away the plates. "Now tell me what you learned yesterday."

She picked at her own lunch, which consisted mostly of fruit. I wondered if this were another of her fertility-inducing fads. The pomegranites suggested I was right.

"I called on Fulvia yesterday evening. As I suspected, she was glad of company. Clodius's old friends are mostly staying away from town, and she won't be received in decent society. Her brother-in-law, Appius, is even making noises about taking the house back."

"Unfortunate woman," I said idly.

"She's brought it on herself. Anyway, she says she was about to give up and go back home to Baiae, but now she's thought better of it since she's to remarry."

"I don't expect to see Antonius back from Gaul anytime soon," I said, raising a cup of her heavily watered wine.

"But she isn't to marry Antonius. She's going to marry that man you asked about this morning: Curio."

I all but choked in midswallow. "What!"

"Exactly," she said, pleased with her timing and effect. "Curio was one of Clodius's friends who stayed in Rome. He's on the rise, which is where Fulvia likes to catch them. He's standing for Tribune of the People, and if he's elected, he can't leave Rome for two consecutive nights during his year in office, so she can't very well leave Rome, can she?"

"But what about her betrothal to Antonius?"

"Neither of them is terribly serious about such things. They are two of a kind. Besides, Antonius is in Gaul while Curio is here. That makes a difference."

I knew Antonius well, and I knew that, if news of losing Fulvia to another man bothered him at all, he'd just console himself by taking another Gallic woman into his tent, to join the five or six who were already there.

"Did you learn anything about her brother, Fulvius?"

"She said that, at home, he'd been a layabout who accomplished nothing. He'd written her some time ago that he intended to come to Rome to become Clodius's client, but Clodius was killed and Fulvius stayed in Baiae. Apparently, if he couldn't get a great man to be his patron, he didn't think he had much chance of rising in Roman politics."

"So why did he come here?"

"She said that a few months ago he wrote her, said he was coming after all, and hinted that he now had powerful patronage."

"But he wouldn't say who it was?"

"He said that she'd learn soon enough. After he moved here he called on her a few times; but there was little affection between them, and he didn't talk about anything important."

"Where was he living?"

"He had a house near the Temple of Tellus," she said. "She never went there."

"Housing in Rome isn't cheap," I said, "even slum housing. Did she know who owned the place?"

"I didn't think to ask her, but if she knows so little about her brother, I would doubt that the name of his landlord would be among her store of facts."

"*If* she was telling you the truth. Somehow, truthfulness is not the quality that first comes to mind when discussing Fulvia."

"Well, it may be true that her evil reputation is exaggerated. I felt rather sorry for her. It is a terrible thing for a woman of her birth, accustomed to every privilege and honor, to be forsaken by her own class. While Clodius was alive she could fancy herself the uncrowned queen of Rome. Now she is a friendless widow."

"Not entirely friendless, if she's to marry this Curio. I think I should talk to her."

Julia's eyes narrowed. "Why?"

"I'm not as sympathetic as you. She might be more forthcoming under more rigorous questioning."

Julia bit into an orange section. "Why should she talk to you at all? You have no official standing, and she may hold it against you that you killed her brother."

"I doubt that. I suspect that she knows perfectly well I did not."

"How are you so sure?"

"I didn't say I was *sure*. I said I *suspect*."

Julia rolled her eyes. Sometimes even she had trouble understanding me.

4

I WANT YOU," I TOLD HERMES, "TO FIND out where Fulvius lived. It was somewhere near the Temple of Tellus. Once you've located the place, find out who owns it. Then report back to me."

"I'll do it," he said. "Are you really going to Clodius's house?"

"Clodius is dead. His widow has a bad reputation, but I don't think she wants to kill me."

"Take some men with you anyway." We stood in my atrium with a crowd of my clients. A lot of them were hard-looking specimens: veterans from my various military postings who had attached themselves to me; farmers from Metellan-dominated areas of the countryside, in town for the elections; a few of Milo's old gang, who needed a patron while he was in exile.

"It wouldn't look good to have them with me in the daytime," I told him. "I won't have the voters thinking I go around in fear of my fellow citizens. I want these men to attend the Plebeian Assembly meeting and shout my praises."

He looked disgusted. "You're getting as bad as Julia. What's more dangerous than your fellow citizens? Just be careful, and keep your weapons handy."

"Did I take you on as a nurse?"

Out in the streets, I felt a pleasant sense of freedom, being on my own for a change. Since returning to Rome, I had been going everywhere amid a cloud of my supporters, constantly campaigning for election. It felt good to be alone. Since the gangs had been broken up and the noncitizens driven from the City, it was considered bad form for a politician to go around with a violent-looking following, although a small bodyguard was permissible. The voters would appreciate my show of bravado in appearing in public without so much as a single slave.

Being under suspicion of murder did not hamper my freedom. This is because Romans are civilized people and don't clap suspects into prison like barbarians. It would take an order of a lawfully convened court even to place me under house arrest.

When I came to the house of the late Publius Clodius Pulcher I thought how strange it was that I could just walk up to the door and knock. There were times when my life would have been forfeit just for showing up in the neighborhood. It was situated in the most fashionable district of the Palatine, just as in Catullus's famous poem: "... five doors up the Clivus Victoriae. . . ."

The janitor who opened up at my knock wasn't the usual aged, used-up slave you usually found performing that task. This one was a stalwart young man with handsome, Cappadocian features, wearing a brief tunic. The housekeeper to whom I gave my name and errand was a raven-haired Greek beauty and all the household slaves, at least in the front of the *domus*, were pretty boys and girls. Some things hadn't changed in this household anyway. Clodia had had a similar liking for beautiful things.

"Please come with me, Senator," the housekeeper said, returning from the inner fastnesses of the mansion. I followed her attractively swaying backside to the peristyle, where rare trees and shrubs grew from giant pots surrounding the pool. The woman showed me to an exquisite bronze table, its fretwork discus supported by three ithyphallic satyrs. The chair was one of three made as a suite with the table, all of the finest Campanian bronzework. Their cushions were stuffed with down and sweet herbs. This was one of those luxurious households Cato was always railing about.

"Please be seated, Senator. My lady will be here presently." I sat and a pair of twin German slave girls brought a pitcher of hammered gold and cups of the same metal, embossed with doves and flowers. The wine was the exquisite Caecuban favored by the Claudian family, wholly unwatered.

While I sipped, admiring the Greek statuary, I tried to guess from which direction Fulvia would make her entrance. Every doorway opening off the peristyle was beautifully decorated and flanked by fine sculpture. Finally I settled on the door with Leda and the swan on one side, Ganymede and the eagle on the other. Both had been executed in scandalous erotic detail and were the most eye-catching works of art within sight. I was right. When she arrived it was between those two statues and for further counterpoint, the pale marble contrasted nicely with her gown.

Leave it to Fulvia to look good in mourning. In tribute to her recently departed brother, she wore a black gown, its fabric sheer to near-transparency, the gatherings of the sleeves drooping so low as to leave her arms and shoulders almost bare.

"Decius Caecilius!" She came forward, one hand extended. "Just yesterday your wife called for the first time in years; today I have the pleasure of your company. Dare I hope this signifies a warming of relations between us?" Her furry voice was as sensuous as her tiny, voluptuous body.

I took her hand. "My feelings for you have always been of the warmest, Fulvia, although your late husband and I had our differences. And speaking of relations, please accept my condolences on the untimely death of your brother."

I fought to suppress the usual effect this woman had on me. Fulvia was in her midtwenties and at the height of her beauty. She was, in fact, one of Rome's great beauties, more so even than Clodia and the equal of Fausta, the daughter of Sulla. But where Fausta's beauty was icily patrician, Fulvia's had a carnality we usually associate with Alexandrian whores and Spanish dancers from Gades. Her abundant, tawny hair; her huge, heavy-lidded gray eyes; her wide, full lips, all held promise of infinite depravity.

"Very kind of you, Decius, but I scarcely knew him." She sat and one of the twins filled a cup for her. In those days women weren't supposed to drink unwatered wine, but they weren't supposed to wear those sheer gowns either. "People are saying you killed him, but I don't believe it. I've heard he was butchered horribly, and I know that you would do a quick, clean job of it."

"You flatter me. Yes, I've never killed a man willingly, but when forced to it I've always gotten the business done with as little fuss as possible."

"I'll have to see to his funeral arrangements. I still have a few friends. One of them is coming here soon to handle the details. I think I'll just have him cremated here and send his ashes back to Baiae for the full funeral treatment and interment in the family tomb. It's on a beautiful site beside the bay."

"That would be best," I told her. "With so few friends and relations here in Rome, he wouldn't get a send-off proper to a man of his ancestry."

"I'm so glad you agree. I have a bad enough reputation without appearing dry-eyed at the funeral. I am really not very good at wailing and clothes rending, although I did my best for poor Clodius."

"That was a noisy funeral, what with the riot and the burning of the Senate house. I'm sorry I missed it." I took another long drink of the Caecuban and held out the cup for a refill. "On a happier note though, I understand congratulations are in order. You are to marry Scribonius Curio?"

"Oh, yes. I know Antonius will be disappointed, but he'll just shrug and wait for me to be widowed again. It happens often when your husband is in politics."

"Too true. I don't envy you if he wins the tribuneship."

She rolled her eyes. "All the gods protect me! I've been a tribune's wife before—people tramping through the house at all hours, stuck here in Rome in the hottest weather, constant political meetings—it's all a great bother, but it establishes a man's political reputation like no other office." Among other things, a Tribune of the People was forbidden to lock or even close the doors of his house. He had to be accessible to the people at any hour.

"So it does. Might I ask how it comes about that you are going to marry this man?"

Fulvia looked as if she needed to give this some real thought. "To be honest, he asked. I haven't been exactly mobbed by suitors lately. Men want me, but they are intimidated by me." She said this as matter-of-factly as she would have if someone remarked upon the color of her eyes. "Or they are afraid of the memory of Clodius—of having to bear comparison with him. That was one thing that attracted me to Antonius—he's afraid of nothing and nobody. Curio is the same way."

"Antonius is rather dense," I told her. "Fearless men often are."

"Curio isn't dense. You haven't met him?"

"Never had the pleasure. I know Cicero regarded him as something of a protégé at one time, thought he possessed great gifts."

"Cicero!" she said with venom. "I hate that man! He pretends to be such a virtuous and pure servant of the Republic, but his brand of politics is no cleaner than Clodius's was. And Clodius really *did* things for the people. Cicero fawns on the aristocrats and acts as their mouthpiece—people who despise him as an out-of-town upstart if he only knew it!"

I was a little taken aback by this sudden fury, but she shed it as quickly as it had appeared.

"Forgive me. I get angry when anyone mentions that man. It wouldn't be so bad if Cicero wasn't such a hypocrite."

"Do you think it was a tribuneship your brother was pursuing when he came to Rome?"

"It might have been. I am sure the action and drama of a tribune's life would have appealed to him far more than the drudgery of a quaestorship." These were the two offices that would boost a man into the Senate.

"But all political offices are costly. He would have needed a wealthy patron to underwrite his expenses, unless he had family money."

"No, our eldest brother, Manius, has control of that. And he's quite happy being one of the biggest frogs in the pond of Baiae."

"Baiae is a wonderful place," I said. "I wonder that any of you left."

"Luxury is good," she said. "Power is better." She took another sip and looked around her. "Luxury with power is best of all."

I could scarcely argue with the logic of that statement. Moments later the comely housekeeper arrived with the news that Fulvia's obsequy-arranging friend was in the atrium.

"Bring him in, Echo. I want Decius Caecilius to meet him."

Moments later a well-favored young man entered the peristyle. "Decius Caecilius," Fulvia said, "I want you to meet Caius Scribonius Curio, my dear friend, future husband, and soon to be Tribune of the People."

I took his hand and we studied each other. Curio was about twenty-five, well built, with sandy hair and bright blue eyes. His hand had broken knuckles and calluses only in the places where weapons-training will put them. His square face was hard and belligerent, which was a good sort of face for a tribune to have in those days. His nose was slightly askew, his ears a bit deformed, and his eyebrows scarred, all marks of the boxing enthusiast. This was something of a rarity among upper-class Romans, who preferred wrestling or armed combat. What he saw I cannot say for certain, but I suspect he classified me as a man approaching his middle years who lived too hard and drank too much. In other words, typical of my generation and class.

"You are a man to whom Fortuna has been generous, if all that I hear is true," I said.

"I've wanted to make your acquaintance for a long time," Curio responded, "but I scarcely expected to find you in this house this day."

"Believe me," I said, "I am not polluted with the blood of Fulvia's brother. I didn't even step in it. I came to ask about him, since I may have to defend myself in court."

"I'm sure Decius didn't do it," Fulvia said. "His reputation is that of a forthright brawler, not a murderer."

"I've heard that manly combat is the technique of heedless youth, careful assassination that of maturity. But I am certain that you are right, my dear. The fact that you entertain Decius in your house proclaims his innocence."

"If you believe it," I said, "why not bring it up at the *contio* this afternoon?"

"I shall do so," he said, smiling.

"Oh, don't," Fulvia said wearily. "Everyone will just take it as further proof that I'm the most disreputable woman in Rome."

"Nonsense," he said. "I've already undertaken to rehabilitate your reputation. I'll lay all your indiscretions at the feet of Clodius and his sisters. You were their helpless, unfortunate victim."

I arched an eyebrow toward Fulvia. She just shrugged. He turned to me.

"Have you any idea why Fulvius chose to attack you? Other than the usual political motives, I mean?"

"None at all. I'd never heard of the man before yesterday. Of course, the City is always full of politically ambitious men, and never more so than at this time of year. Why he should pick me out of all the others he could choose from I can't guess. Give any well-informed Roman a chance to name the most distinguished men of the Republic, and he'll be reeling off names for an hour before he thinks of me."

"You are too modest," Fulvia assured me. "Even if you aren't famous for conquering barbarians, you've always been popular here in the City, both as a public prosecutor and as an administrator. Not as incorruptible as Cato, I understand, but you're believed to be relatively honest; and everyone enjoyed the games you celebrated."

"No one is as incorruptible as Cato, as he'll tell you himself. And if my games were a hit, it's because I enjoy them myself."

"You see?" Curio said. "The people like you because they know you share their tastes. I'm surprised you never sought the tribuneship yourself."

"My family discussed the possibility a few years ago," I told him, "but I was in Gaul during the desired year. I was probably safer there. In Gaul you can recognize your enemies from a distance."

"The tribuneship is not to everyone's taste," Curio said.

"Speaking of that office," I said, "do you know Manilius, the one who's called the *contio* to discuss the murder?" I was curious to hear what Curio had to say about the man.

"A good man. I've been assisting him all year, sort of an apprenticeship prior to taking on the job myself." This was not an uncommon practice. Officials always needed helper, and these were often men in training for the same office. Except for a few public slaves, such as those at the Archive and the Treasury, the Republic supplied no staff to assist the elected officials in their work. Instead, they were expected to supply their own, at their own expense.

"He has only a few days left in office," I said. "I wonder that he wants to take on what could turn into a major case so late."

"His last major act in office is what will stick in peoples' minds at the next elections."

"Where do his ambitions lie?" I asked. "The legions? The courts? Provincial administration?" In earlier times a Roman in public life was expected to be adept at everything. He was supposed to be a soldier, a speaker, a lawyer, a farmer, and many other things. But the Republic had grown huge and complex since the days of our forefathers. It had turned into an Empire, and its public business was too complicated for one man to master it all. The tendency was for men to specialize, so that now we had prominent men who were lawyers undistinguished in war, like Cicero and Hortalus, full-time soldiers like Pompey, and businessmen like Crassus. Caesar was something of a throwback: a man who seemed able to do everything well.

"Manilius acts as if his only ambition is to serve in whatever capacity the Roman people see fit to bestow upon him," Curio said. "This may be sincere or a pose; I don't know him well enough to say. Like most of us he started out as a Tribune of the Soldiers. He was with Gabinius in Syria and Egypt. He seems to have served honorably, but I never heard that he earned great distinction. I get the impression that Gabinius didn't entrust him with as much responsibility as he thought he deserved."

"He was lucky it wasn't Caesar," I said. "Caesar treats his tribunes like none-too-bright schoolboys—tells them to keep their mouths shut and watch the *real* soldiers at work. A tribune can be with Caesar for a year without being given so much as a squadron of cavalry to command."

"Is that because he thinks they're incompetent or because most of them are sons of his political enemies?"

This was a very astute question. Whatever his debts and disreputable history, there was nothing wrong with Curio's political instincts.

"Both, I believe. Everyone knows the contempt in which Caesar holds the Senate. He also makes it a policy to exalt the centurionate and the common soldiers. This reinforces his influence with the *populares*. Of course," I added, "everyone who's ever soldiered knows what an embarrassment an eighteen-year-old tribune can be. They rarely perform as well as young Cassius did in Syria this year."

"That boy could become a power in Rome when he returns," Curio noted. "The Senate may be stingy with the honors it owes him, but he's sure to be a darling of the plebs for that very reason."

"I doubt it," Fulvia said. "I know Cassius. He's a handsome young man, very bright, but as upright and old-fashioned as Cato. He'll side with the aristocrats even while they kick him in the face." There was nothing wrong with Fulvia's evaluation of men either. Cassius did exactly as she predicted.

Our conversation may seem frank and unguarded for two men who did not know each other, but there was nothing truly unguarded about what we said. We both expected to hold office in the following year. We would have to work with one another, so it made sense to feel one another out while we had this opportunity.

"In recent years," Curio said, "you've been known to break with your family's *optimate* stance. Do you intend to switch to the *populares?*"

"I have no faction," I intoned gravely. "I always vote for the good of Rome." This mealy mouthed protestation raised a good laugh. It was what every last politician in Rome always claimed. You never belonged to a faction. Your opponents belonged to factions. Truthfully, I detested the faction politics of the times, but you had to choose one sooner or later. "My family tolerates a little leeway," I went on, more seriously. "After all, we've been anti-Pompeians in the past, but Nepos has never been shut out of family councils even though he's been Pompey's lifelong friend and supporter. If I sometimes lean toward the popular cause, it's always on an issue my family can live with. I suspect that, should it come to a clear break between the factions, I'll side with my family as always."

"That would be a pity," Curio said. "Because the Metelli are sure to stick with the aristocratic side, and the day of the aristocrats is past. Power now lies with the plebs. Clodius knew it, I know it, Caesar most surely knows it."

"And yet I understand that, until very recently, you stood solidly with the *optimates.*"

"For a long time I held a young man's belief in the wisdom of his elders. But we must all grow up sooner or later. Recently, I had a very illuminating talk with Caesar, and I knew it was time to change sides."

"Caesar covered your debts, too, I hear."

"There's no disgrace in that," he said, quite unembarrassed. "Pompey offered to do as much. The disgrace is in accepting a man's patronage and then betraying him. Admit it, Decius Caecilius: Wouldn't it be better for a man like Caesar to manage Rome and Rome's Empire for the good of all citizens, than for a few dozen dwindling old families to run it all for their own benefit, as if Rome were still a little city-state controlled by a few rich farmers?"

"You're not haranguing the *consilium plebis*," I told him. "There is something in what you say, but there's also great danger. The *optimates* often behave foolishly and selfishly, but so do the *populares*. Any degree of mismanagement is better than civil war, which is what we'll have if it comes to a contest between the two. We've had too much of that already."

"So we have," he said reasonably. "Well, let's hope it never comes to that."

We drank to that fond wish, and I rose. "You two have funerary arrangements to attend to so I'll trouble you no longer."

"Let me know how your investigation goes," Curio said. "I'll speak up in the *contio* against your being charged with the murder."

"I thank you for that. I suspect you'll be hearing all about my findings. Fulvia, I thank you for your hospitality at such a difficult time."

"Echo," she called, "the senator is leaving. Decius Caecilius, please call again when you can spend more time."

The shapely Greek saw me to the door, and I found Hermes standing outside. His eyes popped when he saw the housekeeper, and she smiled at him as she closed the door.

"Don't go looking for likely prospects in that house," I warned him.

He sighed. "They say the best-looking women in Rome live in that house."

"I wouldn't bet against it."

"Did you get anything accomplished?" he asked me.

"I've just been talking politics."

"With *Fulvia?*"

We began to walk toward the Temple of Tellus, and Hermes wouldn't tell me what he'd found out until he heard all about my visit.

"Why is this man Curio being so helpful?" Hermes wanted to know.

"He knows I'm in Caesar's good graces and married to his niece. He's Caesar's man now, and he thinks that by siding with me in this odd case he'll be driving me further into Caesar's camp, which is the last place I want to be."

It was not a long walk down the slope of the Palatine, across the Via Sacra, and up the slope of the Oppian Hill toward the temple. The Carinae district had some fine houses in it, and we stopped before one of the more modest of them. It was part of a three-story block, and looming above it could be seen the bronze roof of the temple.

Such buildings were the typical dwellings of Rome's more prosperous inhabitants, those not wealthy enough to own their own homes but able to afford the rent on the better class of apartments.

The poor lived in towering, rickety *insulae* and endured a precarious, dangerous existence without amenities.

"Who owns it?" I asked.

"Claudius Marcellus."

"The consul?"

"No, the one standing for next year's consulship: Caius Claudius, not Marcus Claudius."

"I never have any luck with that family," I complained. "There are entirely too many of them around lately."

"The building is divided into four large apartments, each having three floors. It doesn't have separate, upper-floor apartments rented out to poor families. The ground floor has water piped in. There's a central pool shared by all." A fairly typical arrangement for such a dwelling.

"Prosperous merchants live in houses like this," I said. "How did a penniless political adventurer like Fulvius afford it?"

"That's your specialty," Hermes said. "I just found out what I could about the place."

"Who was your informant?"

He pointed to a barber who had his stool placed on a corner across from the house. The man was shaving a customer while another stood by waiting his turn. Barbers are among the best informants an investigator can have. They often occupy the same spot for many years, they shave most of the men in the neighborhood, they see everything that happens on the street, and they collect all the gossip.

I didn't know a great deal about this particular Claudius Marcellus. He was only a distant relation of Clodius and his sisters, the Claudia Marcella having split off from the Claudia Pulchri back somewhere in the dim mists of antiquity. He was known in the Senate as one of the more virulent anti-Caesarians.

"Let's have a look at the place," I said.

We crossed the street and Hermes rapped on the door. Nobody answered. He gave it a push and it opened easily. He looked at me inquiringly, and I gestured for him to go in. I followed. Hermes vented a shrill whistle. Still no reply.

"Looks like nobody's home," he observed.

"That's odd. In the Forum he seemed to be well-supplied with friends. Why aren't any here, protecting his property? And where are his slaves?" Granted the man was poor, but he would have to be destitute indeed not to have at least a janitor to man the front door and a housekeeper. A bachelor can get along without a cook, relying on street vendors, taverns, and cadging meals. A valet is not absolutely necessary, although a would-be senator cuts a poor figure carrying his own books and papers, and hauling his own towel, oil flask, and scraper to the baths. Three to five household slaves were generally considered the absolute minimum for respectability. I got along for years with only two or three, but I also fell short of most other standards of respectability.

"Maybe he borrowed slaves as he needed them," Hermes said, following my own line of thought. He had been with me so long we thought alike in these matters.

"Probably from the same man who must have let him have this place rent free," I said. "Let's look around."

The place was not palatial, but it was better than the house I lived in when I began my political career. In truth Rome had few truly splendid houses in those days. Even the very wealthy men like Hortalus and Lucullus spent lavishly on their country villas but maintained fairly modest establishments in the City. Voters took it ill when a senator chose to live like a prince. In the City the rule was to spend freely on public works and stingily on yourself. Lucullus had made himself unpopular by building himself a pretentious mansion in the City after his Asian victories. He quickly demolished it and turned the grounds into a public garden, thus restoring his popularity with the plebs.

The triclinium was spacious, with excellent furnishings, as if Fulvius had expected to do a fair amount of entertaining there. The wall-paintings were fine and new, the subject matter patriotic rather than the more fashionable mythological themes. One wall featured the *Oath of the Horatii,* another the colorful story of Mucius Scaevola, a third was Cincinnatus at his plow. The fourth wall was pierced by the door so its decoration was floral.

"Odd decoration for a dining room," Hermes observed. "Where are the feasting gods and goddesses and the satyrs chasing nymphs?"

"Perhaps Fulvius wanted to encourage serious dinner-table discussion," I hazarded. "Nymphs and satyrs are frivolous. Just ask Cato." Cato's prudery was the butt of jokes wherever Romans met.

"If he has old patriots decorating his bedroom we'll know there was something strange about the man," Hermes observed.

"Actually I'm more interested in his papers than in his taste in interior decorating. Let's see what he used for a study."

Not every house had a study. Some men just kept their papers in a chest and did all their reading and writing in the peristyle or a garden. It was commonly thought that reading by any light other than direct sunlight would ruin your eyes. Some sought to further preserve their eyesight by having trained slaves read to them. Some kept secretaries to take dictation and never personally set hand to pen.

Fulvius, as it occurred, had used his bedroom for this purpose. One side of it opened onto a small balcony overlooking the street. This was a common arrangement in multistory houses such as this one. The ground floor contained the atrium, kitchen, and dining room, and opened onto the central garden. It was the public part of the house. The second floor held the family's sleeping quarters, and the third floor was for storage and slaves' quarters. The balcony was another feature common to such houses. It offered a quick escape in case of a fire. All Romans went in dread of fire, and those who lived in the towering *insulae* were the most fearful of all.

The door to the balcony was flanked by a pair of large, latticed windows and beneath one of these was his desk. It was a very fine one, Egyptian work of ebony inlaid with ivory. Next to it was a wooden honeycomb that held scrolls, rolled papers, and wax tablets. A silver-mounted horn tube held reed pens, and a fine crystal stand held different colors of ink in little pots shaped like lotus flowers.

Lying on the desk, half unrolled as if put down in the midst of reading, was a book whose excellent parchment was supple and slightly ragged at the edges, a clear sign that this was a favorite work, often read. It appeared to be a speech or collection of speeches arguing points of law. Such books were the inevitable texts for training aspiring lawyers.

Folded on a cupboard next to the desk lay his wardrobe. Among the tunics, most bore the narrow purple stripe of an *eques*, but two had the broad stripe to which a senator was entitled. There were two togas.

One was white, doubtless the one he'd worn when berating me in the Forum the previous day. The other was the *toga praetexta*, with the broad purple border of curule office.

"He came prepared," I remarked. "And he certainly had confidence. He expected admission to the Senate and a curule chair. Like that Greek athlete who showed up at Olympia with his statue already made. At least he didn't lay in a supply of *triumphator*'s robes. I suppose even his presumption had limits."

"Look at this," Hermes said. Accomplished thief that he was, he'd found a small drawer cleverly hidden among the decorative carvings of the desk. It held a signet ring; a massive thing of solid gold, its surface oddly but attractively granulated. Its large stone was pure sapphire with a Medusa head carved intaglio. It looked to me like Greek work. I examined it briefly and tossed it back to him.

"The man was full of surprises, wasn't he? Can his correspondence be less interesting?" I began to pull papers out and spread them on the desk. "Well, I might have expected it," I said disgustedly.

"That's Greek, isn't it?" said Hermes. He could read and write Latin well enough, but he had never learned to read Greek, although, like me, he could speak conversational Greek passably. Anyone who traveled widely has to learn some Greek, as it is spoken everywhere. But poetic and literary Greek is another matter. Many educated men, like Cicero, were as comfortable with Greek as with their native language, but I was not among them. I could piece my way through a simple letter in Greek if given enough time, but I could see that my schoolboy Greek wouldn't serve me here.

"It isn't just Greek," I told him, "it's in some sort of cipher."

"Someone coming," Hermes muttered. I heard footsteps on the stairs. The noise from the street outside had masked the sounds of someone entering the house. I swept up the documents I'd spread out and stuffed them inside my tunic even as Hermes shut the tiny drawer. By the time the men shouldered their way into the room, we had assumed poses of dignified innocence.

"What are you doing here?" demanded the first one through. He was the red-haired lout, and he wasn't alone. Behind him was the one Hermes had pummeled, and there were others on the stair. "How did you get in?"

"Same as you, through the front door," Hermes said. "It wasn't locked."

"As for what we're doing here," I said, "I came here to see these putative witnesses against me. But we've found no sign that anyone was ever here except Marcus Fulvius, despite your claim to the praetor Juventius this morning." Actually, we had not yet had time to examine the top floor, but by now I was convinced that these witnesses were entirely fictitious.

"You're a liar!" shouted the battered one. "You came here to steal!"

"How about you?" I said, going immediately on the counterattack. "Thought you'd take advantage of your friend's death, did you? Thought you'd just run over here and lift whatever's loose and easily fenced before his relatives showed up, eh? Well, you won't get away with it this time!" Meanwhile, we were sidling toward the door.

"Don't be absurd!" said the red-haired one. "Stop them!"

Immediately, we reversed direction. We had no way of knowing how many might be on the stairway and in the rooms below. I sprang for the balcony as Hermes drew his dagger and covered my retreat. One of the political perquisites of age, dignity, and high office was that you could let someone else do most of your fighting and concentrate on saving your own hide. In my younger days, engaging in street fights was seen as merely one of the ordinary activities of Republican political life. It was, however, thought to be beneath the dignity of a candidate for praetor or consul.

I looked over the low railing, picked the softest-looking patch of pavement below, and—encumbered by my toga—scrambled over the rail, hung by my fingers a moment, then dropped. I landed without incident, grateful not to have slipped in one of the many noxious substances that coat Rome's streets. One good thing about recent sea duty: It keeps the knees supple.

Hermes, show-off that he was, flourished his dagger, gave a last, defiant shout, then actually *leapt* over the railing, dropped ten feet, and landed on the balls of his feet, as easily as a professional tumbler. He grinned at me and resheathed his dagger while passersby gaped. They didn't gape all that much though. Senators flying out of windows and off balconies were not all that rare a sight. Caesar had once flown thus, stark naked with his nose streaming blood, broken by an aggrieved husband.

"What now?" Hermes asked.

"Would've served you right if you'd slipped in a pile of shit," I said, unreasonably jealous that he'd cut so much better a figure than I had in our escape.

"I see no one's pursuing us," he said, casting a wary eye toward the front door of the house.

"It's not what they were there for," I said, "and they don't want to make a public fuss about it right now." I studied the angle of the sun. We still had some hours of daylight left. I patted the front of my tunic, causing a reassuring crackle of papyrus. "I got some of those letters. Let's go find someone who can translate them for us."

"Maybe we can find out about this, too." He made a magician's flourish and the massive signet ring lay in his hand. He'd deftly palmed it as he'd shut the hidden drawer.

"Sometimes," I admitted, "I'm glad I didn't raise you right."

5

THE GOLDSMITHS' QUARTER IN THOSE
days lay in a small block of houses and shops on the Via Nova just
across from the ancient Mugonia Gate, near the eastern end of the Forum. Unlike other quarters of the City, this one had its own wall, low
but strong, its heavy gates guarded by club-wielding slaves whose loy-
alty was guaranteed by their excellent terms of service: five years of
duty followed by freedom and a large enough stake to buy a house or a
small shop. The Goldsmiths' Guild had a special license for their little
fortress and its arrangements, granted by the censors and renewed
every five years as long as anyone could remember. The jewelers and
other dealers in precious materials had similar arrangements with the
censors. Rome was so full of thieves that they needed these special
precautions to practice their trade at all.

The headquarters of the guild was in a modest house just within the main gate. They needed nothing more pretentious because they held their annual banquets at the nearby Temple of the Public Penates.

Next to the old gate Hermes and I paused long enough to buy snacks from a street vendor, our narrow escape having given us an appetite. We bought grilled sausage and onions wrapped in flat bread and doused with *garum*. From another vendor we got cups of cheap wine, and we sat beneath the shade of a fine plane tree to discuss matters before consulting with the goldsmiths.

"The furnishings of that house," I said, "the desk and the inkstand, for instance—those were the sort of things wealthy men give to one another as gifts for Saturnalia or as guest gifts or to celebrate the naming of sons. What was a man like Fulvius doing with such possessions?"

"Maybe they were loaned to him," Hermes said, around a greasy mouthful, which he finally swallowed. "If Marcellus lent him the house, why not the furnishings as well?"

"But why would he do that? Why did he want Fulvius to put up such a fine front?"

"You could go ask him."

"Something tells me that would not be a wise move just now." I weighed the ring in my hand. The fine, strange granulation of its surface gave it an exotic look. I knew I had seen such metal work before, but I did not remember where. "You could buy a decent house with this and have enough left over to staff it with slaves. How did he get it, and why wasn't he wearing it?"

Hermes thought about this. "Could be he was waiting to gain the reputation to go with it, just like the senator's tunic and the *toga praetexta*. A nobody like him standing for tribune or quaestor would look like a fool wearing such a ring. It would be right at home on a praetor's hand."

"That's a thought. It makes me wonder who could dangle such prizes in front of him."

"Caesar could," Hermes said. "Or Pompey. They've both been known to raise obscure men to high office and power."

"Ridiculous!" I said. "Those two would never—"

"I just meant," Hermes went on, "that they are the *type* of men to do such a thing. And there are more ways of rising in the world than through birth or politics. Look at me. All my life I was a slave. Now I am a citizen with the name of a great family, which my descendants will inherit. This happened because *you* wanted it to. The lives of humble men are there for great men to make use of. We needn't wonder that it is done. We just need to discover the reason."

"You're uncommonly thoughtful today," I said, taken a little aback.

"Well, I don't carry your bath things around anymore, so I might as well do some of your thinking for you."

I brushed crumbs from my hands and downed the last of the wine. "Come on, let's see if we can find someone who can tell us about this ring." We gave our cups back to the vendor and walked across the street.

The year's guild master, a man named Laturnus, recognized me the moment I walked in. His office was laid out almost like a shop: a single, long room opening onto a courtyard, the whole upper half of the wall on that side open to admit maximum light. Except for chairs, the only furnishing of the room was a single, long table. It held a balance and selection of official weights, a touchstone, and a case holding samples of pure gold and silver and all the alloys of those metals. I could see that most of the business done here consisted of settling disputes concerning the purity of gold being sold in Rome. There were very strict laws regulating this, and the guild was held responsible for its members' honesty.

"Senator! Or should I say Praetor?" He took my hand and guided me to a comfortable chair. "How good it is to see you!" He was a fat man with keen eyes and nimble hands, both requirements of his craft. "I suppose you've come to discuss next year's legislation?"

My mind, distracted by other matters, failed to grasp his meaning. "Legislation?"

He was puzzled. "Why, yes. You will surely be holding court next year. And we will also have new censors. If Appius Claudius is elected censor, and surely he shall be, he plans to institute a new slate of antiluxury laws. I, and the members of my guild, feel that these laws will be a very bad idea."

"I couldn't agree more," I said. "But the praetors have no power over acts of the censors. Since you goldsmiths deal in the marketplace, your cases are heard by the aediles and they will be enforcing any decrees of the censors."

"Of course, you are right," he said, with a flutter of the fingers, "but the aediles and the praetors often work closely together, as your jurisdictions sometimes overlap."

"Certainly," I said, "and I assure you that I shall look with great leniency on frivolous accusations of luxury-law violations. Somehow I do not believe that the prime threat to the Republic comes from how many rings a man wears or the weight of gold around his wife's neck. I plan to dismiss out of hand all cases except those involving serious crime."

"We shall all be most grateful," he assured me, meaning that he would pass the word and I could expect a fine price break for any jewelry I bought from a guild member.

"Your best bet though," I advised him, "is to cultivate the other censor. He can overrule Appius's acts."

"Oh, believe me, we are doing just that. Calpurnius Piso is most likely to be elected, and he is a man, how shall we say, amenable to persuasion. But he will have very weighty matters on his mind next year, and he may be fully occupied trying to protect his friends whom Appius Claudius plans to expel from the Senate."

"The Senate is in severe need of pruning," I said. "But I've recently spoken with Appius, and he seems far more concerned about the indebtedness of the senatorial class than about luxury per se."

"Let us hope," said Laturnus.

"Now, my friend," I said, "what I came here to inquire about is this." I took the heavy ring from my tunic and handed it to him. "Can you tell me anything about this?"

He took it, stepped closer to the open wall to catch the best light. "A lovely piece. It's very old."

"How can you tell?"

"It's Etruscan work. This granulation of the surface is quite unique, and the art of making it has been lost for generations."

That explained it. I'd seen that surface before, many times, on old bronze lamps and vessels, always of Etruscan make. "Why is it no longer done?"

"It was probably only done by a few families, and the families died out without passing the secret on. The granulation is not chased onto the surface with gravers, as such surfaces are done now. First, they made thousands of minute, gold beads, all exactly the same size. That, too, is a lost art. Then the roughened surface of the piece—the ring, in this case—was prepared with a layer of the finest solder." His voice grew wistful, explaining the arcana of his vocation.

"Then the tiny beads were laid atop the solder, one at a time. This task was so demanding that it is said only children could do it properly. No one older than ten or twelve at the oldest, had the eyesight and the lightness of touch to accomplish it. Then, without disturbing the surface preparation, the piece was put into a furnace. It had to be removed the instant the temperature was perfect. Remove it too soon and the solder would not hold. Leave it too long and the solder would run off, taking the granulation with it. There were a hundred stages at which work this delicate could be ruined. It is amazing that any saw completion at all. But, when done properly, the effect is incomparable. Modern granulation work done with a graver or chisel is gross and coarse by comparison."

"The stone looks Greek," I said.

"It is. But the old Etruscans often incorporated Greek work into their own, just as we do today. Or, this could be a modern stone set into an old Etruscan ring. For that you will need to consult a lapidary. It is not my field."

I took the ring back from him. "Many thanks, Laturnus. I believe that your guild and my future office will enjoy the most excellent of relations." I rose from my chair.

"I rejoice to hear it. Why, if I may ask, is the origin of this ring of interest to you?"

"A matter of an inheritance. Several heirs claiming to be the rightful owner, you know how it goes."

"Alas, so I do."

Back out in the street I checked the angle of the sun. Still plenty of daylight left.

"That was interesting," I said, "but probably irrelevant. Let's go see if the stone has any surprises for us."

We went to the nearby quarter of the lapidaries. Most of the workers in precious substances lived and worked in the same small area near the eastern end of the Forum. Their shops were often located in the Forum itself, but I was looking for a dealer who traveled widely and bought from many sources; one who specialized in sapphires.

A bit of questioning led me to the shop of such a man, a resident alien named Gyges. Despite his Greek name he had a distinctly Syrian look, not an uncommon combination in the eastern coastal cities. I explained what I wanted, and he looked at the stone.

"The stone is from Egypt," he said without hesitation. "Once it had a different shape, but it was cut down and polished flat to prepare it for this carving. That is done a great deal with Egyptian stones. Outside of Egypt, nobody much likes Egyptian jewels. Fortunately, they liked massive, irregular stones, so it is relatively easy to alter them for a more refined taste."

"How old is it?" I asked. "I mean, when was this carving made? Can you tell?"

"It's quite recent. This treatment of the hair—snakes, I should say—was first used by Eunostes of Caria no more than fifty years ago. But this wasn't carved in Caria. The style is that of the Greek cities of southern Italy and Sicily. I am afraid I can't name you a specific lapidary, but I am almost certain that this came from one of the workshops of Croton."

Croton is in Bruttium, of course, but its inhabitants are not Bruttians: they are Greeks. Croton was the home of Pythagoras, who knew things about triangles and music and said people shouldn't eat beans. It was also the home of a great Olympic champion named Milo around five hundred years ago. Lately the place didn't amount to much.

"That doesn't help us greatly," Hermes said as we left.

"You never know what bit of information may come in useful," I assured him. "Now for something that should be truly enlightening, let's go find someone who can decipher these documents."

Rome is full of Greek schoolmasters, most of them penurious. But I needed something better than a man who could drill well-born schoolboys in their alpha-beta-gamma or teach youths of senatorial families to repeat the speeches of Demosthenes. Nor did I want someone who had memorized the entirety of Homer. I spoke of this to Hermes.

"So what are we looking for?" he asked.

"A cipher is no more than a puzzle. Mathematicians like to solve puzzles. We need somebody who is both a Greek scholar and a mathematician."

"I'm game. How do we find one?"

"Let's go ask Asklepiodes. He knows the better-educated Greek community here in the City."

It was not a great walk to the Temple of Aesculapius on Tiber Island. The streets were thinly populated because of the *contio* called by the Tribune Manilius. Those who had not gone to participate went there to watch.

The beautiful temple on its shiplike island was where Asklepiodes practiced and taught in the afternoons. We found him conducting an early evening sacrifice and waited respectfully with our heads covered while he finished the simple, dignified ceremony.

He smiled delightedly when he saw us. "Is someone else dead already?"

"Not this time," I told him. When I explained what I needed, he shook his head in wonderment.

"Your activities are a source of unfailing marvel. Yes, I think I know exactly what you need. Callista is here from Alexandria, giving a course of lectures in the hall adjoining Pompey's Theater."

"Callista?" I said. "This is a woman?"

"Very much so. You have been to Alexandria. You are aware that female scholars and teachers are not at all uncommon there."

"They rarely come to Rome to teach. You think she has the qualifications I need?"

"She is one of the foremost authorities on the Greek language working at the Library, and she is also a mathematician of the Archimedean school. I know of nobody else in Rome who enjoys such distinction."

"I am pressed for time. Would it be excessively rude for me to call on her this evening?"

"Nothing easier," he assured me. "I will take you there myself. It is a short walk from here, just on the other side of the bridge in the Trans-Tiber. And it will be no rudeness at all. In the Alexandrian fashion, she holds an open salon for persons of a scholarly bent. She should be receiving this evening."

"Wonderful. Hermes, go tell my wife that I will be home late this evening, lest she think I've been waylaid and murdered. Tell her I am consulting with a Greek scholar. Don't tell her that it is an Alexandrian woman. This is something I must explain to her in my own fashion. Then rejoin me at the house of Callista. If you run, you should be able to find it before it gets too dark to see."

Asklepiodes explained to him how to find the house and we left the temple, crossing the bridge into the district across the river. A great many foreigners lived in the new district, finding it more congenial both as to accommodation and company. The City proper was crowded, expensive, and full of Romans.

The house of Callista was no more than a hundred paces beyond the bridge, a stroke of luck considering how late the hour was. The sun was almost on the western horizon, and most Romans were already arriving for their dinner engagements, unless the *contio* was running late.

The gatekeeper was not a slave chained to the doorpost as in a great Roman house, but rather an educated servant who recognized both Asklepiodes and my senatorial insignia in a flickering glance. He bowed deeply.

"Learned Doctor, noble Senator, welcome to the house of Callista. My lady entertains a small but distinguished company this evening. She will be so delighted that you have come." He swept before us, and we followed him into a fine courtyard where perhaps ten people sat in a small group, their attention centered on a woman who sat on a small folding chair.

While the servant announced us, I studied the group and saw some faces I knew. Catullus the poet was there, as was Marcus Brutus. Brutus was a pontifex, and as a patrician he was barred from the *contio* that afternoon. He was known for his enthusiasm for Greek philosophy. The rest were men and women of Rome's literary and philosophical community, both Romans and Greeks.

The woman herself rose to greet us. I had rather expected an overeducated crone, but she was a tall, stately woman with the handsome, slightly heavy features so favored by Greek sculptors. Her hair was purest black, divided in the middle and falling over her shoulders. Her gown was as simple and as beautiful as a Doric column. She took Asklepiodes's hand first.

"Welcome, learned Asklepiodes, fountain of medical knowledge." She turned to look at me. "Thrice welcome for bringing the famous Decius Caecilius Metellus the Younger to my house." She released his hand and took mine. "I have hoped for so long to see you, Senator." Her eyes were disconcertingly direct. Not to mention beautiful.

"I am amazed you even know my name, distinguished lady, and I apologize for arriving thus unannounced."

She smiled and she did this, as she did everything else, beautifully. "Oh, but your all-too-brief stay in Alexandria is, shall we say, still remarked upon after nearly eleven years."

"Oh, well," I said, almost blushing, "what's one more riot in Alexandria's long history of them?" The riot had been the least of it.

"Besides, Princess Cleopatra recently spoke of you in the most glowing terms. She said her adventures with you on Cyprus were wonderfully exhilarating."

"Life always seems to be exhilarating around young Cleopatra," I told her. "She has a way of attracting excitement."

"And Ione, the high priestess of the Temple of Aphrodite at Paphos, wrote to me of you. She said that you are the most gifted Roman to come to Cyprus. She believes you to be touched by the gods."

This was getting embarrassing. "I'm just another Roman drudge, trying to do my duty and dodge the odd assassin," I told her.

"Please join our little group," she said. "I believe you must know most of these people."

She introduced them anyway, then Asklepiodes and I took our seats while their discussion continued. Courtesy dictated that I wait until their evening's conversation was concluded before I took my problem to her.

Catullus nudged me in the ribs and said in a stage whisper, "Touched by the gods, eh? Bacchus, I'll bet."

"Venus," I muttered back at him. "Princesses and priestesses find me irresistible." Some of the others turned and frowned at us.

They talked for a long time on some points of philosophy that I couldn't follow, then about the poetry of Pindar, with which I was at least familiar. I kept my mouth shut rather than stress my ignorance.

I must confess that I felt absurdly flattered that this woman knew who I was, had spoken with Cleopatra, and corresponded with Ione about me. Even better, she had not once mentioned my connection to Caesar. By that time I was beginning to feel that, in most peoples' eyes, being married to Caesar's niece was the highest distinction I had achieved.

I was struck by the foolishness of my feelings. Why should I, a widely experienced soldier and magistrate of the greatest republic in the world, feel warmed by the esteem of a foreign woman? After all, she was only a woman. And while we Romans had a grudging admiration, even awe, of the Greeks of former times; we regarded their descendants, our contemporaries, as a pack of foolish degenerates, political imbeciles, and natural-born slaves. We often marveled that the Greeks we saw every day could be even distantly related to Achilles and Agamemnon, or even to the later ones like Pericles, Leonidas, and Miltiades.

Perhaps the truth was that I had grown tired and disillusioned with the Romans of my own class, self-seeking politicians and grasping conquerors who were slowly destroying the Republic more surely than any barbarian enemy could hope to.

Not that I expected to find some cure for our ills in the supposed wisdom of aliens. Many of the more idle and empty-headed members of the senatorial and equestrian orders were forever discovering the answers to the problems that have plagued mankind in the ancient "enlightenment" of Persia or Babylonia or Egypt. They never explain how this wonderful wisdom failed to save those utterly fallen and destroyed civilizations. At least men like Brutus and Cicero chose to admire the relatively rational Greeks, who knew how to carve wonderful statues.

Eventually, people began to rise and take their leave. While Callista bade each good night I spoke briefly with Brutus. He was a man of the highest reputation but far too solemn and serious for my taste. He couldn't decide which direction to spit without wondering how it might reflect on the honor of his ancient family. I thought it a grotesque fixation in one so young. His mother, Servilia, had been one of the great beauties of her generation, and Brutus had inherited some portion of her comeliness, which did not otherwise run in his aptly named family.

"I hope this decision of the *comitia tributa* goes well for you, Senator," Brutus said gravely. He gave the word for the plebeian assembly the slightly contemptuous turn common to patricians. They always preferred the *comitia centuriata*, which was dominated by a handful of great families.

"I daresay their decision will be enlightening," I told him. "This whole business has me utterly mystified. It's true I was a bit rough on certain Romans living in Cyprus, but they were all thieves and plunderers and I can prove it. How this fool Fulvius got killed I have no idea."

"All honest Romans agree that your actions on Cyprus were perfectly just," Brutus said ponderously. "Cato concurs with me on this. The death of this man Fulvius, while unfortunate, is a trifling matter compared with the great dangers before us. Did you know that an invading army is about to descend upon Rome?"

"Really?" I said, doubting his sanity. "Not the Parthians, I hope."

"I almost wish it were. Caesar has given half his legions leave of absence so that they can come to Rome and take part in the election. A rider came in not three hours ago to inform the aediles that the first cohorts would be pitching their tents on the Campus Martius in the morning. The rest will be here within two days."

"That's high-handed behavior even for Caesar," I said. "But as far as I know, it's constitutional. And he can spare them. It's the depth of winter up in Gaul. He can keep his conquests in order with his auxilia." The auxilia were foreigners, allies, and mercenaries. Legionaries, on the other hand, were all citizens, which meant they could all vote. And they would vote for Caesar's favored candidates.

"It's good news for you, I suppose," Brutus grumbled. I was one of those favored candidates.

"I won't be a total hypocrite and claim I don't want their votes," I admitted. "But any army descending on Rome, even a Roman one, is an unsettling concept."

"I rejoice to hear it. But the time must come when men who love the Republic must take action to curb the arrogance of Caesar."

I won't pretend to be an oracle and claim that in these words I perceived a portent of dire deeds to come. Nor did I foresee a bloody Ides of March when I heard Cassius, Casca, Basileus, and all the rest voice similar thoughts in that and future years, all those men who are now so notorious. Half of Rome, it seemed, spoke darkly of the other half, and many important figures jumped nimbly from one side to the other, repeatedly, not least among them the men who later plotted Caesar's death.

Finally only Asklepiodes and I remained of the evening's guests.

"Callista," Asklepiodes said, "my friend the Senator Metellus has a singular problem, its solution requires a combination of skills and talents that I have informed him are possessed in abundance by you alone of all the scholars now resident in Rome." He spoke in Greek, which I could follow well enough.

"How intriguing. I shall seek to vindicate your trust in me." She turned to me and switched to Latin. "And how may I possibly be of help?"

I took out the papers. "These documents were written in cipher by a person whose activities I am investigating. The alphabet used is Greek, although I can't say whether the language thus encoded is Greek or Latin." I handed them to her, and she studied them by the light of a multiwicked lamp.

"Are you certain that it is one of those two languages? I ask because of the extraordinary repetition of the letter delta. The arrangement, even taking into account the common letter substitution of ciphers, doesn't look like either language."

This could mean trouble. "The man in question lived almost all his life in Baiae, which is in Campania. It's conceivable that it's the Oscan dialect that is used. But Oscan has almost the same grammar as Latin, though the vocabulary and pronunciation are different."

She shook her head. "Then that can't be it. Do you know to whom this is written?"

"I have no idea."

"If he turns out to be Syrian or Egyptian, I will be of little use to you, I fear."

"I strongly doubt that the author knew any such language. He was of an old Latin family. His sister has lived in Rome for many years. The family is distinguished but not for scholarship. I would venture to say that he would be lost in any language save Greek or Latin."

"That will simplify things. Would it be possible to leave these letters with me?"

"They are of no use in my possession, and any excuse to call upon you again is welcome."

"You need no excuse, Senator. Please feel free to call upon me anytime. I have no lectures scheduled for tomorrow. I find that election time in Rome is not a good time for much of anything. I'll devote the morning to this. If you can come by tomorrow afternoon, perhaps I'll have made some headway."

"Depend upon it, I'll be here," I told her.

I found Hermes waiting outside. He had brought along a small bodyguard of men from my neighborhood who were under obligation to me.

"I believe the lady is rather taken with you," Asklepiodes said slyly as he took his leave.

"If this were another city, and if I were not as married as I am, I would be greatly taken with her," I said. "But I think I am in enough danger as it is."

"Life's little complexities keep us from growing old too soon," he assured me. "Please keep me informed how this fascinating business progresses."

We walked home without incident, and I dismissed my little guard with my thanks. Julia was waiting up when I went inside.

"I hear you've been up to your old activities," she said, as she took my toga and directed the slaves to lay out a late supper. "It's been a long time since you practiced house breaking and burglary and escaping through the alleys and over rooftops."

"You've been listening to Hermes. That's always a mistake."

"He's acting innocent as a sacrificial lamb. It's the rest of the City buzzing about your activities."

"Oh. Well, gossip is unreliable, you know." I picked up a chicken leg.

"Tell me your news, and I'll tell you mine. And stop evading."

So I began with my visit to Fulvia's house and my encounter with Curio.

"He is a man with a scandalous history," she commented, "but very courageous, and it looks as if he's chosen the right side now. He spoke up for you in the *contio* this evening by the way."

"He said that he would. Tell me about that."

"When you've told me the rest of your day's doings. Have some of that soup. It will keep you from catching cold running around like this in the winter."

Obediently, I sipped at a cup of her grandmother's cold remedy. It was broth of stewed chicken laced with *garum* and vinegar. Not bad, actually. I told her about our visit to the goldsmith's guild and the lapidary.

"That was a waste of time," she commented.

"You never know. Then, of course, I went to get those encoded letters examined by an expert."

"Which one?" she asked.

"Well, I went to Asklepiodes first, and he recommended Callista."

Julia was silent for a moment. "Callista?" The name sounded ominous in her mouth.

"Yes, she's an Alexandrian, quite brilliant in—"

"I know who she is. She's said to be quite beautiful."

"Oh, I don't know about that. Her nose is a little long for my taste. Anyway, I didn't call on her for her looks, but for her expertise in Greek and mathematics."

"You went to the home of a foreign woman at night, without invitation?" The dark clouds were gathering.

"It's a sort of open salon she holds for intellectual sorts." I floundered about for something to allay her suspicions, which were all too justified. "My dear," I said, "Marcus Brutus was there."

The clouds seemed to recede. "Brutus. Well, the gathering must have been respectable anyway."

"Boringly so. Incidentally, Brutus seems to regard Caesar with some hostility." I told her what he had said. Nothing distracted Julia as effectively as an insult to her revered uncle. But she didn't seem concerned.

"Brutus has some foolishly old-fashioned notions. Caesar thinks the world of him. He'll come around. Now tell me what Callista said about the letters."

So I told her what the woman had said. "I'll call on her tomorrow to find out what she's learned."

"Not if you're under arrest, you won't."

"What?" I all but choked on my wine, a light Falernian, as I recall.

"The vote in the *contio* was close, but you are to be tried for the murder of Marcus Fulvius."

"Ridiculous! There is no evidence!"

To my surprise, she leaned over and kissed me tenderly. "Decius, I think I love you most of all when you are being foolish and naive. Surely you understand that you are the only man in Rome who cares about things like evidence. Trials are not about evidence. They are not about guilt or innocence. They are about friends and enemies. Do you have more friends than enemies?"

"I certainly hope so."

"Then you'll probably be vindicated. But you may also find that you have enemies you knew nothing about."

"I've already discovered one: Marcus Fulvius, although he's no longer numbered among the living. And whoever is behind him." Another thought struck me. I told her about Caesar's veterans arriving.

She clapped her hands like a child. "Wonderful! They all know you. We can count on their support." Then she frowned. "But men who've spent years in Gaul won't be in the jury pool."

"What form is the trial to take?"

"You're to be tried before the *concilium plebis,* with a jury of three hundred *equites.*" Very large juries were the rule at that time. It was thought to be difficult to bribe so many people.

"When?"

"On the third day from this."

"What? We only found the bugger dead this morning! It's customary to give an accused man ten days to get his defense together."

"Do you want to be praetor or not? They could delay the election no longer than that. Conviction or acquittal, the election goes ahead in four days."

That was that. Nothing to be done about it. "What was the mood of the crowd? Did your sources say?"

"It's a sideshow to the general spectacle of the elections. You're a popular man with the plebs and nobody knew Fulvius, so there was no crowd baying for your blood. Some good people spoke up for you, and the ones demanding a trial appealed to hatred of the aristocrats."

"Running according to form then," I said, refilling my cup. "What about the Tribune, Manilius? Was he rabble-rousing?"

"From what I heard, he conducted it well, shutting up anyone who spoke too long, putting a quick stop to shouting matches."

"I wonder which side he's on," I said.

"That one is easy," she said. "Until he proves otherwise, consider him your enemy."

6

By morning no lictors had appeared to arrest me, so I presumed I was free to go around as I pleased, which I proceeded to do.

That morning featured a new distraction for the citizens, the arrival of Caesar's men on the Campus Martius. For the moment I was forgotten as everyone flocked out through the northwestern gates to the old drill field to welcome the heroes of Gaul. Being under arms they could not enter the City, but elections were held on the Campus Martius so they didn't have to.

The field had become greatly built up in the last generation, with the homes and businesses around the Circus Flaminius and Pompey's theater complex, which was practically a village in itself, but there was still plenty of ground devoted to military drill. By the time I got there, at least two cohorts' tents were already pitched, and more soldiers were arriving, an endless stream of them coming down the Via Flaminia.

They were veterans and they looked it. Their arms were dingy, their shield covers weather stained, their helmet crests and plumes drooping, their cloaks every shade of red from scarlet to rust brown. But their boots and swords were immaculate, and if their equipment wasn't spruced up for parade, it was in perfect battle order. They looked supremely competent and dangerous.

I went out through the Fontinalis Gate with a knot of fellow senators I'd joined in the Forum.

"Jupiter protect us!" said one, as we caught sight of them. "I am glad to know that Caesar is still north of the Rubicon!"

For some reason, we never feared a Roman army as long as its general was somewhere else. Caesar's imperium ended at the Rubicon. If he crossed it, he would be just another citizen. Or so we thought.

A good-sized fair was taking shape on the Campus Martius that morning, as the itinerant vendors and mountebanks descended upon this cornucopia of soldiery, marched all the way from Gaul with their pay in their purses.

The men themselves were from all over Italy and Sicily, from the tip of Calabria to the northern edge of Umbria. They were the men of the villages and countryside, from towns that had borne Roman citizenship for centuries and others whose fathers had been at war with Rome within living memory. Most of them probably had never laid eyes on Rome.

That was getting to be more and more common of late. In Hannibal's day, the consuls had been able to whistle up ten legions within a day's march of the City, so densely was Latium peopled with prosperous peasant families. Now we had to scour the whole peninsula for enough men to fill that many legions, and few real Romans served except as officers. Perhaps Caesar was right, and someday we would have to recruit Gauls. If he didn't kill them all first, that is.

I searched for familiar faces, but in an army so vast I knew only a relative handful of men. Most of my time in Gaul I had spent in command of *auxilia* or else working in Caesar's headquarters. The first soldiers to arrive belonged to legions that hadn't even been in Gaul when I was last there. The war, originally a fairly modest campaign to support our allies and drive the Germans back beyond the Rhenus, had turned into a vast war of conquest that had spread out to reach the obscure island of Britannia.

Despite their victories, there were no laurels, trophies, or other triumphal insignia in evidence. That would have been too arrogant even for Caesar, and he must have given strict orders for his men to make no such presumptuous display. The Senate still guarded jealously its right to grant or withhold a triumph, and Caesar was not ready to break completely with the Senate. Not yet, anyway.

In fact, as soon as their camp was made, the men made tripods of their spears, leaned their shields against them, put their helmets on the spear points, and stored their armor and swords inside the tents. When they circulated among the crowds, they retained only their military belts and boots as insignia of their status. At this demonstration of goodwill, the most ardent anti-Caesarians breathed a sigh of relief and joined in the general festivity. Thus disarmed, the soldiers were free to enter the City.

The soldiers, like soldiers of all times and places, showed off their awards and souvenirs and loot. Torques—the twisted neck rings worn by all Gallic warriors—were everywhere, from simple bronze pieces worn by the humbler Gauls to magnificent specimens of highly worked gold and silver taken from the necks of chieftains, often by the simple operation of removing the head at the same time. Within days it seemed as if every boy in Rome was wearing a big, bronze ring around his thin neck.

Others displayed beautiful shields of enameled bronze and long, narrow swords that looked exotic to eyes accustomed to the short, broad *gladius*. Gauls are passionately fond of jewelry, and these men had brought back tons of it, as well as yards of extravagantly dyed cloth worked in bewildering patterns of stripes and checks. Rome soon had the most colorful, glittering whores in the world.

I suppose it must have been the same when the Greeks returned from Troy.

"Very clever," remarked Scribonius Libo, another candidate for praetor and a friend of Pompey. "It's just like Caesar to accomplish several things with a single act. First, all these men will weight the polls in favor of his candidates. Second, it will remind everyone of how powerful he has grown. Third, it's a recruiting campaign: these men are proclaiming, 'Look how rich a soldier can become by serving with Caesar.'"

"Caesar uses his resources efficiently," I agreed, "but it's all perfectly legal."

"It shouldn't be," Scribonius grumbled. "We need a law that keeps the legions on the frontiers as long as they're under arms."

There was a lot of such talk in those years. Our old system of raising legions for each new war and then disbanding them upon their return was terribly outdated. We still raised them that way for a really large-scale war like Caesar's, or for an impromptu campaign like that of Crassus against Parthia, but settling the veterans of victorious wars proved to be a perpetual headache. Usually they had no land to return to, much of Italy having been bought up by plantation owners. These, having got the land cheap, were reluctant to see any of it parceled out to veterans. Many of the greatest of these landlords were senators. This was one more way in which my own class was busily cutting its own throat during those years.

The legionaries rarely had any trade save farming or fighting. Since land was scarce, they did their best to stay under arms as long as possible. Some legions had become permanent institutions, passed on from one proconsul to the next, remaining under their standards for twenty years or more. Others, disbanded, stayed together with their arms handy, waiting for the next call to the eagles.

Somehow, we had acquired a class of professional soldiers. They were a constant danger to the stability of the Republic, and Scribonius was not alone in calling for their virtual banishment from Italy, locating them instead in permanent forts along our frontiers. It was an argument with merit, but thus far nobody had the courage or the power to implement such a plan. Pompey could have done it, but his power was heavily invested in the old system. His demobilized veterans were his clients and his power base. He could call them back to arms at any time, and everybody knew it.

What nobody mentioned was the greatest source of wealth for Caesar's rampaging legions: slaves. After the larger battles, in which great numbers of prisoners were taken, Caesar sometimes gave each man a prisoner as a slave, to sell or keep as he saw fit. Of course, men constantly under arms and on the march had little use for slaves and no convenient way to send them home, so they usually sold them immediately to the slave traders who followed the legions like vultures hovering over a battlefield.

These prisoners, I must add, were not captive warriors. Those were regarded as too dangerous for field or domestic service, so they were usually killed on the spot, if they had not killed themselves already to avoid disgrace. Those survivors Caesar selected to fight in his triumphal games were sent to Italy in chains under heavy guard. One need not waste much pity on them. Some of them actually survived the combats and won their freedom. In any case, Gallic warriors had no objection to death in combat. It was work they feared. To men of their class, common labor was unutterably dishonorable and degrading.

The captives were mostly the women and children of the tribe, or people who were already slaves, and these last were the most numerous. Unlike the Germans, among whom all freeborn men were warriors, the Gallic warriors were aristocrats. The bulk of the population were Gauls born to slavery or to a sort of degraded serfdom that was little better.

The upshot of it all was that, once again, Italy was being inundated by a flood of cheap slaves, with consequent effects on the economy and on society in general, making it harder for freeborn Italians to make a living, throwing yet more peasants out of work. It always happened after a big war. You would think we'd learn better, but we never have.

Cato showed up, plodding around barefooted, walking up and down the rows of tents like a new commander on his first inspection. He came to join us where we watched the market taking shape in front of Pompey's Portico, just north of his theater. For once, Cato's ugly face wasn't scowling.

"These are real Roman soldiers," he said approvingly. "These men could have gone toe-to-toe with Hannibal's."

"Hurts to say it, eh, Cato?" said Scribonius Libo.

"The times are decadent," Cato answered, "but there is nothing wrong with Italian manhood. I disapprove of Caesar, and I've never made a secret of it. He is a man with too much ambition and too little respect for the Senate. But he knows how to use an army. He knows how to train and discipline soldiers, too. He doesn't spoil and flatter and bribe them like Pompey."

"You'll notice," I commented, "that they are comporting themselves perfectly. Pompey's veterans have been known to tromp around here at election time fully armed and scowling balefully."

"Caesar just knows how to make a point more tactfully," Scribonius Libo said.

"Decius Caecilius, might I have a word with you?" Cato said, placing his hand on my shoulder in that let's-talk-in-private gesture.

"Certainly."

We walked up the steps of the Portico and into the shade of the colonnade. Its rear wall was beautifully adorned with frescoes. Displaying uncharacteristic taste, Pompey had chosen mythological subjects instead of glorifying his own victories.

"I attended the *contio* yesterday," Cato began. "I think you should challenge its constitutionality. First, it was quite informal. There were no sacrifices, no taking of auguries, so its decisions cannot have the binding power of law."

"By custom," I said, "a *contio* is held to discuss a pending matter and decide whether a meeting of the comitia is called for. Sacrifices and auguries are not necessary."

"Exactly. Yet Manilius proceeded as if he had the power to call for a trial at the *contio*, when it requires a vote in the full comitia to do that. Oh, he was very smooth. He acted like the gravest, most deliberate magistrate since Fabius Cunctator, but his tactics were radical! In the first place, the *comitia tributa* has no right to try a capital case."

"But is it truly a capital case?" I asked. "It's just a common murder. It's not parricide, so there is no sacrilege involved. He wasn't killed by poison or magic. It was nothing but an ordinary stabbing, although it was carried out with rare zeal. It's not as if I was charged with a really serious crime like arson or treason."

"Nonsense! The victim, though obscure, was a man of good family. You, too, are a man of good family and high reputation. If you are not to be tried in one of the standing courts, you should appeal for trial before the whole *comitia centuriata*, with all classes represented, where the tribunes don't control everything."

"There's no time. Not if I'm to stand in the election. If I stall, Manilius and Fulvius's faction will use it as grounds for impeachment and try to keep me from assuming office." A sitting magistrate could not be prosecuted; but if the election itself were to be invalidated, he could be prevented from taking his place.

"Then what will you do? You haven't time to formulate a good defense, and they've had plenty of time to work up their plot, whatever it is."

"I intend to prove myself innocent before it comes to trial."

He looked skeptical. Like Julia, Cato had little faith in the concept of mere innocence.

Foreigners were often mystified by our old Republican system, with its welter of popular assemblies, courts, officials with rival jurisdictions, political factions, and competing *clientela*, but it all made perfect sense to us. Well, almost perfect. As in this case, there was often dispute about anyone's right to do anything.

Over the generations, the various classes had fought over political power; first, patrician against plebeian; then the *nobiles* and senators against the *equites* and lower plebs; until now the classes were hopelessly intertwined. I was a perfect example: a plebeian by birth, a *nobiles* by heritage, having many consuls among my ancestors; an *eques* by property qualification, and a senator by election. I was not a patrician, but by that year the patrician families were all but extinct, and the only exclusive privileges they had left were certain priesthoods, which suited me perfectly. Only a fool wanted to be *Flamen Dialis* or *Rex Sacrorum*.

Most foreigners assumed that the Senate ran things. While the Senate was full of powerful men, its own powers were restricted almost completely to foreign affairs. Cicero got into huge trouble by trying the Catilinarian conspirators in the Senate and executing them without appeal. Even though the immensely conservative Cato fully approved of his actions, Cicero was exiled by the *comitia tributa*, then later recalled by a vote of the *comitia centuriata*.

SPQR, our ancient civic insignia, stood for "the Senate and People of Rome," and we meant it.

Now, of course, it is all changed. Most of the old bodies and institutions remain, but they all just do what the First Citizen tells them to. Once we savaged each other so thoroughly that it is no wonder we were such a terror to our enemies. I fear that Rome has no great future now that it is a monarchy in all but name.

But such thoughts did not disturb me at the time. This accusation of murder was just one more excitement in the general excitement of election time. It was an annoyance, but anything was better than being in Gaul.

"Cato, you recall the crowd that denounced me on the basilica steps yesterday? Were they at the *contio?*"

"They were there. Still denouncing you, too."

"Did they happen to mention that they caught me in the house of Fulvius, rifling through his belongings?"

"Never said a word about it. Oh, there was some gossip going around that you and your boy Hermes were seen leaping from a balcony and running like the Furies were after you, but I've heard that so often that I discounted it. What were you up to?"

"Gathering evidence. The door wasn't locked and no one was there to forbid me to enter, so it wasn't housebreaking. What interests me is that they said nothing about it."

"It does seem odd. What did you find?"

"Nothing immediately useful. But he was living unusually well for a penurious man, in a house owned by Caius Claudius Marcellus."

"A political favor then," he said. "But of what sort? He's an ardent anti-Caesarian, but like you he has a marriage tie with Caesar."

"Really? I was unaware of that."

"Yes, his wife is Octavia. She is a granddaughter of Caesar's sister."

"A great-niece? That's not much of a connection."

"In this case it could be. Caesar has shown great favor toward her brother, young Caius Octavius. If he doesn't breed an heir soon, he may adopt the boy. A few months ago the lad gave the funeral eulogy for his grandmother, Julia. Did a splendid job of it for one so young."

"I've never heard of him," I said. And that was true of most of us. It was just as well for our peace of mind that we didn't know what the future had in store for that particular brat, who was all of twelve years old at the time.

"A couple of years ago, when Caesar and Pompey were patching up one of their breaches, Caesar wanted Octavia to divorce Marcellus and marry Pompey. Caesar would set aside Calpurnia and marry Pompey's daughter. But it didn't work out somehow."

"That must have made for some tense domestic suppers at Caesar's house," I said.

"Why?" Cato was honestly mystified at the suggestion that these women might resent being ordered to divorce and remarry at someone's political whim. Pompey's daughter was married to Faustus Sulla and had two children by him. In the event, Pompey had actually married the daughter of Metellus Scipio. She was the widow of Publius Crassus, who had died with his father at Carrhae. Our political marriages were as complicated as our electoral politics.

"Claudius Marcellus bids fair to be one of next year's consuls," I said. "What is he likely to do?"

"Now that Caesar's soldiers are here, his colleague will be Lucius Aemilius Lepidus Paullus. You've seen the huge renovations going on at the Basilica Aemilia?"

"It's hard to miss."

"Well, Lucius will preside at its rededication, and his name will be carved on it as restorer, but it's Caesar's money that's paid for the work."

Erection or restoration of monuments was enormously important to any man's prestige. Families traditionally saw to the upkeep of the monuments of their ancestors, as witness my new roof on the Porticus Metelli. By restoring the old basilica, Lucius Aemilius not only glorified himself, but he received credit for his piety in honoring his ancestors.

Something else occurred to me. Like many of Rome's older structures, the Basilica Aemilia had more than one name. People sometimes called it the Basilica Fulvia.

IT WAS BARELY NOON WHEN I WENT to the house of Callista. I had intended to call later, but since I might be arrested at anytime I thought it prudent to stop by early. Hermes was with me as usual, and the long walk to the Trans-Tiber took us through an almost deserted Rome because so much of the population had flocked to the Campus Martius to see the soldiers from Gaul. Like most of Caesar's self-glorifying schemes, this one had proved to be a resounding success.

The majordomo greeted me at the door and guided me toward the peristyle garden. From that direction I could hear the sound of feminine voices in conversation. One of them said something, another laughed. Ordinarily I find such sounds pleasant, even soothing. But one of those voices sounded disturbingly familiar.

The two women were seated at a table next to a beautiful pool. One of them, naturally, was Callista. The other was Julia.

"Why, Senator!" Callista exclaimed, "I was not expecting you so early. How wonderful to have you and your lovely wife as my guests at the same time!"

"An unexpected pleasure indeed," I said. "Julia, I am surprised you didn't go out to see all those brawny, sweaty legionaries."

"Oh, soldiers are such a common sight, even my uncle's. But I couldn't pass up a chance to meet the most learned lady in Rome. We have been having the most marvelous discussion on the work of Archimedes."

"I don't doubt it for a moment." During our stay in Alexandria, Julia had dragged me along to see every tiresome philosopher and scholar in that whole overeducated city. She had an enthusiasm for learning that entirely eluded me.

"Once I began to study your documents, Senator," Callista said, "I found myself so enthralled that I quite forgot the time. Eventually, my servants tired of replenishing the lamps and forced me to go to bed. But I was up at dawn and right back to work."

"I never expected such zeal and cannot adequately thank you," I said. "So you now have them translated?"

"I am afraid not. But I have made an excellent beginning. And I've made the most interesting discovery!"

"How so?" I asked, trying to mask my disappointment. Such rapid success was far too much to hope for.

She took the pages from a small chest upon the table. "You recall that I was puzzled by the repetition of the letter delta?"

"Indeed, I do."

"Well, I was in despair when I finally went to bed last night. But

I must have been visited by a god while I slept because when I awoke this morning I knew what it meant. It is something quite unprecedented." She had a look of almost daemonic enthusiasm.

"What might this have been?" I asked her.

"Nothing!"

I was stunned. "I fail to—"

"Let her explain, dear," Julia said. "We've discussed a bit of this, and I want to hear more."

I sat and a servant brought me a cup. "Please do," I urged.

"I know that it sounds absurd, but that delta means nothing at all, and that is what is so exciting. You see, I noticed that the delta was always repeated after a string of other letters, three to eight or so, and that nowhere was a delta doubled. When I woke this morning I realized that whoever encoded these documents intended to simplify decoding by separating the words with the delta, rather the way that some people, when writing, leave a small space between individual words."

"I see," I said. "It seems simple enough."

"It is deceptively simple. But the implications are astounding. It is the use of a symbol to mean nothing at all! I think this is quite unprecedented. There is a subset of philosophy involving the meaning of symbols. I intend to correspond with some philosophers I know to discuss the implications of this. I think it could have great applications in mathematics as well."

"I daresay it could," I said, trying to sound wise. I had no idea what the woman was babbling about. To this day I have no idea. A symbol for nothing? It was as ridiculous as the paradoxes of Zeno.

Julia spoke up. "Callista thinks this might have been the very concept Archimedes was working on when that horrible soldier killed him."

"Well," I said, "that sort of thing happens in a war. He shouldn't have spoken rudely to the man. Callista, were you able to make any other headway on the letters?"

"I am almost certain that the language is common Latin. The

length and arrangement of the words suggest this. I haven't yet discovered the key to the letter substitution though. I had thought it would be simple, but now I am sure it is not. A mind subtle enough to invent this delta symbol probably devised something more complex."

"Maybe," I said, "but you might be giving him too much credit. He may have hit on the delta as a handy way to separate words without giving a consideration to the deeper implications." Whatever on earth those might be, I thought.

"You could be right," she said doubtfully. "Did you happen to see, where you found these documents, any books, poems, other writings?"

"Why?"

"I believe this code employs substitution of one letter for another—in this case each Greek letter stands for a letter of the Latin alphabet—but in order to decipher it, I must have the key."

"Key?" I said. "What might that be?"

"It could be a written instruction, but more likely what has been used will be a well-known book, such as the Homeric poems, Pindar, something like that. If one has the book and knows the system of substitution, decipherment becomes an easy if tedious process."

I was not following this, but I trusted the woman to know what she was talking about.

"Now that I think of it, there were a few scrolls in a holder next to the desk. And one lying on it." I searched my mind for memories of that stimulating afternoon. "The one on the desk was partially unrolled and it looked like it was one he read a lot. You know how it is with a favorite book—the papyrus was like cloth, and the edges had turned fuzzy. But it wasn't some famous work like the *Iliad*."

"It isn't necessary that it be a famous work," Callista said. "Merely that each correspondent have a copy, and the copies must be identical—no copyist's errors, and ideally each line of each column should begin with exactly the same word. Sometimes a letter substitution involves counting inward from the first character in a specific line."

She had lost me again. "Then the books would almost have to come from the same copyist."

"That would be best. What sort of book was it?"

"It was a textbook of court speeches. They're standard teaching tools for the rhetoric schools that specialize in teaching lawyers. They use famous legal speeches, or sometimes hypothetical speeches appropriate for hypothetical cases, to demonstrate how to build logical arguments for or against particular positions. This one seemed to be about points of law—the sort of legal hairsplitting that keeps expert pleaders in demand."

"Law is not a specialty of mine," she said. "Is there a standard text for these things?"

"No, but I happen to know who trained the man in question: Aulus Sulpicius Galba, now duumvir of Baiae."

"And has this man written such a text?" Callista asked. "Almost any book can be used for encoding, and it would make sense for a man to use the work most familiar to him."

"Almost certainly, since he is a law teacher. I could probably find a copy. I might even be able to get the original that I saw yesterday."

"Decius," Julia said, "you will do nothing of the sort. You are far too old for burglary. Send Hermes to steal it."

Callista was looking from one to the other of us as if we were specimens of some exotic beast she was studying. Julia caught her look. "It is quite all right," she assured the woman. "The man is dead."

"Of course it might not be the key," Callista said, "but it seems to be a good candidate for the job, and I have little hope of making a quick translation without it."

"Then I'll get it for you," I said. I turned around. "Where's Hermes?"

"If I know him," Julia said, "he's wherever the best-looking women in this house are kept."

"But that's right in this courtyard," Hermes said gallantly. He was standing just within a doorway that led to a dining room. He had, however, been chatting up a pretty slave girl.

"Curb your insolence," Julia said. "Can you go find us that book without being seen?"

He thought a moment, going over the urban terrain. "I'll bribe my way into one of the houses that opens on another street, then cross the common courtyard. If there's nobody in the house and the book is still there, I'll get it."

"Then go and come back here as quickly as you can—no stopping on the way, mind."

"I shall be as my namesake," he said, hurrying from the poolside as swiftly and silently as a leopard.

"He seems to be a versatile lad," Callista noted with some approval.

"Every politician needs one," I told her.

While we waited for Hermes to return with his loot, we fell to discussing my situation. I told them of my conversation with Cato, about the confusion of marriages and planned marriages that decorated the recent past.

"I know Octavia and her brother only slightly," Julia admitted, referring to the wife of Caius Marcellus. "Caesar's sister, another Julia, married Atius Balbus and their daughter, Atia, married Caius Octavius. The younger Caius Octavius and Octavia are their children. The elder Octavius died some time back. Atia is now married to Lucius Philippus, I believe."

"I know their father," I said. "A few years ago, when Octavius was praetor, Clodius and I brawled our way right into his court. I'd have cut his throat right there in public if the lictors hadn't separated us."

"Just as well you didn't succeed," Julia observed. "I heard there was a Vestal present in the court that day."

"Right," I said. "They'd probably have hurled me off the Tarpeian Rock or tied me in a weighted sack and tossed me off the Sublician Bridge."

"You Romans have such imaginative punishments," Callista said.

"That's nothing," I told her. "You ought to see what we do to parricides or arsonists."

"And yet you are not under arrest even though you are charged with murder."

"We Romans," Julia told her, "have a robust sense of justice. We reserve our harshest punishments for crimes that endanger the whole community. Rome is a firetrap so arson is the most serious of crimes. Treason endangers us all. Sacrilege, parricide, and incest anger the gods and draw the wrath of the immortals upon the whole City."

"Exactly," I put in. "But a grown citizen is expected to be able to take care of himself. If someone tries to kill you, you should kill him first. You're a poor prospect for the legions if you're unable to defend yourself."

"There are exceptions," Julia pointed out. "Murder by subterfuge, especially if poison or magic are involved, are not tolerated. Likewise, violence toward sacrosanct personages, such as Tribunes of the People or Vestals, draws harsh punishment."

"Ordinary senators, on the other hand," I said, "get no such consideration. In really rough times, I've seen as many as half a dozen senators carried dead out of alleys. There are always plenty more where they came from. The Curia is too crowded as it is."

"I see. And these political marriages of yours: Just what is the point of them since they are so easily dissolved?"

"They're traditional," I told her. "They hark back to a day when divorce was much more difficult. At one time only patricians had full citizenship, and they had a special form of marriage—*conferratio*—that was indissoluble. In those days a political marriage genuinely bound the two families."

"We Roman women of the great families put up with a great deal from our men," Julia said. "It is bad enough being pawns in a political game, but it would be nice if we were at least pawns that *counted* for something."

"Between your multiple marriages and divorces, and your habit of adopting each other's sons, I'm surprised you bother with these family names at all. They can hardly have much meaning by this time."

"It is odd, isn't it?" I agreed. "Yet we still behave as if our names were of utmost significance."

"I suspect," Julia put in, "that is because adoption takes place only among a limited number of families, ones that have traditional relationships and a good deal of shared blood."

"That's true," I said. "Metellus Scipio, for instance, is the last of the Cornelia Scipiones, but he is a Metellus on his mother's side, so he's a cousin with or without the name."

"I find it all very confusing," Callista said.

"Be happy that you don't have to worry about such things," Julia advised her.

"Greek women have been known to seek revenge when treated in such a fashion. We remember Medea."

"Upper class Roman wives are usually ready for a change of husbands after a year or two." I saw Julia glowering at me. "There are exceptions, of course."

For another hour or so Julia and Callista talked of philosophical subjects upon which I wisely declined to intrude, save to make occasional noncommittal noises, as if I were following their discussion intently. To my great amazement, Julia seemed to genuinely like the Alexandrian woman. Of course, she had come calling that morning to see what sort of woman I was visiting. She must have been surprised to find a kindred spirit instead of some foreign temptress. Not that Callista wouldn't have made a fine foreign temptress had she chosen to adopt that role.

Then Hermes returned, having flown upon winged heels, as promised. He entered the peristyle with a bulky bundle over one shoulder and grinning like an African ape.

"I told you to bring back that scroll," I told him, "not to sack the house."

"I thought as long as I was taking one book, I might as well take them all."

"There's no stopping a born thief," I said. "Actually, it isn't such a bad idea. One of these others might be the key."

Callista had her servants bring a large table into the peristyle and we spread Hermes's loot out for inspection. There were about fifteen books altogether, some of them being sizable volumes requiring more than one scroll.

"Here's the one you asked for," Hermes said, taking the scroll from inside his tunic.

I unrolled it on the table, and we studied it first. Like most books of better quality, it was written on Alexandrian papyrus of the finest sort. I had seen papyrus being manufactured in Egypt, and it is a most exacting process. The versatile papyrus plant is split open and its pith is peeled away in long strips. A layer of strips is laid side-by-side, slightly overlapped. A second layer is laid atop the first, at right angles to it. This delicate mat is soaked, then pressed between planks with a great weight laid atop the upper plank. The resulting sheet, now bound together firmly by the natural glue in the plant, is placed in the sun to dry and bleach until it is almost white.

The best quality of papyrus is made from the largest plants, so that the fewest strips are needed for the upper surface, the one that is written on. On this surface the strips run in the same direction as the writing. No matter how well the papyrus is rubbed with pumice to obliterate irregularities, the joins between the strips always tend to catch the tip of the pen.

For books of the best sort, the papyrus is trimmed into sheets about ten inches by twelve. They may be written upon as individual sheets, then glued together along their shorter sides into long sheets suitable for binding into scrolls, or they can be purchased ready-made in the form of blank scrolls, ready to be written upon. Each method has advantages and disadvantages, but the latter is now the most common.

While I studied this, Julia and Callista looked over the other books. "I see Cicero here," Julia said, "and Hortalus. Here's a study of the Twelve Tables, together with commentaries and disputes concerning interpretation."

"This," said Callista, "seems to be a text on the use of the Sybilline Books in Roman law, written almost two hundred years ago by one Valgus of Lanuvium."

"Single-minded bastard, wasn't he?" I said. "It sounds like he was planning a Caesar-like conquest of the Roman legal profession."

"Let me see this," Callista said. She began to examine the opening sheets of the scroll. Its first sheet, in the usual fashion, gave the title, *Certain Points of Law,* and its author, who was indeed Aulus Sulpicius Galba. Apparently it was written before he became duumvir of Baiae, for he did not include this dignity among his honors.

It also contained the usual dedication: "This work I dedicate to the immortal gods and the muses, to my revered ancestors, and to my esteemed friends and patrons, Publius Fulvius Flaccus and Sextus Manilius."

"Manilius!" I said. "I knew I'd trip over that name sooner or later."

"It could be a coincidence," Julia said. "It's not an uncommon name."

"When did you start believing in coincidence?" I asked her. "Fulvius and Manilius right here on the same page? That sounds like conspiracy to me. What do you want to bet these two are the fathers of the dead man and our young Tribune of the People?"

"I know better than to take a bet like that."

Callista wasn't interested in the dedication. She was scanning the text with great speed. She was one of those people who could read silently, a talent I have always admired.

"What are you looking for?" I asked her.

"The first sheet that contains every letter in the Latin alphabet. That one is most likely to be the key."

She had lost me again. I rose and beckoned to Hermes. "Ladies, I will take my leave of you now."

"I'll stay here and help Callista with this," Julia said. "What will you do now?"

"I'm going to find out what I can about young Manilius. Come, Hermes."

We left them absorbed in their work, their heads together like two lifelong friends.

7

If ANY ONE PLACE IN ROME COULD BE called the center of government in the old Republic, it would not be the Curia, which was just a place where the Senate met to argue and yell at each other. Nor was it the Septa on the Campus Martius where elections were held. At that time it was little more than a field with barriers to separate the people by tribes, and its informal name of "sheepfold" was quite descriptive.

No, the true center of the Republic was the *Tabularium* on the lower slopes of the Capitoline Hill, where most of the important documents of the City and the Empire were stored. It was our one true government building. Otherwise, we continued our rustic, inconvenient old custom of locating civic functions and offices in temples.

We had the Treasury in Saturn's, although money was coined in that of Juno Moneta. The Temple of Ceres housed the offices of the aediles; treaties and wills were kept in the Temple of Vesta. We declared war at the Temple of Bellona. We used the basilicas to hold courts, but they were used as much for markets and banks. Numerous minor temples housed lesser civic functions.

But the Archive kept the bulk of the records of government, many of them going back centuries. It was staffed by state-owned slaves and freedmen. In those days they were among the very few slaves owned directly by the state, unlike the vast slave bureaucracy that surrounds us now. They were very haughty, self-important slaves, too. The freedmen were even worse.

There was no real system or order to the place. It was not like the great Library at Alexandria where anyone who could read could walk straight to the wing where the work he desired was stored and find it within a few minutes. The Archive slaves simply kept everything in their memories, thus rendering themselves indispensable.

A bit of asking brought me to a warren presided over by a freedman named Androcles. He was not happy to see me. They never were.

"Senator Metellus, is it?" he said, as if merely speaking my name were an intolerable imposition. "I thought the whole City had taken a holiday, all flocking out to the Campus to see the soldiers, as if they've never seen such a prodigy. Well, *some* people still have to work!"

"Excellent," I said, "then you won't mind doing a little work for me."

"What?" He looked as if I had insulted his family, his homeland, and his national gods. "Have you any idea what is demanded of us here? Are you aware that Caesar's new conquests have added not one but three, *three*, mind you, new provinces to the Empire?" His voice had risen to a shout.

"Yes, but—"

"There isn't just to be a Province of Gaul," he went on, ignoring me. "No, that's not good enough for Caesar! There is to be a Province of Belgica, one of Aquitania, and one of Lugdunensis! *Three* brand-new provinces all at once! Oh, it's easy to kill a flock of barbarians and conquer the place, but who do you think has to organize and administer that wilderness? With *three* complete sets of public servants to establish a government, arrange its finances, and keep its records? And we're still getting Cyprus organized. Next thing you know, some fool is going to annex Egypt! Or Britannia!"

"Actually," I said, "it isn't so easy to conquer a new province, and the Senate will see to its administration."

"The Senate? The Senate names provincial governors! They don't do any work! You know that; you're a senator yourself. We have to provide the record keepers, keep the correspondence moving between the provinces and Rome, and build another level of rooms for this place so we can store them all. And do you think the Senate is going to vote us the budget to take care of all this? Hah!"

Hermes stepped forward and took a pouch from within his tunic. When he shook it, it made a musical jingle.

"Well, what is it you want?" Androcles asked, now marginally less hostile.

"I need documents pertaining to the citizenship status of the Tribune of the People Manilius, soon to leave office."

His eyes went wide. "Find documents pertaining to one citizen among all this—"

"Oh, shut up," Hermes said. As a freedman himself he knew all the poses and dodges. "You know perfectly well that you got all that stuff together when Manilius declared himself a candidate. And I happen to know that you keep the records pertaining to all serving magistrates handy because every climbing politician who wants to sue one of them for malfeasance comes here and bribes you for a look at them, just like we're doing. So go get them now."

Androcles glared at him. "I don't have to take that from some jumped-up errand boy! I remember when you carried the Senator's scraper and bath oil, and he was ill-advised to entrust you with those."

I placed an arm around his shoulders. "My friend Androcles, I know how overworked you are, and I, for one, appreciate the toil and stress of your office. Now, as one servant of the Senate and People to another, could you see if you can find these things for me?"

"Well," he said, somewhat mollified, "let me see what's to be found." He stalked off between two stacks of shelves, calling for his slave assistants.

"Always the politician, eh?" Hermes said.

"He's a voter, too, Hermes. Never forget that."

A slave appeared a short time later, holding an armload of scrolls and tablets. "Where do you want these?"

I pointed to one of the tables beneath the latticed windows that lined one of the long, southeast-facing walls. He arranged them neatly and stood back, not letting the documents out of his sight. We began to go over them.

"Publius Manilius Scrofa," Hermes read, "is a native of Rome, born in the Via Sacra district. He is a plebeian of the rural Pinarian Tribe, enrolled in an Equestrian Century. He is twenty-eight years old, unmarried, and has no children."

He read this from the document Manilius filed when he declared himself a candidate. It told me little. He had to be plebeian or he couldn't be a tribune. Nobody who wasn't equestrian could afford public office. All citizens belonged to tribes, and old, respected families always belonged to rural tribes and thought the urban tribes were all riffraff. Via Sacra might put him in Clodius's old camp—he'd been a great hero in the Via Sacra—but not necessarily.

I picked up a document from the last censorship, five years previously. It affirmed that Manilius qualified for the equestrian order, possessing a fortune of 415,000 sesterces. I showed this to Hermes.

"Just over the line for an *eques*," he noted. "That's not much to finance a political career."

"I wonder how his fortune would assess now. A tribune is in a position to make himself rich during his year in office."

"Maybe his father died and he inherited," Hermes pointed out.

"Or he could have borrowed. The censors' assessment is on property.

It doesn't take debt into account. A lot of cash-poor candidates borrow heavily rather than sell their lands and buildings."

"Very true," I said. "But I can't think of any way we can find out. There is no law requiring anyone to disclose the nature of his finances." I pondered this for a moment. "But, to maintain equestrian status, he had to file a list of his landed properties. Let's see what's here. It could tell us something."

We rummaged through the documents until we found a property statement filed with the electoral board that regulated the status of candidates between censorships. The previous year Manilius had listed the same property as during the last censorship, plus a new cash income of one hundred and twenty thousand sesterces per annum from an estate he hadn't possessed then.

"Well, well," I said. "It seems that young Manilius has come into possession of a fine estate in—guess where."

"Baiae?" Hermes answered.

"Where else? Ever since this business started, all roads lead to Baiae."

"Pretty substantial estate, too," Hermes observed, going down the list of its assets. "Two hundred *iugera* of land, divided into plowland, pasture, orchards, and vineyards, as well as a villa with colonnades and formal garden, olive press, wine press, ninety slaves, and twenty tenant families. Plus, it's right on the bay and has its own permanent, stone wharf."

"Not quite princely but very substantial," I noted. "It would be nice to know who owned it before it came into his possession."

"They're all Pompey's clients in the south, aren't they?" Hermes asked.

"Not everyone. And Baiae's become so popular that it's practically neutral ground."

The beautiful little town on the Bay of Neapolis at the southern end of Campania had become the most fashionable resort in Italy. During the hottest months, when Rome became intolerable, most wealthy families abandoned the capital for their country estates. Those who could afford it bought a villa in Baiae as a summer retreat. Cicero had one. So did Lucullus, Pompey, and many others. If you couldn't afford a place there, you tried to cadge an invitation.

"Too bad we don't have a few more days to work on this," Hermes said. "We could go down to Baiae and find out who gave him the estate. It'd be a good excuse for a trip to Baiae, anyway."

"We shouldn't have to go that far."

"Oh? You have a plan?"

"Always. I think we should go call on Caius Claudius Marcellus, brother of our consul and most likely consul for next year."

THE CITY WAS BEGINNING TO GET noisy. The soldiers were pouring in through the gates, flooding the taverns, and beginning to spread their money around. The day had turned into an impromptu holiday. Nobody seemed concerned that I was still running around loose.

The house of the Claudia Marcelli was well up on the Palatine. It was actually a veritable compound, holding the houses of a number of prominent members of that family. By asking, I found the proper door and announced myself. I was conducted into the atrium of a house that was fine but not pretentiously so, with a display of death masks that seemed to go back to the Tarquins. Romans who could boast such ancestry felt little need for greater display. The wealth of a Crassus could not buy lineage like that.

After a short wait, a lady came into the atrium to greet me.

"Welcome, Senator Metellus. I fear that my husband cannot be here to give you a proper greeting." She appeared to be in her early twenties and was therefore far younger than her husband. Nothing unusual about that. Patrician girls were often married off at fifteen or sixteen to politicians in their fifties. She was beautiful in a rather severe way, with hard-planed, regular features. Her clothing was of fine make but proper and old-fashioned. She was as far from Fulvia as she could be and still be Roman.

"What could be more proper than a greeting from the distinguished Lady Octavia?"

"You are diplomatic, but then that is the reputation of your family. My husband is out with the rest of the Senate inspecting my great-uncle's horde."

Her use of the word was not lost on me. "You don't approve of Caesar's sending his soldiers here? They are citizens, after all."

"When I married Caius Claudius I cut my ties with the Julian family. Like my husband and his brother, I perceive Caesar as a potential tyrant."

"But I understand he contemplates adopting your brother."

"I barely know my brother. I haven't seen him since he was an infant." She shook her head. "Forgive me. I forget my manners. Please come in, Senator."

Hermes remained in the atrium. It was just a few paces to the peristyle, where the statues surrounding the pool ran to figures like Camillus, Cincinnatus, and various ancestral Claudians. Not quite as lively as Fulvia's decor. We sat and a slave brought the obligatory watered wine and small loaves. I took enough to satisfy etiquette and determine that the wine was excellent, even though I couldn't identify it.

"Is it possible that I may help you?" she asked.

"Possibly. I am investigating the death of a man named Marcus Fulvius. You may have heard that he was accusing me of corruption, and that I am a suspect in his murder."

She shook her head. "I don't follow City gossip."

"Admirable. I've learned that he was living in a house owned by your husband, a property near the Temple of Tellus. Might you know anything about the man?"

"Like most men of quality, my husband owns a great deal of property both urban and rural. I suppose he must have a hundred residential properties within the old walls alone, and a great deal more outside and across the river. I know very little about them, and I doubt he does. His stewards manage all that for him. State business takes up all his time and energy."

"Service to the Senate and People is a demanding calling. Among his holdings, does he by chance number any estates in Baiae?"

"Why do you ask?" The question was blunt, and her look was direct.

"This man Fulvius was from Baiae, recently arrived in Rome. I wondered if he might be a family client of your husband."

"I know of no family named Fulvius among my husband's *clientela*. I believe the Fulvias are in some way connected to the Claudia Pulchri, but not to the Claudia Marcella."

"I see. Do you know if your husband has dealings with the Tribune of the People, Marcus Manilius?"

"I don't know the man, but my husband stands firmly with the *optimates* and I can hardly imagine him having anything to do with a tribune. Those jumped-up peasants have brought the Republic to the brink of ruin. Sulla should have abolished the office when he had the power to."

"I see I've troubled you needlessly," I said, rising.

"I am truly sorry I couldn't help you, Senator. I do hope you don't think me rude." Her smile was like the smile carved on a statue.

"Not at all. I'll just see if I can locate your husband, our future consul. If I miss him, please extend my regards when he returns home."

"I'll be sure to do so."

I collected Hermes and we left the house.

"Did you catch all that?" I asked him.

"Every word. I didn't think they made Roman matrons like that anymore."

"They don't. I'm sure almost everything she said was a lie."

"That's a relief. A Roman woman who doesn't follow City gossip—it's like saying the sun comes up in the west."

We found a tavern at the base of the Palatine where the soldiers were celebrating among admiring citizenry and took seats outside. The immense bulk of the Circus Maximus reared its arches skyward just a few paces away. An overworked girl brought us a pitcher and cups. It wasn't like the wine served in a great house, but it was adequate.

"What have I taught you about criminal investigations, Hermes?"

"Everyone lies."

"Exactly. What must the investigator do?"

"Sort through the lies to find the truth?"

"That's only part of it. One of the biggest mistakes you can make is to assume that everyone is lying for the same reason. Sometimes they're covering themselves; sometimes they're covering for other people. But sometimes they're hiding something you aren't even looking for. The fact is just about everyone is guilty of *something*, and when someone like me comes snooping around they reflexively assume that they're the target and try to hide their guilt."

"It gets confusing."

"Nothing that can't be solved by a first-class mind and a little inspiration," I assured him. I took another sip of inspiration and pondered for a while. This called for another sip. It really was inferior wine, not nearly as fine as the unknown vintage Octavia had served—

Abruptly, a god (or my special muse) visited me. In moments like this I have a special radiant, or perhaps stunned look. After awhile I noticed that fingers were waving in front of my face.

"Decius," Hermes was asking, "are you still there?"

"Let's order some food," I said. "I'm going to need a little fortification."

Mystified, he fetched flat bread, sausage, and preserved onions from the food counter and brought it to the table. I wasn't really hungry, but I put it away like a starving legionary.

"What's this all about?" Hermes wanted to know.

"We're going to visit the Brotherhood of Bacchus."

He blinked. "The wine merchants?"

"Exactly."

"You intend to get drunk and stay that way until this is all over?"

"A splendid idea, now that you suggest it, but not my intention." I was absurdly pleased with myself.

Hermes shrugged, knowing what I was like in this mood. "Whatever you say."

We left the tavern, rounded the northern end of the Circus, and turned left along the river. This district was devoted to the river trade, a great sprawl of wharves and warehouses with few temples or public buildings. Among the latter was the huge *porticus* of the Aemilian family, where a great deal of the river trade was conducted informally.

The warehouse of the Brotherhood of Bacchus stood between the *porticus* and the river. In the little square between the buildings stood one of my favorite statues in all of Rome. It depicted, about twice life-size, the god Bacchus. He stood in the conventional pose of a Greek god, but this was the Italian Bacchus, not the Greek Dionysus. He was portrayed as a handsome young man, but his features were slightly puffy and pouch eyed, his fine, athlete's body a little potbellied, his smile a bit silly. He looked like Apollo gone to seed. In one hand he held aloft a huge cluster of grapes. In the other, a wine cup. The cup was tilted and the sculptor, with marvelous skill, had depicted a tiny bit of wine slopping over the rim. His pose was a trifle off-balance, his garland of vine leaves just the tiniest bit askew.

"There stands a real Roman god," I said to Hermes. "None of that stuffy, Olympian solemnity about him."

We passed the god and went inside. The interior was cavernous, with massive, wooden racks stretching off in all directions, holding thousands of clay amphorae from every district of the world where grapes grow. The racks were labeled by district and year. Everywhere, slaves in pairs, stripped to loincloths, carried amphorae here and there, bringing them from the boats tied up to the wharf outside or from the racks to wagons waiting in the street out front. Each pair carried a pole on their brawny shoulders, the amphora suspended from the pole by ropes passed through the thick handles molded to each side of its neck. The slaves accomplished this seemingly awkward task with wonderful celerity and skill.

A fat man wearing a toga spotted my senator's stripe and hustled over. "Welcome, Senator. What may the Brotherhood of Bacchus do for you? I am Manius Maelius, steward of the Brotherhood, at your service."

"I'm of a mind to buy some wine for my household. Of course, my steward will be along later to make the purchase, but I want to try the vintage first."

"Of course, of course. What is your pleasure? Here we have wine from Iberia, from Greece and all the islands: Cyprus, Rhodes, Cos, Lesbos—some fine Lesbian just arrived today, Senator—Delian, Cretan, the list goes on. We have Asian, Syrian, Judean, wine from Egypt, from Numidia and Libya and Mauretania, from Cisalpina—"

"My taste runs a bit closer to home," I said, interrupting his circumnavigation of the Middle Sea.

"We have wine from every district of Italy," he assured me. "From Verona, Ravenna, from Luca and Pisae—"

I could see he was starting with the north, so I stopped him again. "Something more southerly, I think."

"Good choice. We bought almost the entire production of Sicily, we have Tarentine and some interesting new products of Venusia—"

"I prefer vineyards north of that area."

He beamed. "Of course, you desire Campanian. The very heart of Italian wine country. Naturally, we have wine from Mount Massicus, especially the always-reliable Falernian, grown on its southern slope. We have wine from Terracina and Formiae, and some rather good Capuan, although its yield has been rather inferior these last years due to excessive rainfall."

Hermes had finally caught on. "The senator has a weakness for the vineyards around the Bay of Neapolis."

The fat man clapped his hands in approval. "Ah, the incomparable slopes of Vesuvius! There is nothing to compare with volcanic soil, a steep slope, and perfect sunshine. Vesuvius is even better than Aetna. We have Stabian, Pompeiian—"

"I think," Hermes said, "if you have some really good product from near, say, Baiae, that you'll make a sale."

"I see that the senator is a real connoisseur. Not many people understand the qualities of Baiaean. Small vineyards, very low yield, so little is exported. Only wealthy vacationers ever try them, and they keep the news to themselves because they don't want a rush to start, driving the price up, as happened with Caecuban a few years ago. It just so happens that we have a few amphorae from a select group of the very best vineyards."

I clapped him on the shoulder. "Lead on, Manius Maelius!"

We took a long walk down the rows of jugs, the skylights admitting the afternoon sun in bars of light divided into small lozenges, the result of the bronze fretwork that protected the warehouse from intruding pigeons.

We ended up in a shed built onto the southern end of the warehouse. It contained no more than a few hundred amphorae, all of them with the characteristic color of Campanian pottery. The racks were labeled by town, the amphorae by vineyard. A single rack bore the name of Baiae.

"We cannot, of course, unseal these amphorae for tasting," Maelius said. "But, since the finest vintages are bought only by persons of quality, we have an arrangement with each vineyard to supply a small quantity of each vintage for tasting purposes." He gestured to a table along one wall. It resembled the serving counter in a wineshop, with jugs resting in holes cut in the table, a dipper and a stack of tiny cups beside each jug.

The steward began at one end of the table. "Now this is from a vineyard owned by ex-consul Cicero himself." He dipped out a cupful and handed it to me ceremoniously.

I sipped. Immediately I knew I was right. It was very similar to the wine Octavia had served. Soil and sunlight will always tell. I reflected that Cicero had never served this vintage when I'd visited him. Keeping it to himself, was he? This confirmation alone would have made the trip a success, but I decided to press my advantage. When the gods have shown you exceptional favor, it makes sense to determine just how much they love you.

"Excellent," I told him, "but not quite what I'm looking for."

I tried one from the Puteoli district, then several others, each time closing in on the bay itself.

"This is an especially fine one, Senator."

He handed me the cup and I tasted. Perfect. It was the very vintage I had tasted earlier that day. My palate is infallible in these matters.

He caught my smile but misinterpreted it. "Ah, I see that this is exactly what you are searching for. Excellent choice, Senator. This wine is from the Baiaean vineyards owned by the great family of Claudius Marcellus."

"The consul?"

He squinted at the label on the jug. "No, this estate is owned by his cousin, Caius Claudius. He is the one standing for next year's consulship." He looked at the rack that held the big amphorae. "You are just in time, Senator."

"How is that?"

"In previous years we've usually managed to get six or seven amphorae from that small estate. This year we got only three and there is one left. Shall I have it set aside for you?"

"Please do so. I'll send my steward to pick it up tomorrow or the next day." We left him beaming.

"Do you really intend to buy it?" Hermes said, as we left. "Julia will have your hide off for buying such expensive wine."

"That's why you are going to pick it up and take it to the country house. It really is excellent wine. Do you know why they only got three amphorae this year?" As we passed Bacchus I kissed my fingertips and touched them to his toes. He must have been the god who sent my inspiration.

Hermes thought a moment. "Because, last year, a part of the estate went to Manilius."

"Exactly."

"But was Manilius being bribed for a specific favor or was it just for his cooperation during his year as tribune?"

"An excellent question. You really are learning how to do this, Hermes. Next year, when I'm praetor, you'll make me a first-class investigator."

"*If* you're praetor next year. If you're *alive* next year, for that matter."

"Such are the vagaries of politics. But the gods are on my side, and maybe they'll continue to favor me." By this time we were past the Porticus Aemilia and turned rightward along the old Servian Wall toward the Ostian Gate.

"What do we know about the Claudia Marcella?" I asked as we passed beneath the portal.

"Not much," Hermes answered. "I've got a feeling we'd have heard a lot about them if we'd spent more time in Rome these last few years."

"That is what I think. We need someone who specializes in gossip, the more scurrilous the better. Not a respectable type, mind you. We can't use anyone whose party affiliation compels him to exalt his own side while defaming the others. We need someone who is shameless about vilifying anyone at all. We need—"

"We need Sallustius."

"Exactly. I loathe the man, but I loathe him for precisely the same qualities I am in need of now. Run on ahead to the Forum, look into the baths. He'll be wherever the news is to be had, maybe out on the Campus Martius where the legionaries are pitching their tents."

"That's a lot of territory to cover," he complained.

"Sallustius won't be hard to spot. When you've located him, come back and find me and lead me to him. I'll be making a more dignified progress toward the Forum. I'll wait for you at the Rostra."

He dashed off and I ambled my way up the old street past the Temple of Flora and around the northern end of the Circus, stopping to chat with citizens as I went. It was still election time after all. Nobody seemed to be disturbed by my suspect status. So far, so good.

The day was getting on, but there was still plenty of daylight left. My head buzzed pleasantly from the recent wine tasting. I always take satisfaction in mixing business with pleasure.

By the time I reached the Rostra, Hermes was standing there, and Sallustius was with him. I put on my biggest, most sincere false smile and took his oily hand and clapped his hairy shoulder.

"Caius Sallustius," I shouted, "you are just the man I wanted to see!"

"So I presumed, since you sent your man to fetch me." He tried for a sardonic smile, but on his face it was merely ugly. "I take it that this has something to do with your current difficulty?"

I gave him a surprised look. "You mean that silly business with the late Fulvius? Not at all! I simply wished to call upon your matchless—ah, scholarship concerning the political personages of our Republic."

"I see," he said, not buying a bit of it. "And just what would you know?"

"Well, since I'm to be one of next year's praetors—"

"Assuming you aren't in exile," he interrupted.

"I wish people would stop saying that. This murder charge is false. Less than nothing."

"Indeed." He put a wealth of disbelief into the word.

"Anyway, it is almost certain that one of next year's consuls will be Caius Claudius Marcellus. It occurs to me that I know very little about the man whom I shall have to work with for the next year. I don't know much about the family, for that matter. They've always been around, but they've become uncommonly prominent of late."

"That," he said, "is because they've made themselves spokesmen for the anti-Caesarian bloc in the Senate."

"I've deduced that much. How did this come about?"

"For one thing, you Metelli abandoned leadership of the anti-tyrannical party."

I winced. That arrow had been straight at the mark. My family's hedging and trimming, once the sign of statesmanlike willingness to compromise, was beginning to look like timidity and weakness.

"So the Claudii have thrust their family forward as champions of good old Republican liberty, eh? They seem to have a lot of people convinced."

"And they're willing to go to extremes to prove it."

We had begun strolling toward the Basilica Aemilia, where the work of restoration went noisily on despite the general holiday atmosphere. Soldiers swarmed everywhere, strutting about to great admiration.

"What sort of extremes?" I asked him.

"Did you hear about the man from Novum Comum?"

The name sounded familiar. "Isn't that one of the colonies Caesar founded in Gaul?"

"It is. Anyway, a few months ago Marcellus—our current consul Marcellus, that is—tried to bring up the prospect of a successor to Caesar in Gaul. This, of course, was opposed, not only by Caesar's faction in the Senate, but by the other consul and by Pompey. One senator who spoke up was from Novum Comum. Marcellus went into an immoderate fury, had his lictors drag the man from the chamber, strip him of his insignia, and scourge him publicly with the rods of their fasces."

I had thought myself numb to enormities, but this left me aghast. "He had a *citizen* publicly flogged?" Heads swiveled to see who was shouting. I went on in a lower voice. "Surely he'll be exiled for this!" That the man had been a senator was a minor matter. By ancient law Roman citizens were not to be publicly flogged or crucified. These punishments were restricted to foreigners and rebellious slaves.

"That is just it. Marcellus proclaimed that Caesar had no right to confer citizenship, and he would recognize no such citizenships, nor would he tolerate any senators sent from any such colonies."

At that time it was customary, when a new colony was enfranchised, to allow a very prominent man of that place to take a seat in the Senate without having first served a quaestorship in Rome.

"And what about Balbus?" I asked. I referred to Lucius Cornelius Balbus, a very prominent senator who, along with two or three others, got his senator's stripe in the same fashion, because he was a friend of Pompey's from Spain. He was no relation to the Atius Balbus who was Caesar's brother-in-law and grandfather of the First Citizen.

"Marcellus isn't picking a fight with Pompey."

I ran a palm over my by now stubbly face. My bright mood of an hour before was gone. "It is worse than I thought," I admitted. "If this keeps up, it will be open war between Caesar and the Senate."

"It's been war for some time."

"I don't mean political dispute, no matter how rambunctious it gets. I mean real war. Next year we could see these soldiers all around us back again, with their shields facing the gates and Caesar behind them on his command platform." Caesar had invented a collapsible platform that could be erected in minutes, so that he could get close to the fighting and still see over the heads of his soldiers.

"Then now is a good time to choose sides, isn't it?" Sallustius said, insinuatingly. I wondered what to read into this. He said almost everything insinuatingly.

"Are you offering me a side to choose?"

"Why," his look was all innocence, "I assumed, because of your family connection and the obvious esteem Caesar holds for you, that you would be firmly in his camp."

This angered me and I was about to snap out something ill-considered when Hermes rapped me sharply over the kidney. Sallustius couldn't see the jab, but I could certainly feel it.

"Isn't that our friend the tribune over there?" Hermes said, nodding toward a little group of men who seemed to be looking over the restoration work. One of them was, indeed, young Tribune Manilius. The other four men were vaguely familiar to me. I knew I had seen their faces in the Senate. Three of them resembled one another strongly, with bushy, brown hair and thick, red noses. They stood just within the portico of the basilica. They all seemed to be arguing about something.

"This is why I led you here," Sallustius said. "I saw them cross the Forum and climb the steps here a bit earlier. You see, of course, the three who look like they hatched from the same egg?"

"Naturally. Is one of them Marcellus?"

"They all are. The one on the left, with the old sword scar on his cheek, is this year's consul, Marcus Claudius Marcellus. The one poking his finger in the tribune's face is his cousin Caius, who is most likely to be next year's consul. The third, who looks like he needs an enema, is Caius's brother, another Marcus Claudius Marcellus. He plans to stand for the consulship the following year."

"And the fifth man?" I asked.

"That is Lucius Aemilius Lepidus Paullus, also standing for next year's consulship, and the man having this basilica restored to the glory of his ancestors."

"With Caesar's money, I hear."

"Caesar is generous to his friends," Sallustius affirmed.

The evidence was apparent everywhere. The walls of the portico were being covered with exquisite mosaics depicting the history of the Aemilian gens back to the days of Romulus, the whole interior was faced with brilliantly colored marble, the old roof tiles had been stripped away and replaced by plates of gleaming bronze. The restored basilica would be the most magnificent public building in Rome, at least until some other politician decided to bankrupt himself for the sake of public adulation.

"This seems like an odd group to see in one place," I observed.

"Odd groupings have become the rule in Rome," Sallustius said.

"Men who were at each other's throats just a few months ago are now comrades-in-arms."

Just then one of the Marcelli noticed us and nudged the others. The consul looked at us and frowned.

"What are you doing here?"

"I thought I'd just pop over and see how the restorations are coming along," I told him. "It looks wonderful, Lucius Aemilius."

He grinned. "I thank you." Then he looked at the consul and glared. "And why are you questioning the right of Decius Caecilius to be here? This is *my* basilica, Consul!"

"He ought to be in prison awaiting trial," the consul Marcellus growled. "The man's a murderer and a disgrace!"

"Not yet proven," Manilius said.

"Who needs proof?" said Caius. "He's the logical choice."

I longed to toss out some remark about that estate in Baiae, just to watch their faces change color. But some things are best kept in reserve.

"The wretch was no loss anyway," Aemilius Paullus put in. "Did you know that he was trying to usurp my basilica?" He waved a beringed hand, taking in all the lavish adornments. Workmen swarmed everywhere, applying the finishing touches to it: bits of gilding here and there, final polishing of the multicolored marble, buffing the thin mica plates set into the clerestory windows. "He waited until all the major work was nearly finished, then he tried to bring up that old claim that it was a Fulvius, not an Aemilius, who built it!"

"It's a valid claim," said the consul Marcellus. "When I was young, I heard it called the Fulvia as often as the Aemilia."

"Nonsense!" Aemilius Paullus cried, going red in the face. "Base calumny! The Fulvians are a family of nobodies who want to steal the glory of a nobler gens! This building is the pride of my family, and it has always been maintained by us!"

This was excellent entertainment, and I believe I was enjoying it as much as Sallustius was.

Hermes whispered in my ear: "Another suspect."

I nodded but said nothing.

"Maintained by you!" Caius Marcellus shouted. "Everyone knows that your great restoration project is the result of the biggest bribe in the history of the Republic! Even now, all over Rome, people are beginning to call this place the Basilica Julia!"

Aemilius Paullus went dead white. "And just what, I pray, am I being bribed to *do?*"

"It is common knowledge," Caius Marcellus sneered, "that you and I will be next year's consuls."

"The two of you have outspent everyone else," Tribune Manilius commented.

"And I," Caius went on, "have pledged to devote myself to recalling Caesar from Gaul and giving his command to a trustworthy man who will draw this endless war to an honorable close. You have been paid handsomely to agitate for an extension of Caesar's command. Dare to deny it!"

"Deny that I support Caesar? Never!" said Aemilius Paullus "He has brought Rome more glory and riches than all the Claudians back to the days of Aeneas! He deserves all the honors the Senate can bestow upon him! As for his gifts to me, such tokens exchanged between men of rank are an ancient custom, one you have practiced assiduously!" He appealed to me. "Decius Caecilius, did Caesar not help cover the debts you assumed as aedile?"

"Actually," I told them, "he offered to cover them all. But I accepted no more of his generosity than my family deemed proper." It seemed that everyone was trying to push me into Caesar's camp.

"You see?" Aemilius Paullus cried. "A man as upright as our next year's praetor, Decius Caecilius, is not ashamed to partake of Caesar's largesse."

"With more moderation than you," said the consul, his exaggerated gaze taking in the lavish restorations. "Don't try to make us out as enemies of the Metelli, Aemilius. We've no argument with them."

The angry, raised voices were attracting attention. People had begun drifting in from the Forum to catch the show. Soon there was a large enough crowd for the infuriated politicians to take notice and moderate their tone. The three Marcelli, accompanied by Manilius, stalked off in a huff.

Aemilius Paullus put a smile back on his face and addressed the minor mob now assembled in the basilica. "Citizens! I welcome all of you warmly, but the workmen are still busy here so I must ask you all to leave for now. But I want you all back here when I rededicate the basilica as soon as I assume office after the election. I shall hold a public banquet to which you and all other citizens are invited."

This got a cheer from the crowd, with Caesar's soldiers cheering loudest. No doubt about it, his election was assured. As soon as the crowd dispersed, Aemilius Paullus came to join us.

"It looks like next year will be an important one, eh, Decius?" he said.

"Lively, anyway. The Senate meetings should be noisy."

"I take it I can count on your support?"

I sidestepped. "I'm just one voice in the Senate. As praetor, I'll have no voice in provincial affairs. You need to talk to next year's tribunes. Caesar's fortunes lie more with the assemblies than with the Senate."

"All too true," Aemilius Paullus grumbled, then he turned to Sallustius. "Have you packed to go yet, Caius Sallustius?"

"Go?"

"Yes, go. I've been talking with Appius Claudius Pulcher, and he's already making his list of men to expel from the Senate when he's censor next year. Your name is on it."

"Expel me?" Sallustius cried, aghast. "On what charge?"

"Immorality, it seems."

"Indeed? Am I so much worse than my colleagues in the Senate?"

"You know that better than I, but Appius doesn't like you, and it's going to be a hard year for men he doesn't like."

"Of what sort of immoralities is Sallustius accused?" I asked. This was something I just had to hear.

"Let's see—as tribune last year he is supposed to have taken bribes to prosecute Milo and oppose Cicero, he maintains his residence in a whorehouse, he looted the Ostian treasury during his quaestorship there, he seduced the wives of at least twenty senators, he likewise seduced a Vestal, he has appeared in the Senate staggering drunk, he dishonored certain statues of the gods during the Floralia, he was seen using weapons in the annual brawl over the head of the October Horse, he employed blackmail to send a naval cutter to Cirta to fetch him fresh oysters—"

"I haven't done half those things!" Sallustius protested.

"Which half?" I asked him.

"This is the basest sort of slander, spread by Caesar's enemies."

"It's enough to get you expelled though," I told him. "If I were you, I'd talk with Calpurnius Piso. He's almost certain to be the other censor, and he's Caesar's father-in-law to boot. If he's obstructive enough, he might be able to keep you in."

"Don't count on that," Aemilius advised. "Piso's wife is one of the ones you're accused of seducing. And you're just one of a very long list Appius has drawn up."

"Who else?" I asked.

"Most prominently, young Curio."

"A serving tribune?" I said. "What does he hope to accomplish?"

"First, he can make Curio's life miserable," Aemilius Paullus pointed out, "even though he can't take immediate action against him. Second, he'll be parceling out the public contracts. Curio has many friends and supporters among the wealthy *publicani*. How many of them do you think will get their contracts granted or renewed under this censorship?"

"That's a powerful weapon all right," I acknowledged.

"And," Aemilius Paullus reminded us, "a tribune must lay down his powers at a specific time—next December to be precise. A censor is under no such obligation. He can stay in office until he judges it to be fulfilled. I think I can predict that Appius will stay in office until he's dealt with all of next year's magistrates who have displeased him."

"Not much chance of keeping my stripe with a quick bribe, then," Sallustius said. "Well, what one set of censors decree, another can set aside. Maybe I won't even have to wait that long."

"How will you accomplish that?" I asked him. Expulsion by the censors usually meant a five-year wait until a more sympathetic pair took office. Then you had to start at the bottom again, getting elected to another quaestorship and serving in that office for a year to qualify for the Senate.

"Appius won't stay in office any longer than it takes him to do as Aemilius Paullus says. He'll have no excuse, and he'll have other things to do. I'll ask Caesar to get me a quaestorship without going through the elections again. He can get the comitia to grant me one by acclamation. He did it for Marcus Antonius. A year of that and I can resume my seat in the Senate." In a few seconds Sallustius had figured out a way to extricate himself from a political predicament that might have discouraged a less flexible man. He was not without talent.

"There, you see?" said Aemilius Lepidus Paullus. "Being a friend of Caesar has its advantages." He lost his smile. "Bribery! As if I would not support Caesar without being bought! The Aemilii and the Julia Caesares have been allies for generations."

I could not vouch for that, but it was clear that the charge of bribery rankled him. Caesar's munificence could be confusing. Sometimes he simply bought a man's allegiance, as had clearly been the case with Curio. But just as often he was generous to a man whose support was already unquestioned.

"How will you handle next year's business?" Sallustius asked him. "It's clear you are going to have a hostile colleague in office."

128

"Much will depend upon how great my support is. I can count upon little from the Senate."

"You can count upon mine," Sallustius said, "but it sounds as if I'll be devoting myself to literary pursuits at my country house."

"Then I shall have to look to the Popular Assemblies, it seems. That's where the real power is these days."

And there it was again: class against class. War was coming.

8

"OCTAVIA SAID SOMETHING IMPORTANT," I told Julia.

"What was it?"

"I don't remember."

"That's a great help." We sat eating dinner while sounds of revelry made their way in through the door and over the walls. Everyone was entertaining Caesar's soldiers, and the party had spilled out into the streets and squares where tables had been set up and the wine flowed. I wished I could be out there with them.

"I mean, I remember everything she said. I just can't put my finger on what did not ring true."

"Sleep on it," Julia advised. "Perhaps, like Callista, you'll be visited by a god who will sort this out for you."

"It could happen," I admitted. "Speaking of that learned lady, did she come up with a solution for the code?"

Julia shook her head. "No, I left her house shortly after you did. I wanted to give her privacy to work on it."

I wondered what the two had really been talking about. Me and my shortcomings, no doubt.

There was a pounding on the door outside and a few moments later my father came in, accompanied by Scipio and Nepos. Julia served wine and retired, none too happy about it. These men were too old-fashioned to talk politics with a woman in the room.

"What have you learned?" Father demanded. I gave a succinct report of my doings, and he made a disgusted sound. "You've wasted your time while we've been lining up support for you."

"No, I find this interesting," said Metellus Scipio. "You've gathered a lot of evidence here and there, Decius. Have you drawn any conclusions?"

"Just a few minor conclusions that may lead to the main one."

"Such as?" said Nepos.

"Fulvius was killed by three or more highly placed men."

"How is that?" Father asked. "The number of weapons says multiple assailants and the bugger was held from behind, I'll grant your Greek friend knows what he's talking about there. What makes you think they were well-born or important and not just street scum?"

"The clumsiness of the execution," I told them. "What grown Roman man doesn't know how to kill a man with a knife? It's part of every soldier's training, and even those who never served in the legions see it done in the arenas, both with straight blades and curved *sicas*. This man was killed by a multitude of shallow cuts, like some wretch executed by an Oriental monarch. And the cuts were administered by straight blades, not well suited to the task."

Scipio nodded. "And a gentleman would never use a *sica*, even to commit murder."

"Precisely. And there was this: Everybody wanted to participate, but nobody wanted to be the one to administer the deathblow."

"You've lost me," Father said.

"We've seen it before," I told them. "The essence of conspiracy is to take part, but also to make sure that the others take an equal part. Look at the absurd lengths to which Catilina's men went to make sure that every one of them was liable to the death penalty. That way nobody could back out, and nobody could squeal on the others."

"So each administers a little bit of the death, eh?" Nepos said.

"Picture yourself as part of such a conspiracy," I began.

"Never!" said Father.

"Bear with me. This is the way I think. If you had conspired with some colleagues to murder a prominent man, would you rush right up and cut his throat, the easiest way to do it? No, because you'd know exactly what the others would do: They'd back away with looks of horror, pointing at you and saying, 'Ohhh, look at what he did!' Imagine how embarrassed you'd be. No, you give the poor bastard a cut, then you back away and make sure that the rest do at least as much. Only then does someone administer the deathblow."

They considered this for a while. They weren't accustomed to my sort of reasoning. Finally, Nepos spoke up.

"I can see men conspiring this way against a really great man, a Pompey or a Caesar. But why a nobody like Marcus Fulvius? He was nothing."

"Yes," I said, "but what might he have *become?*"

"Decius," Scipio said impatiently, "you are not Socrates, and we are certainly not your adoring students. Stop asking questions and give us some answers!"

"Hear, hear!" chimed in the other two. I loved nettling them like this.

"Just this morning, while conferring with the Greek lady who is working on the code for me, we talked about what family names and bloodlines mean to us Romans, to the common plebs no less than to the patricians and the aristocrats. Marcus Fulvius was the brother-in-law of Clodius, whom the commons still mourn. He and his sister, Fulvia, are also the grandchildren of Caius Gracchus. The commons revere nobody the way they revere the name of Caius and Tiberius Gracchus."

"Gracchus!" Father said. "I'd forgotten that. Scipio, what's the connection?" Scipio, with his patrician antecedents, was the acknowledged expert. He could reel off Roman lineages the way most of us could recite the bloodlines of chariot horses.

"The wife of Caius Gracchus was a Licinia, of the Licinius Crassus line. Their daughter was Sempronia and she married—let me see—Fulvius Flaccus. The slut Fulvia and the dead fool must be their children. I think there's another."

"Manius Fulvius," I said. "He's duumvir of Baiae. Now tell me who was the mother of the Gracchi?"

"Cornelia," they all said at once. This took no great feat of memory. Cornelia, mother of the Gracchi, was the most famous Roman mother since Rhea Silvia, mother of Romulus and Remus. Predictably, it was Metellus Scipio who first grasped the implications.

"Jupiter! Cornelia was the daughter of Scipio Africanus, my own ancestor!"

"Exactly," I affirmed. "Marcus Fulvius's brother-in-law was the most popular tribune of his generation. His grandfather was the glorious hero of the plebs. His great grandmother was the most revered woman in Roman history. His great-great grandfather was the man who defeated Hannibal, then was cheated of all his honors by Cato the Censor, the most reactionary aristocrat who ever lived."

I sat back and took a long drink. I needed one. "Picture it: There I am, standing for trial in the court of Juventius. The jury are all members of the equestrian order. Very few members of that body who are not our clients are very friendly toward us in the first place. Marcus Fulvius gets up to introduce himself and reels off that list of recent ancestors and family connections. What happens next?" I looked at them, from one to the other in turn. Father spoke first.

"He steps right into the spot vacated by Clodius."

"And," said Nepos, "he demands to be elected tribune, even though he hasn't served a quaestorship. It's been done before."

Father's scarred face flamed. "This has been going on and we didn't know about it?"

"Why should we?" I asked him. "There's a revolution in the making, and it's directed against people like us."

"Against the Roman Constitution, you mean," Scipio said.

"No, against a few entrenched families that have wielded power for far too long. Who has held power in Rome these thirty years past? Men like Pompey and Crassus, Hortensius Hortalus, Lucullus, families like the Claudia Marcella, and, yes, the Caecilia Metella. All of them supporters of Sulla. The old dictator killed all his enemies and theirs, and left them the Republic to run as they saw fit under his new constitution.

"People are growing tired of them—tired of *us*, I should say. Caesar gained power with the *populares* by identifying himself with his uncle-by-marriage, Marius, the sworn enemy of Sulla. Should it be any surprise that another man would try to do the same by stressing his descent from the Gracchi and Africanus?"

Father surprised me by, for once, not berating me for having such disloyal thoughts. He brooded for a while, then said, "I believe my son is right in this. By whatever pseudo-Greek process of logic, he has found the basis of this threat. But we still don't know who killed this Marcus Fulvius or why. We had the most reason to, and we know we didn't do it." He glared at the others. "We *didn't* do it, did we?"

Nepos and Scipio vigorously denied any involvement. "Face it," Nepos said, "none of us was clever enough even to have seen the threat. We had no reason to kill him until Decius here just explained it, and now he is already dead. But where does Caius Claudius Marcellus fit into this? As you just said, Decius, the Claudia Marcella are old Sullans and they're rabidly against Caesar. Why give patronage to this putative Man of the People?"

"Perhaps," Scipio said, "the Marcelli wanted to raise up a *rival* to Caesar. Fulvius might have drained off some of the popular support Caesar needs to further his ambitions. Clodius was Caesar's tame dog. Fulvius would not have been."

"Very astute," I admitted. "That may very well have been a part of it. It still doesn't explain who killed him."

We pondered that for a while, until we decided that we weren't going to come to any conclusions that night.

At the door Father turned to me and said, "Only you could use an investigation as an excuse for a wine-tasting expedition, and then make it work." I could almost have sworn that I saw him smile.

Julia came to join me as soon as they were gone.

"I suppose you were listening," I said.

"Naturally. Things are beginning to make a sort of sense. Maybe we can get the rest before it's trial time."

"We're running short of sources to investigate," I complained.

"They're all around us."

"What do you mean?"

"How tired are you? Are you up to another expedition tonight?"

"Where are we going?" Ordinarily, Julia was vehemently opposed to all nocturnal wanderings. Rome was a dangerous city, and my reputation was well-earned.

"Not far. The neighbors will be up all night, the wine is flowing freely, and this is the Subura. What better time and place to pick up City gossip?"

Tired though I was, this prospect lent me new energy. "Splendid idea! You get your girl, I'll find Hermes, and we'll go test the waters."

I dashed to my study, bellowing for Hermes. He joined me and I opened the box on my desk, took out my *caestus* and dagger, and tucked them within my tunic. No sense taking any chances. Hermes helped me don the dingy old toga I wore for nocturnal excursions, and I was ready to go.

Julia waited at the door, her head now decently covered by her *palla* and accompanied by Cypria, her maid. We went out into the bustling streets of the Subura.

The festive air was not as extreme as at one of the great celebrations like Saturnalia or Floralia. On those occasions, nobody would be sober and upright at this late hour. The atmosphere was more that of a country village fair, with a great deal of jollity but without the total license of the state-sanctioned orgies.

We received the usual greetings from our neighbors, and we welcomed and praised the soldiers from the district who were visiting their homes, some of them for the first time in years. There were depressingly few of these though. Young City men rarely served in the legions anymore. The legions depended more and more on the Italian *municipia,* the rural citizen communities where life was dull enough to make a soldier's life seem attractive. There was just too much to do in Rome. Life was easy and exciting in the great City. I couldn't blame them. I, too, hated to leave Rome.

The district's innumerable men's clubs and funeral societies stood open, illuminated with candles and lamps. On every corner fragrant smoke rose from charcoal braziers, where vendors served warmed wine and grilled sausages. There were no major temples in the Subura, but many small ones. Fires had been kindled before the altars of these so that the gods of the district could share in the festivities.

Our first stop of the evening was an inn called the Gorgon. It was run by a man named Strabo and his freedwoman wife, Lucia. It had stables where I occasionally boarded horses, and on this night the courtyard framed by the stables and the main building had been filled with tables to accommodate the crowd.

We found places at a table crowded by neighbors and were greeted noisily. Strabo and Lucia bustled over personally to fill our cups.

"Welcome, Senator, my lady!" Strabo cried. "This is even better than the usual election season, isn't it?"

"For us, anyway," Lucia chimed in. "Too bad about this Fulvius business." She didn't seem greatly saddened by my predicament. Not with the business her inn was doing that night.

"Pay it no heed," Strabo advised me. "It will all blow over in a few days."

"In a few days the elections will be over, and I can't get elected with this hanging over me."

"Hadn't thought of that," he admitted.

"It's all the Via Sacrans's doing," Lucia asserted. "Ever since they lost Clodius, they've been looking to do us a bad turn. They know you're our favorite senator."

The Via Sacrans and the Suburans, though fellow Romans, regard each other the way the Spartans and Athenians used to. The rivalry was usually good-natured: shouting at each other in the Circus, where the Suburans supported the Greens and the Via Sacrans the Blues, and the annual fight over the head of the October Horse. But sometimes it erupted into a minor civil war, with scores killed in days of running street fights.

"Does anyone know anything about this man Fulvius?" Julia asked the table at large. It was a long table, and it held a fairly representative sampling of the neighborhood: shopkeepers, idlers, a thief, a Jewish marble merchant, a craftsman or two, even another senator.

This last was a man named Spurius Gavius Albinus, a man of a totally undistinguished Suburan family. Each generation they managed to get one son elected to a quaestorship and thence to a seat in the Senate. He then never held higher office, but membership in the Senate was for life, barring expulsion by the censors. Thus these Gavii retained their status as a senatorial family. The great majority of senators at the time were such men. Only a small group of senatorial families ever held the praetorship, and a smaller group yet, my own included, were consuls.

"Word has it," a shopkeeper said, "that he was being lined up for next year's tribuneship elections."

"Where does this word originate?" Julia asked.

The man looked puzzled. "I don't know. It's just around. Fulvius was going to make a big name for himself by taking on the Metelli."

"I heard," said the thief, "that he had plans to make Pompey's life miserable."

"Pompey?" I said. "The wretch didn't lack ambition."

"Way I heard it," the thief went on, "he figured he had better blood in him than Pompey."

"I knew his father slightly," said the marble merchant. "I travel to Baiae two or three times a year on business." He was a fully Hellenized Jew, meaning that his dress, hair, beard, and adornments were all Greek, and he spoke that language with cultured fluency. He went by the name Philippus. I presume he chose the nane himself, and it was a clever one, being one of the few Roman names of Greek origin.

"He was Fulvius Flaccus, wasn't he?" I inquired.

"Publius Fulvius Flaccus Bambalio," Philippus said, giving it the full treatment. "He and his partner donated a fine Temple of Neptune to the city of Baiae. I furnished it inside and out with beautiful, sea green marble."

"His partner being Sextus Manilius?" I asked.

"No. It was Caius Octavius, the one who was praetor some years ago."

I almost knocked over my cup, but rescued it in time. "Octavius? I'd no idea the man had holdings in Baiae!"

"Oh, yes!" said Senator Gavius. "Octavius served as duumvir one year out of every three. He was one of the town's main benefactors." He added, with a smile of satisfaction, "I go to Baiae often."

Probably because you never do anything for the state, I thought. I might have said something indiscreet, but Julia jumped in at that moment.

"We had heard that Fulvius Flaccus and Sextus Manilius are close friends."

"They are," Gavius said. "Manilius is another of the regular *duumviri* of Baiae. There's a little group of families down there who take the highest offices in turn." He refilled his cup and grinned at me. "Just like here."

"Manilius?" said a copper founder named Glabrio. "Is he any relation to the young tribune?"

"Look!" Julia cried happily, stomping on my foot. "Here's a hero we know back from the war!" It was fortuitous timing. Even without having my foot stomped on, I knew we didn't want to expose this Gordian knot of intrigue before our neighbors.

Entering the courtyard was a family of my clients. In their lead was old Burrus, a veteran of my legion in Spain. Crowned with laurel, in military tunic and belt, was his son Lucius, whom I had last seen in Gaul a couple of years earlier. He had a hand on the shoulder of a nephew who wore one of the Gallic torques that were showing up everywhere. His mother was swathed in what appeared to be about ten yards of vividly checked and striped cloth.

"Patron! Domina!" Lucius said, catching sight of us. I took his hands and saw that he wore silver bracelets on both wrists. Among Roman men, only soldiers wear bracelets, and these are decorations for valor. It was rare for a man so young to wear two of them.

"I see you've been busy." I poured a cup and handed it to him. "Still in the first cohort?"

"I'm an *optio* now, in the *antesignani* of the first cohort."

Old Burrus beamed with pride, and he had reason to. The term is obsolete now, but in those days the *antesignani*, "those who fight before the standards," were the cream of the legions, the bravest of the brave. To be an *optio* over such men was a great honor.

"Amazing! You'll be a centurion in no time!"

"Next year," he said confidently, "when the *primus pilus* retires, then my centurion becomes First Spear, and I step into his place."

This popped my eyes. "That means you'll be a senior centurion without ever having served in the junior centurionate!"

"Caesar knows how to reward the best men," his father said, holding up one of the braceleted wrists for general admiration. "He'd be wearing the *phalerae* if he'd had the rank when he earned these." These formidable decorations, nine massive silver disks worn on a harness, were awarded only to centurions. "As it is, he'll be the youngest man ever to be senior centurion in the Tenth."

"This we must hear about," I said. We made room for them all at the table and spent the next hour or so hearing Lucius Burrus's war stories. And to think that, just a few years before, I had saved this young hero from being executed for murdering his own centurion! It just goes to show that good deeds really are rewarded. Sometimes, anyway.

When the questioning eased up, Lucius turned to me and said, "Father tells me that you and your whole family are under attack."

I gave him a brief rendition of events, the parts that had become public knowledge.

"Pompey's probably behind it," he stated flatly.

"Why do you say that?"

"He isn't supporting us the way he was when the war started. He's jealous of Caesar's success and glory."

"I don't doubt that at all, but I don't see him taking part in something like this. It's too subtle. Pompey's a man of direct action. Besides, how is this supposed to push us into Pompey's camp?"

"I don't know," he admitted, "but it's him. You'll find out." There was no shaking his assurance.

He was getting to be like Julia: Caesar could do no wrong, and Caesar's rivals and enemies were not to be trusted. All of Caesar's soldiers thought and spoke this way. I have never understood why men are so loyal to a man who is getting them killed for his own profit and glory, but they do. To be truthful, there is a great deal about human behavior that I fail to understand. Maybe philosophers know, but I am too old to take up philosophy now. Besides, I suspect that most philosophers are frauds and fools.

Later, Julia and I wandered over to the little Temple of Mercury that stood just behind our house.

"There's another name that's turned up too many times," I said to her as we walked, "Octavius."

"He was just a common political nonentity," she said. "He made it as high as praetor, but he never achieved any real distinction. I think he died last year or the year before. But you're right. A name that comes up twice when you are investigating a conspiracy has to be suspicious. Just this morning we were talking with Callista about his daughter and her marriage to Caius Marcellus—"

"That's it!" I exclaimed, just as we turned the corner next to the little temple. Its altar fire still burned high, attended by a couple of sleepy-looking priests. They glanced our way at the sound of my cry.

"Keep your voice down. That's what?"

"What Octavia said that was important and I couldn't remember. She said she hadn't seen her brother since he was an infant."

"Yes, so?"

"Earlier this morning I talked with Cato. He says that, a few months ago, the younger Caius Octavius gave the funeral eulogy for his grandmother, Julia, the sister of Caesar. Is Octavia saying that she didn't attend *her own grandmother's* funeral?"

"Decius! Sometimes you really are inspired! I attended that funeral. She was my aunt, after all, and I was there with all the Julia Caesares. I heard the boy speak, and it was excellently done for one so young. It was while you were still on Cyprus."

"And was Octavia there?"

"She was. So why is she lying about it now? Why does she want to pretend she has nothing to do with her brother?"

"I intend to find out."

9

THE NIGHT HAD BEEN A LONG ONE, but I woke early and fully alert for a change. Time was getting short, and I had none of it to waste. I rousted Hermes, and Julia and the slaves got me presentable and out the door before full daylight broke over the City.

"To the Archive again, Hermes," I said.

"Again?"

"Yes. Today, it's the Land Registry."

This was located on the ground floor with several of its rooms dug back into the side of the Capitoline Hill. Since nothing was more important than ownership of landed property, these documents got the most stringent protection from fire.

In charge of this department was an old freedman from Athens named Polyneices. We found him at his desk in the gloomy interior of the huge building. He was white as a grub from spending his days entombed within the sacred soil beneath the Capitol. The only illumination came from oil lamps that burned in locked lanterns with lenses of inch-thick glass. The lamps had to be lighted outside, then locked before being carried within. To kindle a light within these rooms meant crucifixion for a slave, beheading for a free man.

"This is most irregular," Polyneices said, not quite as peevishly as Androcles, whose offices were two floors above.

"What constitutes regularity in this place?" I asked him. "I just need to find the title history of a piece of City real estate. It's a tedious job, I'll grant you that, but I'll make it worth your while. Don't bother trying to tell me you're unbribable. You are a Greek, after all."

"Do I look like I need money?" he asked. "I've already paid for my funeral, and I've bought a very decent tomb for my family out on the Via Tiburtina."

"Everybody needs money!" Hermes protested.

"Not necessarily," I said. "However, I shall be praetor next year, and very few men never need a favor, if not for themselves, then for some family member. How about it, Polyneices? I am sure you are all very respectable people, but surely you have the odd scapegrace, the inevitable ne'er-do-well, among your kin? My own father has bailed me out of the lockup more than once in my young and foolish days."

He thought, stroking his jaw in that odd Greek fashion. "Well, I do have a grandson who causes me to lose sleep. He's caused his mother endless worry, and he's getting old enough to get into serious trouble."

"If he's arrested in the coming year, have his mother call on me and remind me that he's your grandson. I'll let him off for a first offense, as long as it doesn't involve bloodshed or robbing a temple."

"Oh, he wouldn't do anything that serious, Senator. Just youthful foolishness. Let me see what I can do for you." He disappeared into the gloom of the underground chambers like one of Pluto's minions.

"Will you really let him off?" Hermes wanted to know.

"Surely. If it *is* just youthful foolishness, the scare will do him a great deal of good. If he's a born offender, he'll be back and I won't spare him a second time."

A short while later, Polyneices emerged with a deed engraved on plates of copper. Some old Roman families used these copper plates as further insurance against fire, water, hungry insects, and simple age. Lead plates were sometimes used for this purpose, but lead melts at a low temperature, making it a false economy. Copper is more expensive, but it lasts forever. I carried the plates to the doorway, where enough light made its way in for me to read them.

The deeds were for the house lived in by the late Fulvius and owned by Caius Claudius Marcellus. But Marcellus had owned it only for the last four years. Before that, the owner was Caius Octavius.

"How was this property transferred from Octavius to Marcellus?" I asked Polyneices. "Was it purchased? A gift?"

"I have no idea, Senator. The law requires a record of transfer of ownership, but it does not require disclosure of the manner of transfer. Caius Octavius states that this property now belongs to Marcellus and he appends his seal. That is it. I would not want to be the one to ask such a man to furnish particulars."

"True," I said. "Aristocrats are touchy when vulgar subjects like money are brought up. They love to acquire it, but they hate to talk about it. I don't suppose you might have records of holdings in Baiae here?"

"Are you joking, Senator? Deeds pertaining to the City and surrounding countryside give us enough trouble. We need a new *tabularium* as it is. No, I'm afraid you'll have to go to Baiae if you want to see those deeds." A malicious gleam came into his eye. "You plan to be consul in a few years don't you, Senator? You could make your name immortal by giving us a new archive. You could call it the *Tabularia Caecilia Metella.* The land just above this building is wide open. Caesar is going to give us a huge new basilica, you know. It will be called the Basilica Julia, and it will be the largest building in Rome. But your *tabularium* will be on higher ground and will look more impressive."

144

"If I get a chance to loot Parthia in my propraetorian year, I'll consider it. But if I give the City an archive, I'll have it organized like the Museum in Alexandria. It will put memorizers like you out of work."

"What do I care? I'll be retired by then."

Outside, Hermes and I watched the Forum warm up in the morning sunlight.

"I suppose we could try the censor's records again," Hermes said. "Caius Octavius might have declared ownership of that estate in Baiae, if it was his."

"It might be a lot of work for nothing," I told him. "He needn't have declared every last thing he owned, just enough to prove his status and fitness for office. His City property alone should have been plenty for that. In any case, what we need to know now isn't who owned which property when. It's what the connection might be."

Hermes leaned with his elbow on the railing in front of the *Tabularium*, his chin cupped in one palm, looking like one of the Greek gods pondering the fate of mortals. He had grown into a truly handsome young man.

"It seems to me," he began, "that the last few years everyone is for either Caesar or Pompey. Marcellus hates Caesar. But Octavius? Like you, he married Caesar's niece. Then he gave his daughter in marriage to Marcellus."

"Octavia," I said, "claims that she has cut her ties to the Julians, but she is lying. Why?"

"Let's consider it," he said, "but let's not think on empty stomachs."

"Excellent idea."

We went down to one of the little side streets off the Vicus Iugarius where one of our favorite food stalls was located. At the counter we got steaming bowls of fish stew laced with *garum* and cups of heated sour wine, heavily watered and lightly spiced. It was eye-opening food, guaranteed to leave you wide awake and ready to face the most tedious

Senate meeting. Hermes and I took our breakfast outside and dished up the sour, vinegary stew with pieces of flat bread.

"Are you serious about building a new *tabularium?*" Hermes asked, crumbs falling from his lips.

"If I build anything, that's what it will be. The City really doesn't need a new temple. Pompey's Theater will hold most of the population. We don't need a new bridge. What we really need is an efficient way to store records. But I doubt I'll ever be rich enough to do it." I took a sip of wine and winced at its bite. "Actually, I think this whole practice has gotten out of hand."

"What do you mean?"

"I mean, great men go out and loot the world. Then they come back home and build great monuments to themselves and slather their names all over them and then bask in the honor of it all."

"Hasn't it always been that way?"

"Yes, and that's the problem. We're lords of the world, and we still act like the big frogs of little Greek city-states, putting up statues of ourselves and calling it immortality."

"But what else are we going to do?"

"I don't know," I admitted. "But it's wasteful. There ought to be something better we could do with our loot. As it is, what we end up with are cheap slaves and expensive monuments, the occasional spectacle, and public banquets."

"You like spectacles and public banquets."

"Doesn't everybody? But they're unproductive."

"Now you're talking like a merchant. This isn't helping to solve our problem." He handed his now-empty bowl to a boy who added it to a stack of them he held nested in one arm.

"Sometimes you have to get your mind off the problem if you're ever going to get it solved."

"I've been considering something," Hermes said, now handing his empty cup to a little girl who was gathering them.

"Tell me." I gave her my own crockery.

"The day before yesterday, when we went on our little burglary expedition, we wondered why there were no slaves in the house. I said they'd probably belonged to whoever lent Fulvius the house."

"I remember."

"We now know that the house was owned in turn by Octavius and Caius Marcellus. They've probably gone back to their own households. Octavius is dead, so the slaves are unlikely to be his. I can go back to the house of Marcellus. I might be able to induce some of them to talk."

"Octavia impressed me as the sort of woman who keeps the household staff confined to the house and hard at work at all hours."

"There are ways," he assured me. Having been a slave himself, he knew all about these things.

"Then go there." I divided my money with him for a bribe fund. "I am going to Callista's. If I'm not there when you are done, look for me in the Forum. I'm to be tried tomorrow and the election is the day after, so I have to act like a defendant and a candidate, making friends and collecting votes."

I FOUND CALLISTA IN HER COURT-yard, surrounded by stacks of books and four or five assistants—and Julia. My wife seemed to have developed a special sense for detecting when I was about to call upon an attractive woman.

"How goes the work?" I asked.

"Wonderfully!" Callista said, with a flushed expression most women reserve for activities of a more intimate sort. "I've made a reliable interpretation of at least six of the Greek letters!"

"Just six?"

"With these, I'll have the rest figured out in no time!" she cried happily.

"No time is exactly what I have," I told her.

"Nonsense," Julia said. "We have all day today, and tonight if need be. That's plenty of time."

147

"So, what have we learned?"

"I've conferred with a number of scholars here in Rome," Callista said, "and several of them have lent me their relevant books." She gestured to the heaps of papyrus leaves and scrolls that overloaded her desks and tables. She took up a tiny scroll and held it like a trophy. "This one proved to be extremely important."

"How so?"

"It's from the collection of Xenophanes of Thebes. He is the architect who designed Pompey's theater complex on the Campus Martius. Being an architect, he is an avid scholar of geometry. This book is by a Pythagorean philosopher named Aristobulus."

"I've met Pythagoreans," I told her. "There are even a few senators who follow that sect. They are very boring people, with all their talk of transmigration of souls and their stupid dietary practices."

"Don't be obtuse, Decius," Julia said. "Just listen."

"I apologize. Please go on." I knew better than to ignore that tone of voice.

"Aristobulus," Callista continued, "is a scholar of the symbolic use of numbers and symbols. He is an advocate of a concept called the 'unknown quantity.' It is an extremely obscure and arcane field of study. Pythagoreans, with their mystical leanings, are about the only scholars who give it any serious attention. As far as I know, Aristobulus is the only one now working on the problem."

She had lost me again, but I thought I understood her drift. "You think this has something to do with that—what did you call it?—that 'symbol for nothing?'"

"Aristobulus uses the delta as his shorthand symbol for the unknown quantity. It is only a short step from that to a symbol for nothing at all."

"This is making me dizzy," I said, "but I trust your comprehensive knowledge of your field."

I took the little scroll from her hand. It was finely made, enclosed in a leather tube with an ivory tag depending from one of the terminals.

Written on the ivory in tiny, precise Greek letters, was the name of the author: Aristobulus of Croton.

My scalp prickled. Croton. Where had I heard that name spoken recently? Since this business had begun, my days had been so packed with events that I was beginning to lose track of who had told me what. To a Roman public man, educated to commit vast quantities of minutiae to memory, the sensation was disorienting.

"Decius?" Julia said. "You're getting that look again."

"What look?" Callista asked.

"The hit-on-the-head-with-the-sacrificial-hammer look," my wife elucidated.

"I think he looks like a Dionysian reveler in a state of *ektasis*, the mind completely out of the body."

"Isn't that something like *enthousiasmos?*" my loving Julia inquired.

"No, that's possession by the god. He'd be much more lively."

"Instead of talking about me as if I weren't here," I said, "you could give me some help. I'm trying to remember where I heard Croton spoken of recently."

"There was some question whether you *were* here," Julia said. "And how can we help you remember? We weren't there when it happened."

"Let's consider how the subject might have arisen," Callista said. "For what is the city of Croton famed? It was the home of Pythagoras, naturally."

"Let's see"—Julia mused—"Croton? Athletes. Jewelers."

"That's it! The day before yesterday, Hermes and I found a seal ring in Fulvius's desk. The lapidary I consulted said that the carving on the stone was in the style of the Greek cities of southern Italy. He was pretty certain that it was from Croton."

"I love this sort of logic!" Callista said happily. "I know that applied logic is rather disreputable, but I find this exhilarating. But what is this about a ring?"

So I told her about this minor theft. What with murder and burglary and conspiracy and intrigues of one sort or another, it occurred to me that the felonies were beginning to pile up.

"If this conspiracy was hatched in Baiae as you think," Callista said, "where originates the connection with Croton? The two towns are not close."

"Baiae is about midway between Rome and Croton," Julia put in. "It's a substantial trip in both directions."

"The conspirators," I said, "wanted a code. As I've mentioned, certain senators follow the teachings of Pythagoras—not these men, of course, but one of them might have heard of Aristobulus in conversation. Or, who knows, one of them might have spent some time in Croton and studied with the man and knew of his theories. In any case, they probably hired him to devise this cipher for them. For a good fee, he would have been happy to go up to Baiae to confer with them."

"But why a *ring* from Croton?" Julia asked.

"This business is full of little anomalies. But I doubt that it's a coincidence. There are no coincidences in a conspiracy."

"That sounds like a quote from Euripides," Callista said.

"I don't cadge from Greek playwrights," I told her. "What do you know about this man Aristobulus other than what you've already told us?"

"Virtually nothing. He's quite obscure. He never taught at the Museum, or in the other schools of Alexandria, or I would have heard about it. I could make inquiries in the Greek community here."

"No, please, there's no time for that. I'll talk with Asklepiodes. He travels all over Italy with Statilius's troupe, and he loves to hobnob with the scholarly crowd wherever he goes. If he's been to Croton he may know Aristobulus."

"Excellent idea," Julia said. "Why don't you go along and do just that so that we can work on this code."

I can take a hint.

of the Statilian school. Supervising the diet of the gladiators was one of his duties. Satisfied that all was in order, he led me to his spacious surgery, a room so draped with weapons that it looked more like a Temple of Mars than a medical facility.

"More bodies to examine?" he asked me.

"Not this time. Do your travels ever take you to Croton?"

"Usually once each year. The city and its district are Greek, so there is not as much demand for gladiators as in Rome and Campania, but the city authorities sponsor a modest show each fall. What is your interest in Croton?"

"In your travels there, did you ever meet a mathematician named Aristobulus?"

His face, usually so maddeningly serene, showed genuine surprise. "Why, yes. Whenever I am in Croton, I attend the weekly dinner and symposium of the Greek Philosophical Club. Croton has a small but distinguished community of scholars, as you might expect of the home of Pythagoras. He was always there until—well, Croton is all the way down in Bruttium. How is it that you are investigating his case?"

Now it was my turn to look astonished. "His case? What do you mean?"

"He was murdered earlier this year. You mean you aren't investigating? Since you always seem to be around wherever there is a murder, I supposed—"

"Murdered? I first heard of the man less than an hour ago, in connection with the case in which I am embroiled, and now you tell me he was murdered! How—"

Asklepiodes held up a hand for silence. "Let's not confuse one another further." He pointed to the chairs that flanked a table by a window. "Have a seat." He clapped his hands and one of his silent Egyptians appeared. He said something incomprehensible to the man, then took the chair opposite mine. "I've sent him for some wine. My very best wine because I know you speak most easily with proper lubrication."

"That is thoughtful of you, old friend." I am sure I had that hammered look again. I do not object to things moving fast, but they shouldn't move in so many directions. The wine came and it was, indeed, excellent.

While I sipped I looked out the window, which overlooked the training yard. About a hundred men were practicing noisily with sword and shield, some paired in the traditional way with a lightly armored man bearing a big shield fighting another who carried a small shield but wore more protective armor. But many were Gauls plying their national weapons: a long, narrow, oval shield and a long sword, with no armor at all except for a simple, pot-shaped helmet. Such men were appearing in the arenas in ever-greater numbers. It was easier to let them fight as they were accustomed to than to try to teach them to fight like civilized swordsmen.

As I pondered this sight and tried to calculate odds for the next big *munera*, I told Asklepiodes of the latest twists in my case. He listened with rapt attention and when I finished, he clapped his hands and chuckled as if he'd attended the cleverest comedy ever written by Aristophanes.

"I rejoice that someone is getting some amusement from my plight," I said, with perhaps too much heat for one drinking my host's excellent wine.

"But this is so splendid!" Asklepiodes said, not at all abashed. "Over the years you have investigated hundreds of murders"—a gross exaggeration, but he was a Greek—"and I have aided you in many of these. But this is the first to involve scholarship, mathematics, a cipher—it is all just wonderful! Now, let me tell you what I know."

"Please do." I helped myself to some more of his speech lubrication.

"Aristobulus—he didn't call himself 'of Croton' at home since they are all from Croton there—"

"That is understood."

"Aristobulus was a small man, advancing in years but not in fortune. He wore rather shabby clothes, but he tried to pretend that this was a virtue, as philosophers so often do. He was not argumentative, neither was he talkative. Rather, he was aloof, as if the company were unworthy of him. But I learned that he never passed up one of these weekly dinners, which were not paid for by subscription from the members of the club but by the testaments of wealthy members in times past."

"I never knew a philosopher to turn down a free meal," I said, nodding.

"Anyway, when the time came for the symposium after dinner, Aristobulus drank his share and more, and he grew more talkative. This often consisted of boasting about his discoveries in the mathematical field. He had some rather radical ideas, as the learned lady has tried, without success, to explain to you."

"I never claimed to understand mathematics. When I had charge of the Treasury I had slaves and freedmen for that, fortunately."

"He was never mocked by the rest of the company, but he was regarded with, shall we say, a healthy scepticism," Asklepeodes commented. "The last time I attended that gathering but one was the last time I saw him alive—he was better-dressed." He paused and took a sip, waiting for my reaction. Asklepiodes always did that.

"Well? What did this signify?" I was never good at restraining my impatience.

"He did not precisely boast, but he hinted heavily that he had acquired a patron, a highly placed person who understood the importance of his work. His clothes were not gaudy, you understand. He adhered to the principles of philosophical simplicity. But they were new and of excellent quality. And, for the first time since I had known him, he wore jewelry: a ring." That maddening pause again.

"Ring! What sort of ring? Quit stalling!"

"There was a massive seal ring on the index finger of his right hand. Eumolpus the Cynic, a rather acerbic gentleman as you might gather from his appellation, took note of this new adornment and made comment that it contrasted oddly with Aristobulus's customary, not to say flaunted, austerity. Aristobulus replied that it was a gift from his patron, that he used it as a seal on all his correspondence with this mysterious benefactor, and that he must wear it as a symbol of their mutual pledge."

"Did you get a good look? Can you describe it?"

"As it occurs, Aristobulus reclined to my immediate left during that banquet, and I was able to examine the ring closely. It was of massive gold and had an exotic, finely granulated surface. It was set with a handsome sapphire. I have spent much of my life in Egypt, and I know Egyptian stone when I see it. It was carved intaglio with a *gorgoneion*."

This was more than I had expected. "Did he say anything else? Anything that might identify his patron or the business they had together?"

"Nothing definite," Asklepiodes said. "And you must remember that I was not giving this matter any special attention. I was far more involved with my more congenial friends. I do remember that he hinted his patron was a powerful Roman, not a Greek, and that the man was interested in 'the truly important things,' by which I presume he meant the arcane field of mathematics that consumed him."

"If so," I said, "he was flattering himself. Philosophers are prone to do that in my experience. His patron was interested in one thing only: an unbreakable cipher he could use to keep secret his doings and those of his coconspirators. Aristobulus's absurd 'symbol for nothing' was used for no greater purpose than separating the words in a text. He might as well have simply left a space between the words."

"That might have made the code easier to break," Asklepiodes pointed out. "As it is, a mind less penetrating than Callista's might never have divined the implication. Then the code would have been truly incomprehensible."

"I suppose so. Anyway, how did the man come to be murdered?"

"When I accompanied the troupe to Croton two months ago, I attended the club dinner as usual. Aristobulus had never been my favorite among that company so it was only after the dinner and well into the drinking bout that I noticed he was not there. I asked where he might be, and the others said he had been murdered and were surprised that I had not known about it. Apparently the killing gained some degree of notoriety in the southern part of the peninsula.

"In any case, it seems that Aristobulus had left on a rather sudden trip to Baiae—"

"Baiae!" I cried triumphantly.

"Yes, I thought that would get your attention."

"You have it already! Go on!"

"Calm yourself, my friend. Unrequitable passion has a deleterious effect on the bodily humors. He must have completed his journey to Baiae because he was on the road south, returning to Croton, when he was fallen upon and slain," Asklepiodes said.

"'Fallen upon'?"

"Yes, it appeared to be the work of bandits. They've become rare in the vicinity of Rome, but southern Italy is infested with them."

"It always has been. Southern Italy is more like Africa than civilized Latium." I wasn't being quite fair to our southern brethren. Southern Italy was full of desperate, dangerous men because the peasants of that region were the most thoroughly ruined in the peninsula. The entirety of the land south of Capua and the whole island of Sicily had been turned into latifundia. Land that had supported thousands of peasant families had been converted into a few vast plantations worked by cheap slaves, leaving the dispossessed farmers to fend for themselves.

"So," I went on, "how is it that the murder was attributed to bandits? I don't suppose anyone came forward to confess?"

"Of course not. When does anyone confess to a crime save under

155

torture or when caught in the act? But, according to those who found his body, it bore all the signs of a bandit attack: He was discovered stripped to the skin, even his sandals taken. Also missing was the hired donkey he had been riding."

"How was he dispatched?"

"Stabbed through the body. That is all I know of his fatal wound. Had I been able to examine the corpse, I might have discovered many revealing details. But he had been cremated more than a month prior to my visit. Apparently, it never occurred to the authorities to inquire into the incident. Bandit attacks are so common in the region that they saw no reason for an investigation."

"And he was traveling alone? Not even a slave or two?"

"Apparently. As a penurious man of simple habits, he had only a rather elderly housekeeper."

I mused for a while, studying the weapons on the wall. "Stabbed, eh? And through the body? Bandits usually favor a club to subdue their prey. It gets less blood on the clothes."

"They might have forced him to strip before giving him his passage on the ferryboat."

"Then why not cut his throat? It is the swiftest and surest method for dispatching a man with a knife. I'll tell you why: These people can't shake off their aristocratic habits. They want to make it look like bandits did it, but they have to stab their victim from in front, like gentlemen."

"A strange sort of oversight, one would think," Asklepiodes commented.

"They intend never to be called to account for their crimes," I said. "It is to maintain their own good opinion of themselves and each other that they commit murder as if they were soldiers striking down an enemy. Doubtless these men tell each other that they are acting out of patriotic motives."

"'Patriotic'?" Asklepiodes gestured with his beautifully manicured hands like an actor in a comedy who is at his wit's end. "But this is so puzzling. Not only killing a very obscure Greek philosopher from patriotic motives but constructing so elaborate a conspiracy to prevent one man from attaining the office of praetor. I hope you are not offended that I wonder at this."

"Oh, I'm under no such delusion. I am just the immediate and rather a minor target, I'm afraid. These men have designs on the whole Republic."

"Ah," he said, with satisfaction. "That is on a scale rather more grand. To my poor mind, though, the details remain wreathed in obscurity."

"They are not very plain to me either, but I think I am beginning to see where this is all headed. Three men named Claudius Marcellus, two brothers and a cousin, are pushing us toward civil war. One of them is this year's consul, another will be next year's, the third will very likely be consul the year after. They are doing everything in their power to turn the whole Senate against Caesar. This is a plot made simpler by the fact that Caesar does so little to ingratiate himself with that body.

"Like good generals, these Claudii are making long-range war plans. They've assembled their forces, and probably not only in the Senate but all over our Empire. They've agitated among the people but without great success. The plebs love Caesar." I thought about that for a moment. "They've probably had more success in the south. Their base is in Baiae, and the southern part of the peninsula is almost solidly for Pompey. His veterans have settled there.

"But their most forward-looking policy has been to arrange for a truly ingenious cipher to keep all their conspiratorial correspondence secret. I know of no other planners, military or civil, who have taken such a precaution."

"It is not characteristic of you Romans," Asklepiodes agreed. "Your flair for careful planning is, of course, world-famed. But you are not known for your subtlety. This is almost, how should I put this? Almost Greek."

"Exactly. You know, I can't begin to count how many conspiracies and even military operations I know of that have come to grief because correspondence, reports, or dispatches have been intercepted. The Catilinarian conspirators were so inept that the most illustrious men actually appended their personal signatures and seals to letters sent to prospective allies."

"Perhaps you Romans have not been literate long enough to understand the perils hidden in the written word. The great kings of Persia have been using ciphers for centuries, although I confess I have no idea how such codes work."

"I just wish I knew whether Pompey is involved. I rather doubt it. Subtlety was never his style."

At that moment Hermes burst in, breathing hard, sweating and grinning. "Oh, good! I've caught you before you could get away!"

"You've learned something important?" I turned to Asklepiodes. "I sent him to the house of Caius Marcellus to bribe some information out of the man's slaves."

"I may have, but that's not why I ran all the way to Callista's and then here. You've got to come to the Forum. There's a show going on there you won't want to miss!"

"What?" I was totally mystified.

"Last night someone attacked Curio and tried to murder him!"

"Is he dead?" I got to my feet. This had to be tied to my own difficulties.

"No, just knocked about and cut up a bit. But the real show is Fulvia. She's gone down to the Forum like a blood-soaked Fury, and she's baying for vengeance."

"Jupiter preserve us all," I groaned. "The last time Fulvia put on a show, the mob burned the Curia and half the buildings around it."

"This I must see," Asklepiodes said, gleefully. "Let's take my litter. I can get us there far more speedily than the two of you can make it on foot."

10

ORDINARILY, A LITTER GETS YOU where you are going no more quickly than if you had walked. It just gets you there in style and much cleaner than if you had braved Rome's unsanitary streets. The litter of Asklepiodes was different.

First, there were his bearers. They were all powerful men and trained runners. The physician often had to rush to the site of an emergency and did not want to waste time. He used eight of them, instead of the more common four or six, so that each would bear a lighter load. Perhaps even more important, though, was the flying wedge of gladiators that cleared the way before us. Rome's narrow streets were easily jammed, and they tended to get more so as you approached the Forum, especially if there was something interesting happening there, as there was on this morning.

For obvious reasons the gladiators of Statilius Taurus prized their surgeon and were always willing to do anything to keep him happy. Up front we had a dozen of them, all huge men who positively loved hard, physical contact. Thus we were able to cross the City at a running pace.

"All right," I said to Hermes, as we lounged behind the closed curtains, "tell me what you learned."

Hermes mopped his face with a fold of his tunic. His sweat was testimony to his exertions that morning. He was in superb physical shape, and it took a strenuous sprint to bring perspiration to his brow.

"I managed to catch some of Caius Claudius's slaves on their way to the fruit and vegetable market. One of them was the cook who had been assigned to the house of Fulvius. There were six of them assigned, and I was lucky to catch this one because the others were all Syrians barely able to understand Latin."

"Didn't I tell you these were careful plotters?" I said to Asklepiodes. "The slaves they lent their man were foreign, so that they wouldn't be able to understand or repeat what they overheard. Too many people blab as if their slaves weren't there."

Hermes nodded agreement. "But the cook had to know Latin because she had to do the marketing. Unfortunately, she was mostly confined to the kitchen and didn't hear much. But the man had callers at all hours of day and night, and the conversations out front got pretty heated."

"Had she any idea who the visitors were?"

"She said they mostly had low-class accents, but a few were high class, and it was most often those voices she heard arguing."

"She didn't hear any details of their conversations at all?"

"None she was willing to talk about. Remember, she is still a slave."

A slave's lot is not a happy one in cases of this sort. They can only testify under torture, and a slave who voluntarily testifies against his master can look forward to a short and miserable life. I recalled that, after the killing of Clodius, Milo freed all the slaves who had been with him, ostensibly as a reward for saving him from Clodius (as if Titus Milo ever needed saving from anybody) but actually so that they could not be put to torture in the trial he knew was coming.

"Well, what *did* you learn?" I demanded impatiently.

"Three days ago, late in the evening, a slave came from the home of Caius Marcellus and told the slaves in Fulvius's house that they were to gather whatever personal belongings they had there and return to their master's house at once. Fulvius wasn't there, and neither was anyone else."

Three days ago meant the night before we had found Fulvius murdered. "You say a slave summoned them? Was it the steward?"

"No. She said it was one of Octavia's staff, a man from her old household before she married Marcellus."

"Were the other slaves part of Octavia's staff or dowry?"

"From the way she talked, they were all Marcellus's property. Do you think it's important?"

"Hermes, in this case, *nothing* is too trivial to have significance. Octavia is neck deep in this matter, I'm sure of it. But that doesn't mean she is playing the same game as her husband."

The Greek sighed. "Sometimes I wish I were a playwright. This has the dimensions of high tragedy and the complications of low farce."

"Yes, well, that's politics for you," I muttered, half distracted. We were getting near the Forum, and I drew a curtain aside to see what was ahead. There was certainly a lot of noise coming from that direction.

We had taken the most direct route from the *ludus:* across the Sublician Bridge and through the Forum Boarium, and along the Vicus Tuscus to where it crossed the Via Nova and ended between the Basilica Sempronia and the Temple of Castor and Pollux, near the western end of the Forum. Ahead and to our left I could see the greatest concentration of the crowd, and from that direction came the greatest noise.

"Is that the lady?" Asklepiodes asked.

"The one and only Fulvia," I said with a sinking heart.

She was on the Rostra, a tiny form still clad in black, gesturing wildly. I saw white-clad men, most likely senators, trying to scale the platform, but other men were pushing them back. I wondered who, with the old gangs broken up, had the insolence to manhandle the Senate.

"I need to get closer," I said.

"Get us up to the Rostra, lads!" Asklepiodes cried.

"Whatever you say, Doctor!" yelled one. "Let's go!" And in a blur of flying fists and elbows, the crowd parted magically before us. Within what seemed like only seconds, we were before the railing of the Rostra, its age-darkened ships' rams looming ominously above. In front and to both sides stood a cluster of senators, lictors, and other attendants trying to shout down the furious woman who harangued the mob from above. I now saw that the men who controlled access to the speaker's platform wore military belts and boots.

"Oh, no!" I cried, appalled. "She's got Caesar's soldiers supporting her and laying hands on the Senate!"

Up on the platform, Fulvia was putting on an amazing show. Her pale hair streamed wildly, tears flowed down her swollen cheeks, her face was scarlet with rage, her mouth was drawn into a long, vertical rectangle, like that on a tragic mask. Also, her sheer, black clothing was in such disarray that she was in imminent danger of losing the upper half entirely.

"Slaves! Cowards! Spineless slugs!" she screamed. "How can you call yourselves Romans? They came to slaughter the man who would be your tribune! They feared him because they knew he would be the defender of your liberties! They fell upon him and now he lies at death's door because he wanted to be *your* champion! How can you allow them to live?"

Cato made his way to the litter. Hermes and I stood outside,

Asklepiodes remained within. The gladiators stood around us in a protective circle. They made way for Cato's senatorial insignia.

"Quite a show, eh, Decius?" he said disgustedly. "Just when we had the City about cleaned up, this had to happen."

"Does anybody know what's going on?" I asked him.

"Just that Curio's been seriously wounded. That wild woman got up on the Rostra and started screeching less than an hour ago. A pack of Caesar's boys were here in the Forum, and they appointed themselves her bodyguard because Caesar's told them Curio is his man and they were to vote for him. Now she has them so wrought up they're putting violent hands on senators and lictors who are trying to silence her. How are we going to get this ugly mob calmed down?"

I looked all about and thought fast. Fortunately, thinking fast was one of my specialties. "Where are the consuls?"

"Nowhere to be found, naturally," Cato said.

"I see a cluster of twelve lictors over there," I said, pointing toward the southern end of the Rostra. "Are they Pompey's?" Only consuls and proconsuls were entitled to twelve lictors.

"Yes, he got here a few minutes ago."

"Good. The crowd will quiet down enough to listen to him. Tell him to call attention to me—send his lictors to arrest me or something. I think I can get them calmed."

Cato rushed off in the direction of the lictors. I hoped Pompey would move quickly, because Fulvia was reaching the flamboyant climax of her oration.

"Romans! Look at me!" Here she seized the neckline of her sheer, black gown and ripped downward. The flimsy cloth shredded away from her and left her nude from the waist up. The shouting died down to a murmur, punctuated by groans and a few low whistles. My own jaw dropped along with the rest. This was a spectacle worthy of traveling a long way to see. She began to beat with her tiny fists against her by no means tiny breasts.

"Do you not know who your enemies are? These cruel and self-ish aristocrats murdered your greatest defenders, the brothers Grac-chi! Caius Gracchus was my own grandfather!" Like many another good rabble-rouser, she spoke of the aristocrats as if she weren't one herself.

"They murdered my husband! Milo and his gang, protected by their friends in the Senate, slew my darling Clodius, who championed you like a god! Yet Milo lives! His followers slunk from the city like chastised children instead of being hurled from the Tarpeian Rock!" Here she swung her arm to point at that prominence atop the Capitol, throwing her own prominences into bold relief. "They walked away alive, and you did nothing! And you call yourselves Romans!" Her face flushed so dark I expected her to go into seizures.

"Now," she went on, "they have struck down my betrothed, as if they must widow me twice! How long will you allow your champions to be murdered, Romans? How long before you see who your enemy is and burn this corrupt city to ashes? Tear down this rotten sink of mur-der and greed and plow up the ground and sow it with salt so that noth-ing will grow here again, as my great grandfather did to Carthage back when there were *men* in Rome!"

Now I could understand how she had induced Clodius's supporters into using the Curia for his funeral pyre. I was about ready to torch a tem-ple for her myself. Actually, it was her great-great-grandfather's adopted son who wrecked Carthage so thoroughly, but she wasn't going to pass up a chance for a fine rhetorical flourish over a carping detail like that.

The crowd was about to go into full roar once more when Pompey ascended the steps at the north side of the Rostra, alone, not even a single lictor with him. The soldiers at the top of the steps looked at one another, suddenly uncertain what to do. Tossing an ordinary senator off the platform was one thing. Laying hands on Gnaeus Pompeius Magnus was quite another. He stopped near the top and jabbed a finger toward Fulvia.

"Get down from there, you shameless, indecent woman! I'll not have—" Then he pretended to catch sight of me for the first time. His eyes went wide and his scandalized expression gave way to one of rage. The change of expression was broad and obvious, just as we were all taught to do in the schools of rhetoric. His accusing finger swung, slowly and deliberately, toward me. Just as he planned it, every gaze in the Forum swung away from Fulvia and toward me.

"Decius Caecilius Metellus the Younger!" he shouted, that parade-ground voice echoing back from every public building for a quarter mile in all directions. "What do you mean coming to this place with a pack of killers? I expelled all such gangs from the City and forbade them to return upon pain of death! Answer me if you value your life!" The silence in the Forum was now total. Even Fulvia looked stunned, about to collapse from her excess of passion.

"Give me a boost, boys," I said quietly. Two of the gladiators stooped, grasped me about the knees and raised me to their shoulders as easily as lifting a wineskin. With my feet planted firmly on their brawny shoulders, I made a rhetorical gesture as broad as his own, easily visible in the farthest reaches of the Forum, one arm extended, the other hand clasped to my breast, fingers spread, as if I were clutching a heart stirred to the highest pitch by the terrible events of the moment.

"Proconsul!" I cried, pitching my voice slightly lower than his famous bellow. "Word came to me that my good friend, Scribonius Curio, had been attacked and lay terribly wounded! Frantic with concern, I ran to the *ludus* of Statilius Taurus, there to summon the one man who can save our beloved future tribune. In this litter—" here I gestured gracefully toward the little conveyance below me—"is the great Asklepiodes, acknowledged from here to Alexandria as the foremost expert in the world on the subject of wounds made with weapons! These men are no criminal gang, Proconsul. They are *his* escort, come hither at peril of your wrath to speed the great physician's way to the side of the wounded Curio. Every man of them owes his life to Asklepiodes, who can cure wounds lesser physicians would give up as hopeless!"

The gladiators began to tug their tunics up and down and sideways to show off for general admiration the terrible scars of the numerous wounds Asklepiodes had stitched up for them. People began edging closer for a better look.

"Splendid, Metellus!" Pompey shouted. "I forgive them their intrusion just so they leave as soon as their duty is done.

Citizens!" He threw wide his arms. "Stand not in the way of the great physician! He must fly at once to the side of Curio!"

The crowd began to mill about uncertainly. Most of them had no idea which direction the litter needed to go so they couldn't very well get out of its way. For the moment their attention was off Fulvia.

"Put me down," I ordered.

Cato hustled back. "The wretch is at Fulvia's house. As likely a place as any to be assaulted."

I leaned into the litter. "That's where Clodius used to live. You know how to get there, don't you?"

"All Rome knows that address," he assured me. "This has been most enjoyable, and if I may be of help, next year's tribune will owe me a favor." With that he was hoisted aloft and carried off.

I dashed up the steps. A soldier I knew slightly from the Gallic war recognized me and stepped aside. "Good day, Captain. We kept anyone from disturbing the lady because we thought that's what Caesar would want us to do. He said to support Curio."

"I doubt he had this in mind, but it looks like no harm done. You men get back to your carousing." I rushed to Fulvia's side, pulled off my toga and draped it over her white shoulders. Her whole upper body jerked rhythmically, as if she were sobbing, but no sobs came from her. Then I understood why she kept quiet while Pompey and I distracted the mob: The moment she stopped screaming she had gone into convulsive hiccups.

I patted her on the back as I led her from the Rostra. After a while the hiccups subsided and she could talk.

"They waited for him outside my house. *My house*, Decius!" As if she would have been less offended had they picked some other street.

"It is because they knew he was to be found there. How badly is he hurt?"

"I left him weak and bleeding badly. I know you think I'm heartless for leaving him there and coming down here, but my personal physician is with him. You needn't have brought your Greek. It was very thoughtful of you though."

"It was the least I could do."

"It was just *too much!*" she went on, getting her breath back as I led her down the steps with an arm about her shoulders. "I mean, first Grandfather and Great-Uncle Tiberius, then Clodius, now Curio! Are they determined to leave me entirely bereft?" It did not escape me that she had not included her late brother among those for whom she grieved.

"Fulvia," I said soothingly, "you are a high-born Roman lady, and you must learn to accept the fact that, in the course of your life, about half your menfolk are going to die violently."

I looked around and what I saw wasn't greatly reassuring. Everywhere there were senators, many of them pointing and glaring at Fulvia. But even more of them were frowning in the direction of the soldiers, and the words I overheard weren't pretty. They would not soon forget that Caesar's legionaries had shown such insolence and disrespect toward senators and had handled them violently.

As for the soldiers, those tough, battle-scarred men seemed not at all abashed by this senatorial hostility. They looked as if they had rather enjoyed the little tussle and were now back to basking in the admiration of the populace. The plebs and a few senators who were Caesar's supporters saluted Fulvia respectfully. It had been a bravura performance. After this, the upcoming elections were sure to be anticlimactic.

"You weren't entirely candid with me, Fulvia," I chided her. "You said you had no gift for public speaking."

"It isn't from training or inclination," she said. "It is just that sometimes I get so *angry!* It isn't rhetorical polish you hear, it's passion."

"Well, we're all doomed if you ever take it up as a profession." I saw someone coming toward us like a thundercloud. "Uh-oh, here comes Pompey. Let me talk to him, keep your eyes modestly downcast and your mouth shut."

"Why? Do you think I should be afraid of him?"

Pompey gave me a curt nod. "That was excellently done, Metellus. We tend to forget how dangerous it is, having so many people in the City as we do at this time of year." He turned his glowering countenance toward Fulvia. "As for you, you indecent young woman, it is your great luck that I choose not to have you arrested for creating a public scandal. It is a pity that you're a widow because by rights your father or husband should flog you like a rebellious slave. As it is, I ought to—"

She raised her blotched, tear-stained face and stared him fearlessly in the eyes. "Why don't you go screw yourself, you pompous, jumped-up toad! And by what right do you address a single word to me? You have no imperium here in Italy, only in Spain. You are only allowed your lictors by courtesy. Everyone else in Rome has gotten used to jumping when Pompey speaks, but I don't! Now step aside and keep out of my way or I'll set my slaves on you." As if she had any with her.

Pompey looked as if someone had dropped an anvil on his head. Everyone within hearing range gasped, scandalized and delighted. When he had his voice back, Pompey spoke to me.

"Metellus, get this woman to her home and chain her up. The Republic is not safe while she's walking around loose." He whirled around and stalked off, his spine actually trembling with fury. People sprang from his path as if they'd discovered hot coals under their feet.

"You don't take advice very well, do you, Fulvia?" I said.

"Never. Escort me home, Decius."

Like a deferential valet, I obeyed her. Hermes joined us, smiling hugely. A day like this didn't come along very often. And I was pondering this new side of Fulvia. I had known her, slightly, for years, but only as a member of that almost laboriously scandalous social set headed by Clodius and Clodia. This fearless, determined woman who could not be cowed or intimidated was new to me.

As we crossed the Forum from west to east, headed toward the Palatine and her home, we acquired an escort of citizens, among them a number of Caesar's soldiers. It was the last thing I wanted, but it was unavoidable. Romans prized this means of showing their support for someone they respected, and a great man sometimes found himself embarrassed by a self-appointed escort of thousands. By the time we reached the Clivus Victoriae there were several hundred in our train, and nobody seemed to think it odd that I, Clodius's deadly enemy, was taking his widow home.

At her door Fulvia thanked them graciously, feigning hoarseness to avoid a prolonged oration. Then she went inside, closely followed by Hermes and me. As soon as the door was closed behind us she turned and removed my toga.

"Here, Decius, and I thank you for the loan."

I took it from her hands and, with Hermes, goggled as she went about the atrium, calling for her slaves. We were seeing only what the whole city of Rome had just seen, but somehow, in this private setting, it seemed far more intimate. Her slaves, frightened and astonished, hustled her into the rear of the house while she called for her wardrobe mistress and her cosmetician and her hairdresser.

"Well," Hermes said, "we don't get to see something like that very often."

"As well for our hearts that we don't," I told him. "My own is near apoplexy as it is. Now, where is Curio? I want a few words with him."

"I saw Asklepiodes's litter up the street by a fountain, with the bearers and the fighters lounging around it, so he must be here somewhere."

I caught sight of Echo, the comely Greek housekeeper, and beckoned her over. She led us to a bedroom that opened off the peristyle, where Asklepiodes stood by a bandaged Curio, while a man in Syrian robes looked on with disapproval. This had to be Fulvia's personal physician, resentful at being usurped by the illustrious Greek.

"Decius Caecilius!" Curio said, seeming quite spirited for a man at death's door. "How good of you to come. My new friend, Asklepiodes, tells me that my betrothed took my injury rather too much to heart."

"You would have enjoyed the spectacle," I told him. "I hope someday she will perform my funeral oration. I'd like to be remembered for something. I take it that the severity of your wounds is not as great as has been feared? If so, I rejoice at the news."

"No, I'm fine, but don't tell anybody. This will do me endless credit at the election." He wore a bandage around his temples and some blood was seeping through it. "The scalp wound made it look bad. You know how copiously they bleed. The rogues set upon me as soon as I stepped out the doorway, and when I staggered back inside I looked like I'd been through a *taurobolium*." He referred to the odd initiation ceremony practiced by the Phrygian cult of Mithras. New members pledge themselves to the god by standing in a pit covered by a bronze grate. A bull is led onto the grate and its throat cut, showering the novices with its blood.

"How many were there? Did you get a good look at them?"

"It was only beginning to get light. To be truthful I was still half asleep and a little the worse for last night's drinking and—well, other things. I think there were three of them, armed with daggers and clubs."

"I am surprised you are still alive," I told him.

"It was dark, and I think they had been indulging in wine more heavily than I. They got in each other's way, and I am handy with my fists. I've trained as a boxer all my life. I like it better than swordplay. They probably thought they *had* killed me. These two physicians, with the best of intentions, have striven to finish the job. Each insists his methods are foolproof."

"A poultice of herbs is always the best for such wounds," the Syrian said, heatedly. "With a proper prophylactic spell, it unfailingly halts the bleeding and protects from infection."

"I fear that my esteemed colleague," Asklepiodes said affably, "is more conversant with headaches and menstrual cramps than with wounds. A thorough washing with boiled, sour wine and a tight compress to hold the edges of the laceration together will protect the wound, promote quick healing with minimal scarring, and reduce the danger of infection."

"Asklepiodes has my vote," I said. "He's put a mile of stitches in my hide, and I'm still here."

"And now," the Greek said, "I can do no more here, so I bid you all good day. Just change the dressing every day, and you should have no more trouble."

Curio thanked him, and, as he left, I saw him whisper something to Hermes. The young man nodded.

"I'm sorry that Fulvia got so overwrought," Curio said. "But I was a frightening sight, and she's an excitable woman." He looked at the heap of bloody clothes on the floor and shook his head. "My best toga and tunic. They look like someone mopped the floor of a slaughterhouse with them."

"I imagine Fulvia has plenty of men's clothes you can wear. Clodius liked to affect workingmen's garb, but I know that he had decent clothes that he wore to banquets and Senate meetings."

"I suppose so." Curio seemed unhurt except for the head wound.

"So who do you think they were?" I asked. "Such assaults seem to be all the fashion lately."

"Do you mean, do I think they were the same ones who killed Fulvia's brother? I doubt it."

"Why do you say that?"

"Because those men would have done a better job of it. They made sure Fulvius was very thoroughly dead, then they dragged his corpse all the way to the basilica steps. There was a certain amount of planning, determination, and skill involved there. No, I imagine it was somebody with a personal grudge. I've made enemies like the rest of us."

Fulvia came in, now decently gowned, her hair dressed, and the facial evidence of her recent fury reduced by cosmetics to a slight puffiness around the eyes. It spoke well for the efficiency of her slaves that they had wrought such change in so short a time.

"Why, Caius," she said to Curio, "you look much better than I had expected."

"Please don't sound so disappointed, my dear. I told you before you stormed out that it was not all that serious."

"But you men *always* talk like that! Clodius used to come home bleeding like the loser at a *munera* and tell me that the barber nicked him. I've seen men with their guts hanging out insisting they were merely scratched. I thought I'd probably find you dead when I got back here!"

"You got yourself freshly made up and dressed in your finest first, though, didn't you?" he noted.

"Don't try my patience!" she was beginning to get wrought up again.

Curio stood and took her in his arms. "Now, now, let's not get excited. It's all just the little hazards of life in Rome these days. Things will quiet down after the election." He looked at me and made a significant gesture of the eyebrows, indicating the door.

"Well, all seems under control here," I said. "I'll just take my leave of you. Curio, congratulations again on your survival. Fulvia, thank you for a wonderful entertainment this morning. It will be long remembered."

I beat a hasty retreat, Hermes following close on my heels. As we left the house, he touched my arm.

"Before he left, Asklepiodes said you're to meet him at the altar of Hercules."

"I saw him speak in your ear. Let's go learn what he's discovered."

The altar of Hercules was on the western side of the Forum Boarium, near the Sublician Bridge. There we found the physician lounging at his ease, still in his litter, with his bearers squatting all around it. The gladiators had apparently been dismissed. The old cattle market, besides selling livestock and meat, was the business place for some of Rome's best food vendors, and Asklepiodes had availed himself of their wares while he waited for me.

"Ah, Decius, good. I did not think you would tarry long. Have a seat and help me finish this excellent lunch. You too, Hermes. I bought enough for five men."

I climbed into the litter and relaxed on the cushions. Hermes remained standing outside. Between Asklepiodes and me lay a platter of flat bread two feet wide, heaped with street-vendor delicacies, the best to be had. I took a skewer of tender quail grilled over charcoal and Hermes picked up a river fish caught that morning and steamed in a wrapping of pickled vine leaves.

"You are being even more generous than usual today, old friend," I told him. "I will not forget it. Now, what were you able to deduce from Curio's wounds? Did they tell you something significant about his attackers?"

"There was only one wound," he said, "and it told me a great deal indeed. Your friend Curio was not attacked. The wound was self-inflicted."

Hermes pounded me on the back, as I choked on delicious quail meat. Asklepiodes looked upon the effect of his pronouncement with deep satisfaction. There were times when I would have liked to strangle him. He handed me a cup of excellent Falernian, and I forgave him.

"Explain," I said, when I could speak again.

"When I arrived—and this was only a short time before your own advent upon the scene—Curio lay on that bed, his hands clasped to his bloody head, writhing about like a condemned man being flogged with chains. He and that Syrian quack were astonished and alarmed when I showed up. When I went to examine the wounded man, the Syrian tried to restrain me forcibly. Luckily, my medical specialty being what it is, I know a great deal more about force than he."

I nodded, remembering his many demonstrations of homicidal technique, some of which had left marks on me for weeks.

"I called for a basin and cloth, something oddly missing from the room, and cleaned Curio's head. His attitude changed swiftly. He began to make light of the wound and say that Fulvia's physician was being entirely too excitable, that he was no more than stunned by the blow to his head. Are you aware of something called the 'coward's blow?'"

"I think I've heard it mentioned among the sporting crowd. Something to do with throwing a fight, isn't it?"

"It comes from the early days of pugilism. In the earliest times, boxers were amateurs—aristocratic athletes like the other contenders in the Olympics and the rest of the Greek games. But, in time, there arose a class of professional pugilists, and people began to bet heavily on the outcome of the fights, even as they do today. Various ruses were developed to rig the outcome, and one of these was the coward's blow.

"Any scalp wound bleeds freely. The skin is stretched thin as vellum over the skull and is plentifully supplied with blood vessels. There is a spot"—he tapped a place on his own pate, about five inches above his right eyebrow—"which, when nicked, guarantees an especially generous effusion of blood. By prearrangement, one boxer would aim a punch at his opponent's head. The other would duck in the usual fashion but not quite enough. The tip of one of the *caestus* spikes would open a cut on that spot, and the blood would flow as from an upended bucket. The prearranged loser would drop as if slain, and the wagers would be paid. As an added bonus, once the place has been spiked a few times, all that is needed to reopen it is a tap, so the ruse can be repeated endlessly, always before a new audience."

"And this is the wound you found on Curio?" I asked.

"It was done with a dagger, and at the precise angle that would be made by a right-handed man cutting himself, but it was the coward's blow—a trifling laceration done by a man who knew exactly where to cut for the most dramatic effect."

I nodded. "I saw the boxer's marks on his face when I first met him, and just now he said that he was a lifelong enthusiast of the sport. He would know how that cut is delivered. He made a quick recovery when you found him out though. He acted as if he had never thought the wound was serious and he carried it off well."

"Do you think the lady Fulvia was party to the ruse?" Asklepiodes asked.

I was pondering that one myself. "No, I think not. I would certainly never put such a subterfuge past her, but her outburst in the Forum this morning was genuine. It could not have been faked unless she's an actress of surpassing merit. I believe Curio left her house this morning before daylight, waited until the janitor shut the door, took out his dagger and cut himself, waited until he was well-soaked with blood, then raised a huge noise, as if he were being murdered. The janitor reopened the door, and Curio staggered back inside. He'd probably made arrangements with the Syrian beforehand to keep the true nature of his wound secret."

"That would have been prudent," Asklepiodes agreed.

"He probably didn't expect Fulvia to erupt like Aetna though, or he would have had his supporters in the Forum ready to further his plans, whatever they may be. And, of course, he had no way to anticipate another physician coming to examine him. He had to make the best of it and play the scene to the best effect he could."

"Just what *is* his plan?" Hermes wondered aloud. He took from the platter a pastry of mashed figs cooked with honey and nuts.

"I intend to find out," I told him. "But that isn't the question uppermost in my mind at the moment."

"Oh?" Asklepiodes said. "What question troubles you more?"

"How did Curio know that Fulvius was killed elsewhere and carried to the basilica steps? That is a detail I've mentioned to very few people, and Caius Scribonius Curio isn't one of them." I took a slice of fish pie. The way things were going, who knew when I would next have a chance to eat? It is always best to be prepared.

11

"DID FULVIA REALLY STRIP NAKED right atop the rostra in front of the whole public?" Julia wanted to know.

"Only half naked. I think stripping to the waist as a display of grief is a Greek custom."

"When did Fulvia turn into a Greek? She only did it because she thinks she has plenty to show off."

"Now that you mention it, the condition wasn't at all unbecoming, though pity wasn't the reaction she evoked." Julia and I had encountered one another at our house, where I had gone to get my bath gear. She had just come from Callista's to change clothes for an afternoon ceremony at the Temple of Vesta. Then it would be back to Callista's to work on that code.

"You were eager enough to escort her home, I hear." She looked radiant and deceptively benevolent in Vestal white.

"And a good thing I did. Listen to what I learned there." As usual, Julia couldn't stay angry when she was hearing really scabrous gossip and shady intrigue. She seemed thoroughly edified by my recitation.

"What an indiscreet pair," she said, shaking her head. "And what does Curio intend by this ludicrous charade?"

"Not so ludicrous," I told her. "He has the whole City believing he was almost assassinated, and I'd believe it, too, if I hadn't seen the evidence and heard what Asklepiodes had to say. With the elections just the day after tomorrow, the sympathy vote could just push him over the top in a tightly contested election."

"Sad to say, that is the most innocent explanation you can think of."

"Unfortunately. And I am now sure that he had some knowledge of Fulvius's murder. But was it prior or post, and was he personally involved?"

"Would Fulvia marry her brother's murderer? That would be rich even for her."

"Not everybody knows what everybody else is doing in this tangle of deceptions," I sighed. "So far we have Fulvius, the Marcelli, Octavia, Curio, Tribune Manilius, and even Fulvia herself, and every one of them may be playing a different game. Some of them may not be involved at all, although I wouldn't put any money on that proposition."

She looked at the satchel of towels, oil flasks, and scrapers on the table. "Which bath are you going to? The Licinia?"

"No, the one near the old Senate house. The other senators will be gathering there, and I want to sample the climate. Have you made any further progress on the code?"

"Two more characters. Some whole words are turning up, though it's too soon to try to make any sense out of the documents. It's the most enthralling work I've ever done. I'd still be there if I didn't absolutely have to go to the temple this afternoon. Callista thinks we can have it broken by nightfall."

"Wonderful. Send word to me as soon as you have them translated. I'm afraid I have no idea where I'll be."

"Wherever it is, go easy on the wine. You need all your wits about you just now." She swept out like a white cloud.

"Big chance of that," Hermes said, when she was gone.

"Oh, I don't know. I'm thinking of reforming." Hermes wisely said nothing.

It was still only early afternoon, which seemed unbelievable so eventful had the day been. Men were just beginning to gather at the baths. The one I favored was just off the Forum. Although it was less luxurious than the newer *balnea*, it was favored by men of power in Rome, the senators and the untitled but wealthy *equites*.

For a change, I soaked in the hot bath and just listened to them talk for a while. Naturally, almost all the talk was about Fulvia's performance that morning, and the "attack" on Curio. Naturally, Fulvia got the bulk of the attention. Some claimed to be shocked and scandalized; some were merely amused. All agreed that she had made a fabulous sight, and those few who hadn't been there were much aggrieved at having missed the show.

"What's this about Curio being a champion of the plebs?" asked a crusty old senator. "I thought he was one of us!" Us being the aristocrats, the *optimates*, the men who sometimes styled themselves *boni*, the best.

"That's what I thought," said another. Apparently, Curio's defection to Caesar's camp was so recent that many senators hadn't gotten the news yet.

"Oh, yes," an *eques* affirmed. "It seems he's as two-faced as Janus. He'll spend his year pushing Caesar's interests if he gets elected."

"And now it looks as if he's marrying Clodius Pulcher's widow," said a young senator, who wore a dreamy expression. "It's going to be a little hard on his dignity when he gets up to interpose his veto, knowing that we've all seen his wife naked."

"He doesn't seem to be a man easily embarrassed," said the *eques*.

"Who tried to kill him?" I threw the question out at random, my eyes half shut, as if I were almost asleep. I didn't want to take part in the conversation, but I was curious to hear opinion taken from the common store. Sometimes this sort of thing can be more revealing than the informed opinion of insiders.

"Same bunch who killed that fellow, what's-his-name, Fulvius," the young senator opined.

"I'll wager it's Pompey's doing," said the *eques*. Pompey was not at all popular with men of his class, who tended to favor Caesar.

"Why?" asked the old senator. "Aren't Pompey and Caesar still pretending to be friends? Since that dog Clodius was killed, Caesar's had no flunky to run the city for him. Young Curio's father was a good man. He was one of *us!* This boy won't be near the rabble-rouser Clodius was. Why should Pompey want him dead?"

"Besides," the young senator put in, "if there's one thing Pompey knows how to accomplish well, it's killing people. He wouldn't send incompetents to have a man done away with. He'd send a few of his old centurions, men who know how to do their master's bidding and keep their mouths shut about it afterward."

"Whoever it was," said a voice I recognized, "they certainly got that wild woman excited." Sallustius Crispus lowered himself into the bath. I hadn't seen him come in. "She might have gotten another riot going except for one thing."

"What's that?" asked the *eques*.

"Didn't anybody notice?" Sallustius said, grinning. "She never said just *who* she wanted killed—because she didn't know."

"Sounded to me like she wanted the heads of the whole Senate hung up on the Rostra," the young senator said.

"A rhetorical excess, I'm sure." Sallustius caught sight of me then, or pretended to. "Why, Decius Caecilius, I seem to run into you wherever I go."

"He's standing for praetor," somebody said. "There's no getting away from a candidate."

"He'd wear his *toga candida* in the bath, if he could get away with it," said another, amid general laughter. That was fine with me. The last thing I wanted at that moment was to be taken too seriously. Gradually the talk turned to other things. As I expected, Sallustius was there when I resumed my clothing.

"All right, Sallustius, you've been dying to say something. What is it?"

"Our friend Curio, of course, is saying nothing about the men who attacked him, save that they were inept. His friends and supporters, however, are not so reticent."

"Oh? What are they saying?"

"That it was not Curio's enemies who attacked him, that it was Caesar's enemies."

"I see. Supporting Caesar has exposed him to attack from the vile and underhanded *optimates*, eh?"

"Oh, yes. Very much so. And what a brave man he is to have survived the attack. How becomingly modest to act as if it were a trifling brawl, instead of the Homeric combat his friends are describing this very day. I saw him just a little while ago in the Forum, his head wrapped in a blood-soaked bandage."

I had to smile. Curio's little charade seemed to be working splendidly. Had I not so inopportunely sent Asklepiodes to tend to him, he probably would have had himself carried to the Forum on a litter, looking ready to expire but proclaiming himself to be prepared to take office and serve the People of Rome despite his near-mortal injuries.

We walked out of the dressing room and out into the pillared arcade that fronted the *balnea*. Beyond the steps, between the walls of two temples, we could see a small part of the Forum, including the old sundial from Syracuse. People continued to climb the steps in search of a bath, many of them senators. I was obliged to nod and greet most of them in passing but managed to handle our conversation in the meantime.

"So this raises not only his own standing, but Caesar's as well?"

"As if he needed it. You escorted Fulvia home, did you not? How did you find Curio?"

"Just as she described him: poor man was at death's door, bleeding like he'd been beheaded. I was in the act of sticking a denarius under his tongue when he revived and begged to return to his public duties." I was probably enjoying this too much. I have a tendency to do that. Sallustius certainly took it wrong.

"I see. Then you have finally got off the fence and declared for Caesar? Good choice. You won't regret it."

"Nothing of the sort! And don't go around telling anybody that I'm in Caesar's camp because I'm not!"

He winked. "Of course, I understand perfectly." Sometimes I truly hated the man.

"So how do you interpret this business?" I asked.

"I find myself wondering a few things. For instance, how did these attackers know to ambush Curio outside Fulvia's door?"

"They intend to marry. It's no secret and one really doesn't expect a woman like Fulvia to wait until the vows have been made and the hymns to Hymenaeus have been sung."

"That is so," he said, nodding sagely. "Yet a good many people have not yet heard of these proposed nuptials. Most of us were still under the impression that Clodius's widow was to marry Marcus Antonius, even now earning laurels in Gaul. Most of Curio's friends do not yet know. How did his enemies come to learn of it?"

"I'm sure I haven't the foggiest," I told him. Guarding Curio's secrets was no concern of mine, but something made me unwilling to communicate anything to Sallustius.

"In fact," he went on relentlessly, "last night I attended a meeting of, shall we say, the inner circle of Caesar's supporters here in Rome at the house of Caius Antonius the quaestor and brother of Marcus Antonius. Do you know him?"

"Who can avoid knowing the brothers Antonius? They're always either committing some crime or prosecuting somebody else for doing the same. For a pair of disreputable drunks, they're a lot of fun, most of the time. Your meeting must have been enjoyable."

"Oh, it was all very serious for a change," he said. "We discussed how we were going to manage the voting now that Caesar's men are here. A great many of those soldiers have never even seen Rome, much less voted in an election here, so there was much discussion about how to see that all runs smoothly. Curio was there, among others."

"I would expect him to be, now that he's changed sides."

"Yes, just so. After the meeting, a crowd of us walked through the City, each man leaving the group as we neared his home. As it happened, we passed right by Curio's door. He left us there, nowhere near the Clivus Victoriae. He gave us no indication that he feared attack either."

"No doubt he didn't wish to besmirch his future bride's reputation." I said this with a straight face.

"That must have been it. Once we were safely away, he tiptoed his way through Rome's night-darkened streets and was seen by his enemies, who have a batlike ability to find their prey in the dark. They decided to let him spend a last night with his beloved before attacking, possibly as a courtesy."

I spread my hands in a gesture of helplessness. "The world teems with mysteries. Personally, I wonder how the ocean stays where it is. Why doesn't it run off the edge of the world?"

"You should ask that Alexandrian woman you've been visiting. She is said to be a great scholar."

Trust Sallustius to jab at you from an unexpected direction. Talking with him was like fighting with a left-handed swordsman. I thought I kept my face impassive, being well schooled in that art, but he was as perceptive as he was devious.

"We've discussed mathematics and language," I said. "The subject of cosmology has never come up. Now that you mention it, I must remember to ask."

"She's a great beauty, too. I've attended her salon on a number of occasions. Your taste in women is, as always, impeccable."

"Oh, she and Julia are great friends. Whatever poor reputation I have stems from my young and foolish days."

"Really? Since Fulvius made his denunciation three days ago, everyone assumes you seduced, or were seduced by, Princess Cleopatra."

"She's just a girl. Besides, she's royalty and I am a mere Roman senator. And a plebeian at that." I thought I was restraining my temper admirably.

"Oh, come now, Decius. Nothing is beneath the dignity of Egyptian royalty, everyone knows that."

I glanced at the angle of the sun. It was just past midafternoon. The old sundial we looted from Syracuse two hundred years before would show the hour to be the sixth, possibly the seventh. It always gave the time incorrectly, but it would be somewhere in that region.

"Sallustius, I am sure that this is taking us someplace, but I can't imagine where."

"I would truly love to have your personal account of Catilina's conspiracy. I believe you know things nobody else does."

"You've asked me about it often enough."

"Suppose I had something to trade? Something of great interest to you right now? Something of vital importance to your career and possibly to your continued existence? Might that not be worth your helpful cooperation?"

I considered this. It did not come unexpectedly. Collecting secrets was the breath of life to Sallustius. Trading them was his passion. He would not make such a proposition idly. I knew he must truly believe he had something worth my granting him an interview about that unhappy experience. He knew the value of information the way a slave trader knew the value of his human livestock.

"All right," I said after due consideration. "If you truly know something I don't know already, you shall have your interview. But it will have to be after this business is settled and the elections are over."

"That is understood," he said, nodding and grinning like an ape. "You'll have a few days between the election and the day you assume office." Like everyone else, he knew that, barring death or conviction, I would be elected praetor.

"Done. What do you know?"

"Let's find a quiet place to talk."

We left the steps of the *balnea* and passed between the two temples into the Forum. A short walk brought us to the Temple of Saturn. On this day and at this hour it was deserted except for its slaves, who were busy decorating it for the upcoming Saturnalia celebrations. The archaic, blackened image of the god, holding his golden sickle, his legs wrapped in woolen bands, ignored us as we entered the dimness of his home.

"This is where it started, by the way," I said.

"What started?"

"My involvement in Catilina's conspiracy."

"In the Temple of Saturn? But of course," Sallustius said. "You were Treasury quaestor that year. How could I have forgotten?"

"That's for later. What do you have for me?"

We walked past the ornate podium that held military standards. In some years they stood like a dense forest, topped with eagles, boars, bears, spread hands, and other emblems of military units great and small. That year it consisted mainly of empty sockets. So many units had been activated that the only standards left were those of obsolete organizations, the phalanxes and maniples of previous centuries. One section had been covered with a black cloth. There had stood the eagles lost by Crassus at Carrhae. The cloth would remain, an emblem of dishonor, until the eagles were taken back from the Parthians.

Beyond this podium was a broad, marble desk used by the Treasury quaestors and their staffs on days of official business. Ranged around it were wooden chairs with wicker seats. We pulled out two chairs and sat, alone in the quiet dimness of the old temple. Only faint sounds of activity made their way through the open doors.

Sallustius arranged his toga, took his time getting comfortable, laced his fingers over his small but distinguished paunch, and began. "Does it ever strike you, Decius, how few the great families have become?"

"This is oblique, even for you. Get to the point."

"Bear with me. I am a historian, and I take a long view of things. Like most of your class, you are a man of direct action and only take heed of what lies directly in front of you at the moment. You pay little attention to what stretches far behind and of what lies ahead."

I sighed. This was going to take awhile. "I may be more perceptive than you think, but tell it as you like."

"The great old patrician families, the Cornelii, the Fabii, and such, have been dying out generation by generation. They are infertile. More and more they rely on adoption. Or else they fall into poverty because patricians are barred from trade and business. Their only legitimate sources of income come from the land, which is no longer adequate. Public office is expensive, as you know all too well. The Senate takes its new members mainly from the wealthy *equites* now," Sallustius began.

"You're not telling me anything I don't know."

"Of course not. Everybody knows this. They just don't take the trouble to extrapolate the consequences. Rome is a Republic, Decius, but it is far from being a democracy. Roman voters are profoundly conservative, and for centuries they have elected their leaders from a tiny clique of families. New Men like Cicero can be discounted. They have been too few to matter.

"The resulting order has been rough but relatively stable. There have been challenges—such as the upheaval of the Gracchi, the rebellion of Sertorius, Catilina's abortive coup—but overall the order of things has been stable. But that order has been upset over the last three generations by a succession of military strongmen: Marius, Sulla, Pompey, and now Caesar have arisen to upset the order of things.

"It is our own fault, of course. We give our generals godlike powers within their theaters of war and their provinces. Then we expect them to come meekly home and behave like Republican statesmen. It is human nature to love power once one has tasted it, and few have tasted of power as deeply as Caesar or Pompey. Men hate to give power back to whoever bestowed it. They want to keep it for life, and they want to pass it on to their sons as if it were any other inheritance.

"Marius was a jumped-up peasant, he died mad and his children amounted to nothing. Sulla produced twin children late in life. He was old and dying and he knew it. He could have no important part in the upbringing of his son so he reluctantly but sensibly retired to private life after years of absolute power."

"Considering Sulla's proclivities," I said, "it's remarkable he produced any heirs at all."

Sallustius shrugged off this non sequitur. "Pompey is another man of no family. His father came from nothing, and his sons are of no consequence. He has had a remarkable career, but it's over, and he has no future did he but know it.

"Caesar is the man of the hour. His family is incredibly ancient—all the way back to Aeneas and the goddess Venus, if you care to believe his propaganda, but still the most ancient of all Roman families by any interpretation. He is a patrician, one of the few left in Roman politics. He is immensely popular with the commons. He is the most astoundingly successful general since Scipio Africanus. He is now rich beyond imagining. How old is Caius Julius?"

The sudden question took me a little aback. "About fifty, I think."

"Exactly. Julius Caesar is fifty years old, and he has no heir. He has—what?—ten, perhaps fifteen vigorous years left to him? He has attained the years where men begin aging fast. If Calpurnia were to present him with a son tomorrow—a great unlikelihood since she is here in Rome, not pregnant, and he is in Gaul—he might live to see the boy perform his manhood ceremony, perhaps see him off to his first military tribuneship. He will never live long enough to guide a son's career to the higher realms of imperium."

I shifted uncomfortably in my wicker-bottomed chair. "What's all this talk of heirs have to do with anything? Only monarchs need to worry about passing their powers on to heirs."

Sallustius nodded solemnly. "Exactly. Caesar's probable heir is at the center of your problems."

I was beginning to seriously doubt his sanity. "Are you talking about young what's-his-name? Little Caius Octavius?"

He spread his hands in a gesture of satisfaction. "Who else? He's about twelve years old and a precocious twelve at that. Already proven himself as a public speaker by delivering his grandmother's eulogy. You missed that, Decius, but I can tell you that it went down *very* well with the commons. When Caesar comes home next year or the year after, he's going to keep that boy close and teach him all he needs to know about being a Caesar. His real father is dead; his stepfather is an old man who will be more than amenable to the adoption."

"Being Caesar's heir, even were it to happen, won't make him or anyone else a prince," I said.

"You are behind the times, Decius. It will mean exactly that." Sallustius said this flatly, without flourishes and without his customary insinuation. He said it like an historian adding a fact to a book. "What is a prince, anyway? A prince is a human being with a pedigree, like a champion racehorse. The pedigree of the Julii is the highest to be had. That family is surrounded by a unique aura that separates it even from the other patrician gens."

I was persuaded but unconvinced. "Ancient is the word for them. How many great Caesars have their been? Not many in recent centuries. Caesar's father was the first of that family to reach the consulship in ages."

"But the commons have never lost their reverence for them. It was why they were happy to have Caesar as *Pontifex Maximus* when he was little more than a boy."

"He bribed his way into that office!" I protested.

"Of course, but it pleased the people no end. They like knowing that a Julian is arbitrating between them and the gods. And," Sallustius leaned forward for emphasis, "if they respect the Julian men, they absolutely adore the women. Why this should be I don't know. It must be some religious impulse every Roman absorbs with his mother's milk. You weren't in Rome when Caesar's daughter died, were you?"

"No, I was still in Gaul."

"You've never seen such a spectacle. She died in childbirth, as so often happens to Julian women—" Realizing the thoughtlessness of his words, he stopped abruptly. Sallustius had forgotten he was talking to someone married to a Julian. "Forgive me, Decius, I did not—"

I waved it off. "Please continue."

"Very well. When Julia died, Pompey did not have to feign his mourning. He truly loved the girl and was heartbroken. But you cannot imagine how the people reacted. I have never seen anything like it. They dared to bring her body here for cremation." He pointed through the doorway. "Right in the middle of the Forum, where the kings were cremated in the old days. They put her ashes in a grave on the Campus Martius, among the heroes of Rome. No woman has ever before been so honored. The people were honoring neither Pompey, (her husband) nor Caesar (her father). It was purely for love of Julia. Although they barely knew her, she was the most beloved woman in all Rome."

He leaned back again. "This boy, this Octavius, comes from that family. His grandmother was a Julia. The day will come when his ancestry will be important."

"Before he gets my support, he'd better have a lot more to offer than he has now," I grumbled, wondering where all this was leading.

"But will *your* support be of any value to him?" Sallustius asked.

"Eh? Explain yourself."

"I know, Decius, that you are a man without personal vanity, and that your own ambitions are modest, limited to praetorian office."

This was not quite accurate. I fully intended, someday, to be consul. I just wanted it to be in a year without turmoil, allowing me to busy myself with routine duties such as presiding over the Senate and making speeches nobody would have cause to remember. I certainly did not deceive myself into thinking I was a great leader of legions. In the severely limited range of my ambitions, Sallustius evaluated accurately what my family considered my political laziness.

"Nonetheless," he went on, "you can hardly imagine a time when your opinion and support will not carry weight because of who you are: a Caecilius Metellus."

"It goes without saying." I was not as complacent as I was trying to sound. I had grave fears for the future of my family, but I did not want to give them voice in front of one of Rome's less discreet persons.

"Your family's constant trimming and fence-mending have earned it a great many enemies. They married a daughter to a son of Marcus Crassus, they married another to a son of Pompey, they married you to Caesar's niece, all while opposing these men in the Senate and the assemblies. I realize that they have done all these things in order to *avoid* making powerful, implacable enemies, but the time is past for such tactics." Sallustius asked, "You are familiar with the old saw about there being three categories of friends?"

I quoted: "My friend, my friend's friend, my enemy's enemy."

"It is your family's mistake that in holding to this course they have sought to be none of these things. It has made them *everybody's* enemy." I was about to protest, but he held up a hand. "Bear with me, please. You've been away from Rome too much in recent years, and the great men of your family seem to listen only to each other.

"I, on the other hand, listen to everybody. I go everywhere in Rome, from the lowest lupanar and drinking club to the houses of the greatest men. I even attend intellectual salons like those of your new friend Callista. And it may not seem likely to you, but I spend most of my time listening, not talking."

"That *is* difficult to picture," I acknowledged.

"That is because you are too easily swayed by personalities and surface appearances," said Sallustius. "Unlike your elders, you make friends and enemies far too easily and often for the wrong reasons. For—what? twenty years?—Titus Milo has been one of your closest friends. For about as long, Clodius was your deadliest enemy. Why is that? The pair of them were never more than political gangsters with not an ounce of moral difference between them."

"But I *like* Milo," I explained. "I always have. Whereas I detested Clodius from the moment I laid eyes on him."

"And that," he said, with exaggerated patience, "is why you're such a political imbecile." Sallustius wasn't the first to say this, so I took no offense. "Men like Caesar and Curio don't allow such petty considerations to influence the clarity of their political aims."

"I suspect that this is why the Senate will never appoint me dictator," I said.

"Decius, I would hate to lose you. Aside from being a good prospect as a Caesarian, you are certainly one of the more interesting and unusual figures in our public life. But I fear you will not be among us for long if you fail to acknowledge the desperation of your peers. All of them: your family, the Claudians, both Marcelli and Pulchri, the Cornelians and Pompey, and the rest, they are all second- and third-raters. And they have been fighting and plotting and bleeding themselves white against *each other!* Now in Caesar, they are up against a man of the first class, and they have no idea what to do. They are all so jealous of each other that they will never agree on a policy. They have no man of comparable worth to rally behind. In their blind panic they will bring on a civil war they cannot win."

"It needn't come to that," I said. "I know Caesar well. He is arrogant and ambitious, but he is not reckless. He has little personal respect for the Senate, but he is respectful of its institutions. He did not initiate this series of extraordinary commands. Marius began that more than half a century ago. Sulla, Pompey, and others have taken full advantage of them; Caesar has just been better at it. In following precedent, he's adhered strictly to the Constitution. I don't believe that he will take up arms against the Senate. He is no Sulla." Even as I said it, I had doubts. What did I really know of Caesar? What did anybody know? "I don't feel like arguing about this. I seem to have this same argument with my wife every day lately."

"You should listen to her," Sallustius said. "She's a Caesar."

"So she may be descended from a goddess, but she isn't one herself, anymore than her Uncle Caius Julius is a—Did you say you've been *everyplace* these months I've been away?"

"I was wondering how long it would take to work its way into your brain. I was going to let you have one more good rant before repeating it. I knew you would take more satisfaction in working it out for yourself."

"And did your researches among Rome's political plotters take you to the house of Marcus Fulvius?"

"Oh, yes. And it was a very inspiring setting for mapping out the glorious future of Rome, with its patriotic wall decorations and, well, you've been there I understand."

"I have. Were you invited or did you just barge in after your inimitable fashion?"

"I was invited to dinner, along with several other senators and *equites* prominent in the assemblies. Curio was there, by the way. He was still with the *optimates* at the time, but was perceived to be wavering."

"I take it that this assemblage was not random."

"By no means. I noted at once that all the guests formed, you might say, a community of predicament."

I mulled over what I knew of Marcus Fulvius and Curio so unalike in most ways. "Would indebtedness be the common denominator?"

"Very good! Yes, our host was most commiserative. He lamented that this was how a few wealthy men and bankers had gained such undue influence in Roman political life. Office is so ruinously expensive these days, and the only way a man of modest means can hope to be of service to the Senate and People is to go into debt."

"Might I hazard the speculation that he had an answer to this vexing problem?"

"But of course. And there was none of that Catilinarian foolishness; no suggestion that you should go out and murder your father or set fire to the Circus. Marcus Fulvius and his patrons had a simple and somewhat drastic solution: cancellation of debts."

"Stop." I put out a hand. "Just hold it there for a moment. We have been talking thus far about reactionary aristocrats. A blanket cancellation of debt is radical beyond the most outrageous of radical policies. Even the Gracchi couldn't manage it when they were trying to save the ruined farmers. Lucullus signed his own political death warrant when he tried to alleviate the tax-debt burden of the Asian cities. How did this nobody from Baiae propose to do what nobody has yet managed?"

"Oh, there would have to be proscriptions, of course. Unlike Sulla's, though, these would fall most heavily upon the *equites*, particularly the bankers. The Senate and the bulk of the commons would hardly suffer at all. It's not as far-fetched as it sounds and not all that repugnant. After all, do you know anybody who really *likes* bankers?"

"Only a dictator can proscribe." I was beyond astonishment.

"Proscription is nowhere in the Constitution, although it happens when a tyrant seizes power. So there is nothing that says it is a power reserved solely for a dictator. A really powerful cabal could carry it off."

"Sallustius, surely you could not have believed that this—"

"Did I say I believed him?" He looked truly insulted. "Give me credit for some political good sense. I know a crackpot when I see one. When I hear one, at any rate."

"And yet he had backing."

"Certainly."

"I know already that the house he lived in belonged to Caius Claudius Marcellus."

"Really? I did not know that, although it's not much of a surprise. I would have thought one of the other Claudii though. Caius is not the most ardent of them. His brother and cousin are far more forceful."

"They're also the most dismal of conservatives. Where did all this radical claptrap come from?"

"A good question. I pondered it at great length, as it occured." He leaned back in his chair, and I prepared myself to sit through a lecture. Sallustius would have to show off his political acumen. I would just have to let him. His knowledge of Roman political life, both high and low, was comprehensive. And he was no fool.

"First of all, any who took this scheme seriously had to suffer from a political blindness exceeding even that of your family. They think they are still fighting the social struggles of two hundred years ago, patrician against plebeian, *nobiles* against peasants. Back then the *equites* formed a tiny class of prosperous farmers who could afford to show up at the yearly muster with a horse.

"But the *equites* have been quietly growing in wealth and power, and now they are, in fact, the real power brokers of the Republic. If you want to stand for high office, they are the people who can lend you the money to do it. Once you are in office, it is understood that you are in a position to do them favors. Who, for instance, will be collecting the revenues for all those new provinces Caesar has been adding to our Empire?"

"*Publicani,* of course. The tax farmers."

"Exactly the people Lucullus alienated to his own political hurt. Caesar will not make that mistake. He knows where the power lies in Rome. He secured his own position through the assemblies not the Senate. The *optimates* think of themselves as Rome's rightfully privileged class. They see ranged against them the *populares,* whom they perceive as a penniless rabble led by demagogues like Clodius and Caesar. They forget that the *populares* also include most of Rome's millionaires. Their well-bred contempt for mere money precludes their giving this bloc serious consideration."

I thought this over. "So Pompey and his supporters are out. Pompey is far from politically astute, but he understands the power of the *equites*. He rose from that class himself."

"Oh, Pompey would never touch anything as foolish as this. And Caesar is not only friendly toward them, he is extraordinarily reluctant to see citizens executed. He'll kill barbarians in droves, but he is reluctant to see even his mortal enemies killed."

"So who?"

"Aren't you interested in knowing what subject was *not* discussed?" asked Sallustius.

My patience was thinning fast, but he had a point. I was being slow that day. "All right. Did he discuss an attack on the Metelli?"

"Didn't breathe a word of it. In fact, he hinted heavily that your family would be one of the many great ones who would be solidly behind him. After all, what he proposed was a return of the ever-popular Golden age, when Rome was ruled by the best men, when proper aristocrats drew their modest wealth from the good soil of Italy, when commoners knew their place, and base tradesmen did not flout their ill-grubbed money before their betters."

"Does anyone really believe there was ever such a time?" I asked. "Well, I suppose Cato does. You don't suppose— No, even Cato isn't that loony, and he all but slapped Fulvius in the face when the man confronted me. So what brought about this change?"

"I am guessing that Fulvius changed patrons," Sallustius said. "None of that crowd who have been howling for your blood were present when I visited his house. They seem to be mostly old Clodians, not at all the sort who would want a restoration of the old aristocracy, much as they might despise bankers and moneylenders."

"All right," I said, throwing up my hands. "What are you telling me? I am thoroughly confused, and my time is running short. I go on trial tomorrow, and I would really like to be able to demonstrate that I am not guilty of murder."

"It's the boy, Decius."

"That child is all of twelve years old! Just being able to deliver a competent eulogy doesn't qualify him for high-stakes political intrigue!"

"So who is behind him?" Sallustius said, as insinuatingly as always. "You know Cicero's dictum: *A cui bono?* To whom goes the benefit? Who is behind him? Who stands to gain if he becomes Caesar's heir? Who would absolutely *not* want to see Fulvius's silly plan come to anything? Assuming, as we both do, that the various Claudii Marcelli bankrolled him and put him up to it in the first place as a means to undermine Caesar, who would be in a position to know what was going on in that house?"

A few things fell into place. "Octavia."

He nodded. "The boy's sister and wife of Caius Claudius Marcellus. Who was their father?"

"The elder Caius Octavius."

"And what do we know about him?"

"He was praetor a few years back," I said, searching my memory. "I believe he was the first of his family to reach the praetorship. He did a decent job of governing Macedonia as his propraetorian province. Nobody accused him of corruption."

"Yes, by all accounts a good and honorable man. Do you know who his forebears were?"

"My wife keeps excellent track of these things," I said. "I don't."

"The family is from Velitrae, in the Volscian country. His father was a banker of that city. He married his son to Atia, the daughter of Caesar's sister, who was the wife of Atius Balbus, another banker of Velitrae. Balbus was of great aid to Caesar in his penurious years. So Caesar's probable heir and his sister's are the grandchildren of bankers on both sides. Think of it: An attack on bankers, an attack on Caesar's power base—these things would not be to the advantage of Octavia's little brother."

"So you think she subverted Marcus Fulvius, drew him away from her husband and the other Marcelli? But how?"

He slapped his hands against his knees and rose from his chair. "I didn't say I knew everything. I'm just telling you where you should be looking. You are the one who is supposed to be good at this sort of thing."

I rose as well. "I thank you for this information, Sallustius." I tried not to make it sound too grudging. "This has been most illuminating, and you shall have your interview."

"If you live," he said cheerily.

We went outside and stood for a moment in the shade of the great portico. Off to the east end of the portico we could see the whole length of the Forum. Out there, near the meeting place of the comitia, I saw a man with his head turbanned in bloodstained bandages, surrounded by a crowd of belligerent-faced men, some of them wielding staves and cudgels.

"Curio has acquired protectors," I noted.

Sallustius smiled benignly. "Are you familiar with the story of Pisistratus?"

"All I remember is that he was tyrant of Athens." We walked down the steps and turned toward the Forum.

"He was a politician and soldier of some account, but merely one among many such. One day he appeared in the agora heavily bandaged, and claimed that he had been set upon by ruffians in the hire of the aristocrats. He petitioned the assembly to be allowed a bodyguard of armed men, and this was granted in an access of antiaristocratic fervor. Somehow this bodyguard kept growing until Pisistratus completely overawed the citizenry and eventually made himself tyrant, which position he enjoyed for a good many years."

Sallustius turned to me and smiled again, less benignly this time. "It is the opinion of all rational historians that the wounds suffered by Pisistratus were self-inflicted."

"Our friend Curio would never do anything so underhanded," I asserted. Then we both had a good laugh over that one.

Sallustius wandered off and left me with some heavy thoughts to ponder. I shook hands and cadged votes bemusedly for a while, assessing the possibilities in the light of this new evidence, if evidence it was, and not just some fancy of Sallustius, who was never above playing his own political games.

The sun was just touching the rooftops on the west side of the Forum when a Greek slave boy ran up to me.

"You are the Senator Metellus?" he asked with a heavy Alexandrian accent.

"I'm one of them. Decius the Younger by name."

"My mistress, Callista, sends you this."

He handed me a folded piece of papyrus. I opened it and saw a single, oversized Greek letter: Delta. Below that, in small, neat letters, was a single Latin word: Done.

12

I FOUND THE TWO OF THEM, JULIA AND Callista, relaxing amid a great litter of papers and scrolls, looking absurdly happy and satisfied with themselves. They were celebrating with a bit of wine, which they were drinking from, of all things, Thracian rhytons; those strange drinking horns made of silver with the bases in the form of animal or human heads. Callista beamed at me and handed me one. Its horn part was delicately fluted, the base representing a ram, its curling horns and dense wool exquisitely molded.

"Bit of a departure from philosophical simplicity," I noted. I took a sip and tried not to wince. It was one of those Greek wines flavored with resin that I have always found disagreeable.

"They were a gift from a Thracian nobleman who attended a course of my lectures at the Museum," Callista said. "I only bring them out for special occasions."

"Well, if this isn't a special occasion," I said, "then I don't know what constitutes one. Breaking a code is a unique sort of accomplishment."

"I don't know when I've enjoyed anything so much," she said, with apparent sincerity.

"What have you learned?" I asked.

Julia took up a small sheaf of papers. "We could have hoped for more. No names of the conspirators were used, probably for security's sake, but probably also because they were scarcely needed, since only a tiny circle of plotters were involved. Also they are not dated. Again because the participants would know when they were written and received. These were never intended for future reference."

"Marcus Fulvius intended to use them in the future," I said.

"How so?" Julia asked.

"That he intended to use them at some future date I deduce from the fact that he didn't destroy them after reading, which is what you usually do with incriminating documents. As to his motive, since he intended to be a great man, he may have wanted them for his memoirs, which he fancied would have an audience. Or, more likely, he may have intended to use them for blackmail purposes, or as insurance in case the others should someday turn against him, as I now believe they did."

"I never would have thought of those things," Callista admitted, "yet I find your logic impeccable, and your grasp of the various possible alternatives comprehensive. Most people who have not been trained in philosophy and logic form a single opinion, usually based on prejudice or emotion, and adhere to it stubbornly."

"This is what makes my husband the—singular sort of person he is," said my loving wife.

"But he employs his gift in a unique way," said Callista. "Give me a problem of mathematics, of the nature of the universe, of natural history, or the nature of beauty, and I will bring to bear upon it all the resources of five hundred years of philosophical thought, from Heraclitus to the present day. But, confronted with the problems of human passion, of ambition, greed, lust for power, jealousy, and simple stupidity, I am as helpless as a child. Such things do not yield to analysis and philosophical rigor."

"That," Julia told her, "is because you have lived your life in an elevated world of the mind, where thought is the highest joy. Decius, to the contrary, is intimately familiar with all these things."

"Well, what do we have here?" I asked, a little put out at Julia's fulsome praise of the philosophical world. I had spent some time at the Museum of Alexandria and so had she. Among the teachers there we had found no shortage of pettiness, jealousy, and ambition.

"We've sorted these into what seem to be chronological order," Callista said crisply. She took a sheet from Julia. "This one I've put first because the original showed signs of awkwardness in using the cipher. The ones I've assigned a later date show far greater assurance in the execution."

"That makes sense," I allowed. I took the sheet and read. It began without the usual preamble: "From so-and-so to his esteemed friend so-and-so, greeting." Instead, it got down to business in the first line.

> Our supporters are in place and have their orders. They will assist you in any way you wish, as in locating and inviting the subjects for each of your meetings, accompanying you to the Forum, etc. From receipt of this message you are not to approach us in public or in private. If you encounter one of us in a public place, there can be no more than an exchange of civilities. In public, for now, we are mere acquaintances whose families are vaguely connected. For your first gathering you will invite the following men whose sympathies we deem to be in accord with our program:

There followed a list of seven names. Those I recognized were low-level senators, two of them relatively well-known malcontents who continualy courted attention by berating the greatest men. They were tolerated because of tradition and because we liked to let the public think that the Senate is an assembly of equals, as in the good old days. When the plebs saw nonentities like these haranguing Caesar or Pompey, Cato or Cicero, to his face, right up on the Rostra, it gave everyone a sense of participation and the comforting and very deceptive feeling that Rome was in no danger of succumbing to tyranny.

"The next few," Callista said, "are very brief and mostly list the guests he is to invite to each new meeting." She showed me these and each of them gave a list of seven names, along with assurances that all was proceeding splendidly.

"Always seven names," I muttered.

"What was that?" Julia queried.

"Wait awhile," I said, studying the lists. "Things are beginning to shape up."

"I love it when he's like this," Julia said.

"He is communicating with his muse," Callista affirmed.

I ordinarily resent it when people talk about me as if I were not present, but this time I was too preoccupied to take umbrage. As the messages progressed according to Callista's chronological table, the names of the senators and others got less safe. More prominent men began to show up, men known to have reservations about the trend of Roman politics, but not radical. Some names began to be repeated. These must have been the ones inclined to fall in with Fulvius's crackpot scheme. I mentioned this to the two women.

"That makes sense," Callista commented.

"The *equites*," I said, "at least those whose names I recognize, are not in the banking or moneylending fraternity. Most seem to be members of prominent business families. These are probably men who have squandered their wealth and are in danger of being degraded from equestrian status."

"I notice," said Julia, "that while some of these names are prominantly anti-Pompey or anti-Caesar, none are famously pro-Pompey or pro-Caesar."

"Very astute, my dear. No, these are mostly malcontents, those perpetually jealous of the great men but adhering to none of them. You may also notice that none of Cato's patriotic little band are here either. And this despite the fact that Fulvius's walls were decorated with their favorite historical patriots."

Julia thought about that for a moment. "Those men are veritable ancestor worshippers, but they are also against any sort of tyrant."

I put down the papers for a moment and gestured to a nearby slave, who refilled my rhyton. I no longer even noticed the resinous taste. My mind was working like one of those German ale vats, where little clumps of spirit-inspired particles swarm around like bees.

"Do you recall what I told you about the wardrobe Hermes and I found in Fulvius's house?" I looked around. "By the way, where is Hermes? I haven't seen him all afternoon."

"He said he had to go locate some people, and he'd catch up to you later. As I recall you found some equestrian tunics, some senatorial tunics, a plain, white toga, and a *toga praetexta*."

"Very good. At the time this told me that the man had vaunting, presumptuous ambitions. He was ready to assume a seat in the Senate and curule office. What escaped me at the time was what was *not* there."

"This being?" Julia queried.

"He had no *toga candida* and no *toga trabea*." I caught Callista's quizzical look and elucidated. "The *candida* is the specially whitened toga we wear when standing for office. The *trabea* is a striped robe worn by augurs and some orders of priesthood."

"He could have had the plain toga whitened," Julia said.

"That would have left him with no toga for everyday purposes: Senate meetings and sacrifices and such." More and more in those days, Roman men were discarding the toga except for formal occasions.

"So what do you deduce from this?" Callista wanted to know.

"First of all, that he expected to get a Senate seat, and even curule office, without standing for election."

"Only a dictator can place a man in the Senate without election. At the very least it takes a vote of the full Senate."

"Exactly."

"Why not a priestly robe?" Callista asked.

"Most colleges of priesthood are filled by co-option. A priesthood is held for life. On the death of, say, an augur, the College of Augurs meets and votes in a new member. Likewise with most other priesthoods. A flamen can be appointed by a dictator, but they have to be patricians, and Fulvius didn't qualify. Certain positions, such as *Pontifex Maximus,* are elective. But once elected, the pontificate is for life. The men behind Marcus Fulvius promised him a Senate seat and a curule office without having to stand for election. They couldn't make him an augur or a pontifex, so they didn't bother making the offer."

"So somebody intended to become dictator," Julia said, "and Marcus Fulvius was going to help him do it. But who? Pompey's supporters have been trying to get a dictatorship for him as long as I can remember, but Fulvius approached none of them."

"The Claudii Marcelli," I said, "have been fomenting political hysteria in Rome. They've got everybody thinking that we are about to be tyrannized by either Caesar or Pompey. And they've been successful in this. Nobody seems to notice that Caesar is a prodigiously successful and ambitious but meticulously constitutional proconsul, and Pompey is a used-up old man content to rest on his laurels. They have us all drawing our swords against phantoms."

"And they planned to overthrow the government with a clown like this *Fulvius?*" Julia said, incredulous.

"He's just the one we've discovered," I told her. "They didn't put in this much planning, hire Aristobulus to concoct their code, and then kill Fulvius just to control one man to agitate among the debtors and malcontents. They must have other agents, probably far more important than Fulvius."

"You said something about there being seven names on each list," Callista said. "What is the significance of this?"

"The meetings were conventional dinner parties," I explained. "His triclinium was set up for it, with all those patriotic paintings. The couches were arranged according to strict form, as to location and size. For centuries we've always followed the custom of nine at dinner. He would have adhered to that. Seven guests each time. Fulvius made eight. Who was the ninth man?"

"This will bear some thought," Julia said. "What did you learn at the baths?"

I told them about my little foray, and what Sallustius had told me about the meeting he had attended at the house of Fulvius.

"Sallustius was holding something back," Julia said. "He didn't give you the names of the other attendees."

"Even Sallustius can be discreet at times. He knew that if he named names and I used this in a prosecution or denunciation, each of them would know which gathering it was and who had blabbed. That could mean death or permanent exile for him. And he went to only one dinner party, so he could not have known that one of the guests was a permanent fixture at these meetings. The significance would have escaped him."

Julia scanned the names, her lips forming each one as she read it, barely voicing them. "What other names do we *not* see on these lists, now that we are thinking in negatives? I don't see either Curio or Manilius. These were written well before Curio declared for Caesar, and he was known for his indebtedness. Why not him? And Manilius was a tribune. Who better to rouse the mob against the moneylenders? They would have seemed natural targets for this scheme."

"I am not satisfied with Fulvia's story that she had nothing to do with her brother while he was in Rome. She might have known about Curio's defection ahead of time and told him. As for Manilius, he's shown no signs of exceptional radicalism. Curio says the two of them cooperated during his tribuneship."

"There is the matter of that estate he suddenly came into," Julia pointed out.

"The Claudii Marcelli have plans, and some of them are even constitutional. It's never a bad idea to have a Tribune of the People in your pocket. It's done all the time."

"Or," said Callista, "either one of them could have been the ninth man."

Julia smiled at her. "Now you're beginning to think like a Roman."

"By next year," I went on, spinning out my speculations, "or maybe the year after, I believe they intend to declare both Caesar and Pompey to be enemies of the state and get the Senate to name one of themselves dictator. That one will name one of the others his Master of Horse."

"How can they do that?" Julia said, heatedly.

"I don't know, but they will provoke Caesar in some fashion, offer him some insult that he can't allow to pass. They want to force him into a move that they'll be able to take before the Senate as proof that the state is under attack and call for an Ultimate Decree of the Senate."

"I don't understand," Callista said. "I thought a dictator was a usurper, like a Greek tyrant. And what is this—cavalry commander?"

"Among us," Julia explained, "dictator is a constitutional office. In time of deadly national danger, such as a foreign invasion, when our division of powers is too slow and clumsy to meet the emergency, the Senate can direct the consuls to name a dictator.

The dictator in turn names another man to be his Master of Horse. This is an ancient title for his second in command, who will carry out his orders."

"The dictator," I went on, "has full imperium. He does not share it with a colleague, and his acts are not subject to tribunal veto. He is attended by twenty-four lictors, the number of both consuls combined. The dictatorship is what we call an 'unaccountable' office. Alone of all Roman magistrates, when he leaves office he cannot be called to account for his acts. He can order *anything,* including the execution without trial of citizens. He can declare war on his own initiative. There is no limit to his power save one."

"What is that?" Callista asked.

"Time. A dictatorship is held for six months, and then the dictator must step down. Sulla's dictatorship was unconstitutional. It was a military coup. There weren't enough senators in Rome to pass a resolution of dictatorship. Once in power he doubled the size of the Senate to pack it with his flunkies, and then had them keep voting him back in as dictator. He held the office for three years and didn't step down until he was too sick to go on. This sort of thing is why we so seldom appoint a dictator."

"It would take great fear to make the Senate do it now," Julia said.

"People are ripe for it," I pointed out. "You've heard all the scare talk, seen all the line drawing that's been going on. Agitation to cancel debts and perhaps massacre the bankers and money lenders would add fuel to the fire nicely."

"But something happened," Julia said.

"Yes, something caused Fulvius to swerve from the path that had been laid out for him and instead attack the Metelli through me."

"Look at this one," Callista said, handing me a translated page. "It is one of the last."

You are to stop this foolishness. Your support is withdrawn. We have called back our men, and they will no longer aid you. Render an accounting for your actions at once or face the consequences.

"This does sound impatient," I said.

"And this is the last one." Callista handed me the page.

I am sending you more slaves for your household and more men for your protection and support. They are rough, but trustworthy. As long as you remember the terms of our bargain and adhere strictly to them, you will achieve your ambitions and will have nothing to fear from me. Do not try to contact me. I will send someone for you should we need to meet.

"This last message differed from the others," Callista said. "It is written in a woman's hand."

"Are you sure?" I asked.

"Oh, yes. The differences are quite distinct."

"Fulvia?" Julia said.

"Not Fulvia, though she is probably involved. This was written by Octavia."

"Octavia?" Julia said.

I told them about the heavy hints Sallustius had dropped concerning the wife of Caius Claudius Marcellus and her little brother.

"When I met with her yesterday," I paused. Could it have been just yesterday? "When I talked with her yesterday, she was a little too emphatic in proclaiming that she had cut her ties with the Julian family, that she thought Julius Caesar was a potential tyrant, that she had nothing to do with the Fulvians, that she had no knowledge of her husband's affairs, that she hadn't even seen her brother since he was an infant, and she didn't follow City gossip. Is such a thing believable?"

"Not in our family," Julia said. "I think Sallustius is right. He's a weasel, but he knows his subject. Caius Marcellus does nothing without her knowledge. She knew all about this plot, and she even learned their code. She knows what futile bunglers her husband and his kinsmen are. She knows that Julius Caesar is destined to be the greatest man in Rome, and she wants to make her brother his heir."

She said this with a bitterness that surprised me. Then I understood that she had hoped that a son of ours would be Caesar's heir. It seemed that the gods had other plans.

"So Octavia subverted the plot?" Callista asked. "How could she do this? What lever did she apply to move Fulvius more to her liking?" Even in asking this she used an analogy from Archimedean mechanics.

"It's unlikely that she was able to promise him greater rewards than he already expected," I said. "So it must have been blackmail."

"She couldn't have accused him of political scheming," Julia said. "Everybody does that anyway."

"No, Octavia threatened to expose him for the murder of Aristo-bulus. The Marcelli wanted the Greek out of their way, and they wanted to bind Fulvius more tightly to themselves, so they sent him to do their dirty work."

"What proof?" Julia asked.

"It must have been the ring. The Marcelli wanted the ring back. It was the only thing that connected them to Aristobulus. Fulvius killed Aristobulus and delivered the ring. Octavia got hold of it and showed it to Fulvius. She'll have had some sort of written evidence connecting him to the crime, but she concealed the ring in the desk her husband lent to Fulvius. Anytime she wanted, Octavia could have some ambitious friend, Curio, for instance, accuse him and demand an investigation. The *iudex* appointed to investigate would get an oppor-tune tip as to where to find the ring. Those men who caught Hermes and me going through Fulvius's belongings, it was the ring they'd come for. The Marcelli weren't concerned about the papers because they were in cipher. But Octavia wanted that ring back."

"And where did Octavia get those men?" Julia asked. "She culti-vates her reputation for virtue the way Hortalus cultivates his fish ponds."

"She got them from Fulvia. One way or another, those two women have been plotting together. Clodius's widow has retained some control over his supporters, who are Caesarians to a man. It may have irritated Fulvia that her brother was working with the other side. Octavia pre-sented her with a way to control him."

"How could she have exposed him without incriminating her husband?" Julia asked.

"Either the Marcelli have very carefully kept their own hands clean," I said, "or else she just didn't care. Remember our conversa-tion here yesterday when I mentioned that Caesar wanted Octavia to divorce Caius Claudius Marcellus and marry Pompey? I had assumed that she was mortally offended and detested Caesar for demanding that she leave her husband. It was probably Caius who refused."

"Why did she set Fulvius to attack you?" Callista wanted to know.

"I'd like to believe I'm important enough to be at the center of all this," I said, "but the sad truth is, I'm nothing. But my family is still extremely influential in the Senate and the assemblies, and they're turning more and more against Caesar. She had a tool in Marcus Fulvius, and she set him to undermining the Metelli. I was standing for curule office and was a convenient target. I was just back from a foreign command, and nothing is more common than to accuse such a man of corruption overseas. Remember, he had that fine pedigree to flaunt before the public just prior to election time. We speculated that he might have been fishing for a tribuneship by acclamation. If Fulvia had all the old Clodians primed to agitate for him in the *consilium plebis*, they might have carried it off. Then he'd be untouchable for a year."

"But how would he have produced his witnesses?" Julia asked.

"Oh, he might have had some people lined up to commit perjury, and it may have been enough just to throw the election into disorder. He might have accused me of bribing away his witnesses or murdering them or something. Enough to get me barred from the election anyway. That would mean one less Metellus holding an important office next year. But something went wrong. The Marcelli, never quick-thinking men, realized what he was up to. Octavia got her slaves out of the house, maybe even warned Fulvius. He put on a dingy, old freedman's toga and tried to get away, but they caught him and killed him. Then they dumped him on the steps of the basilica."

"Do you think the various Marcelli, Marcus, Caius, and Marcus, actually killed him with their own hands?" Julia wanted to know. I explained to them Asklepiodes's analysis of the wounds, and the conclusions I had drawn from them.

"Decius Caecilius," Callista said, with what seemed to be unfeigned admiration, "I believe you have invented a whole, unique subset of philosophy! Have you ever considered writing a book about this? I am sure that you would be much in demand for lectures at the Museum in Alexandria."

For a moment I wasn't certain that I had heard her correctly. "Are you serious?"

"I am always serious about philosophical matters," she assured me.

I glanced toward Julia. She was looking away, intently studying the fretwork that tastefully graced one of the walls.

"I shall have to give that some thought," I said. "After all, I'll have to have *something* to do during the occasional exile from Rome." Another thought occurred to me. "Speaking of philosophical things, Callista, I've always wondered why the ocean doesn't run off the edge of the world, taking Our Sea with it, out through the Gates of Hercules."

"The world is a sphere," she asserted, "floating in space, so there is no place for the ocean to run off to. This was proven by Eratosthenes almost two hundred years ago."

"I see. Well, that answers that." It made at least as much sense as a symbol for nothing.

"Getting back to our problem," Julia said. "Do you think the Marcelli killed Fulvius with their own hands, and more to the point, can you prove it?" My Julia was always the practical one.

"I simply cannot believe," Callista said, "that your political intrigues can get this complicated! It makes the struggles of the old Greek city-states seem laughably simpleminded."

"It wasn't intended to be this way," I told her. "This was to be a rather ordinary power play, but it got out of hand. These are not very acute people. As Sallustius characterized them: a crew of second raters. They tried something too difficult for them to control; one of them didn't even know that his own wife was in the other camp and spying on all their doings. They chose a badly flawed tool in Fulvius, and everybody lied to everyone else and to me. What should have been a clean, discreet operation turned into a tangled mess that called for murder and then a cover-up, which, in turn, called for a false accusation against me. And all this was begun by men of consular standing. It's really very depressing."

"However this turns out," Julia said, "I am going to write to Caesar this evening. He has to know what is going on behind his back here in Rome."

"Probably a good idea," I agreed. "But I have a feeling that very little goes on in Rome that Caesar doesn't know about. I assisted him with his correspondence back at the beginning of the war, remember? He has more friends sending him news and gossip than Cicero. But do go ahead. It will at least set his mind at ease about us. I'll send him a full report after I've wrapped up this business."

"Why, Decius!" Julia said happily. "I believe this is the first time you've acknowledged that Caesar is the real authority in Rome."

"It seems inevitable now," I admitted. "I've seen too much of the quality of the men ranged against him. Don't celebrate prematurely though. By the time I write that report, I'll be praetor, or I'll be in exile. The first prospect is the ideal one; the second is better than the third."

"What is the third?" Callista asked.

"Third, I'll be dead and won't get a chance to write the report."

For a while we discussed my best course of action. I was to go on trial in the morning and we went over my defense, the most likely attacks I would face, and my best counterattacks. Julia's mind for this sort of political-judicial warfare was as fine as that of any professional lawyer in Rome. She lacked only the rhetorical training to be a first-rate advocate. That, and the fact that women couldn't argue in court.

It was well past dusk when Hermes arrived.

"Where have you been?" I demanded.

"Finding people. We've come to escort you home." He was quite unabashed, and I didn't feel like berating him as he deserved. Besides, he usually knew what he was doing.

"Who is we?" I asked.

"Some friends."

Julia and I rose. "Callista," I said to the Alexandrian, "I cannot thank you enough. I sought an advisor and found a friend. If all goes well tomorrow and the next day, I shall be one of next year's praetors. It may be that I will be praetor *peregrinus,* in charge of cases involving resident aliens. If in that office or in any other way I can be of assistance to you, please do not hesitate to call upon me."

Julia gave her a parting embrace. "My husband is not always perfectly rational, but he means that. And please don't wait to have some sort of problem to call on us."

"Just knowing that I have the friendship of the two of you is more than adequate recompense for this small service, which truly was not a service but a pleasure. The thrill of intellectual accomplishment is its own recompense."

We stepped outside into the dimness. "What a gracious lady," Julia said. "For once I can only commend your judgment in seeking out a foreign woman."

"That's good of you, my sweet. Hermes, who are all these men?" I could just make out the forms of some twenty or thirty men crowding the street. One held a small torch that did not yield enough light to reveal more than that. The others brought out torches and ignited them from that one. Soon I could see an abundance of military belts and high-strapped, hobnailed military boots, and men with hard limbs and harder faces, all deeply tanned.

"Evening, Senator, my lady," said young Burrus, *decurio* of the Tenth Legion.

"Hermes, I can't have this!" I protested. "These are all Caesar's men! I won't have people thinking I'm taking Caesar's side against the others, that I'm—" I mumbled the last few words because Julia placed her fingers across my lips.

"Decius," she said, "be quiet."

"You put him up to this!" I said, astonished.

"I didn't have to. We discussed how to keep you from getting yourself killed with this absurd neutrality, and Hermes suggested this. I concurred."

"The time is past for neutrality," Hermes told me, this boy who used to carry my bath implements and run my errands. "Let people say

213

what they will. These men are here by *their own choice* whether you want them or not, and they will keep you safe in spite of yourself until this business is over. Remember, in the City they aren't Caesar's soldiers, they are citizens and voters and they can do as they like."

I sighed, knowing defeat when it was staring me in the face. I was as much in Caesar's camp now as if I had been in his army in Gaul.

"Let's go home," I said.

13

WE LEFT MY HOUSE IN THE PEARLY light of earliest dawn. When I stepped from my gate onto the street, it was already packed with my supporters. The occasion was too serious and solemn for a cheer, but I heard a collective murmur of approbation from them.

As soon as I was in the street, I was surrounded by soldiers. This we had discussed the night before, and as much as I hated to look like I went in fear of my fellow citizens, I could not reasonably object to this precaution. There was a very real possibility that the Marcelli, or Octavia, might decide to spare themselves embarrassment by hiring someone to slip a dagger between my ribs before I could reach the trial site.

Hermes accompanied me, positioned to my left rear, the most likely approach for a right-handed assailant. Before me stretched a wedge of soldiers. At the tip of the wedge were young Lucius Burrus and his father. Old Burrus had chosen to wear his military decorations, of which he had earned a cartload: silver bracelets, torques, *phalerae*, even a civic crown. Armed soldiers could not enter the City, but I had the toughest-looking pack of unarmed soldiers south of the Padus. Stretching far behind was a great mob of my clients, my neighbors, and other supporters.

"Well," I said, "barring rooftop archers, I should make it to the Forum alive."

"Archers," muttered a nearby soldier. "I knew we should've brought shields."

"Let's be off," I said.

The mass of humanity began its stately pace down the narrow street, toward the Clivus Suburanus, which would take us to the Forum. Julia and the household staff would follow as soon as the street was halfway cleared.

I wore my best toga, not my *candida*. It might look presumptuous, to show up at a trial wearing a chalked-up toga. Besides, proper rhetorical form called for a lot of broad gesticulation, and that could raise great clouds of chalk dust, an undignified sight. I was impeccably barbered and had spent the previous hour in breathing exercises, practicing my gestures, and gargling hot, vinegared water, things I hadn't done in years. For once I wasn't carrying weapons. It might be awkward if my dagger or *caestus* should clatter to the podium at the peak of a dramatic gesture. Instead, Hermes carried them for me.

When we reached the Forum, the crowd was already gathering. The trial was to be held in the old Forum's largest open space, at the western end between the Basilica Aemilia and the Basilica Sempronia. There the magistrate's platform, recently restored and adorned by Caesar, stood ready for a trial before the *comitia tributa*. This meant that, instead of the center of the platform being dominated by a praetor in his curule chair, we would be facing the Tribunes of the People, who by custom would be seated on a single bench. Since none of the presiding officials held imperium, there were no lictors on the podium. Behind the platform, on the Basilica Aemilia side, towered the wooden bleachers erected for the three hundred *equites* who would be my jury.

The Metelli were already gathering by the western end of the podium: my father, Creticus, Nepos, and Metellus Scipio, accompanied by their huge rabble of supporters, along with many friends and colleagues, some of them personally devoted to the Metelli, others merely opposed to the same people. Cato was there, and I welcomed his support as heartily as I disliked him personally.

To the other side, I saw a great pack forming, many of them old Clodians hoping to witness my downfall, some of them the men I had seen with Marcus Fulvius. I was curious to see whether any of the Marcelli would make an appearance among them, but I saw none of them. Perhaps it was too early. Or perhaps they were having second thoughts about the whole affair.

Father looked disgusted when I walked up, surrounded by my entourage.

"Did you have to show up like an invading army?" he spat.

"No choice. They've appointed themselves my bodyguard." I scanned the bleachers, where the jury, wearing their narrow-striped tunics, were only beginning to take their places. The podium was as yet deserted. "Is there someplace where we can discuss this business before the proceedings begin?"

"It's a little late for discussion," Father said, "but if you've anything to tell us, just have your little army give us some space."

So the soldiers formed a ring around us and held the crowd back. Scipio gave me a quick rundown of the day's procedure.

"Cato will lead off. He's not a member of the family and is known to oppose us on many policies, so he'll be respected as an impartial speaker. He'll challenge the constitutionality of this court so we'll have groundwork laid for a retrial if you should be convicted. That will mean you can't stand for election tomorrow, but there will be other years.

Then he'll laud your good character and defame the late Marcus Fulvius. Then he'll introduce the speakers, all of them prominent men, who will shout what a wonderful person you are.

"It will then be the other side's turn to bring on the accusations against you."

"Who is to prosecute?" I asked.

"Manilius himself," said Creticus.

"What? A serving tribune? Is that legal?" This I had not anticipated.

"Apparently there is no law that specifically forbids such a thing," Cato told me. "Tribunes are usually too busy for such activities, but this is Manilius's last day in office, and the exposure will benefit his campaign for the aedileship."

"What did you want to tell us?" Father said. "Time is short."

So I began a precise description of my findings. Before I was halfway through, their fallen faces told me that this was not going down well. Father cut me off with a short, savage gesture.

"Cease this nonsense! A secret code? A Greek mathematician, and a woman at that? Are you mad?"

"A conspiracy among three of the most prominent men of the state?" Scipio cried, going scarlet. "One of them a sitting consul! Another almost certain to be elected consul for next year?"

"And," Nepos said pitilessly, "yet another plot on behalf of a twelve-year-old boy? And concocted by a Julian woman?" He turned to Father. "Cut-nose, maybe we'd be best advised to get up there, declare him insane, and hustle him out of Rome as quickly as possible."

"Nonsense," Cato said, calmly for once. "I've seen him like this before. He'll get over it. Decius, forget all this drivel, even if it's true. You have no evidence, no witnesses. For legal purposes, none of it happened. We'll do this the old-fashioned way, the way our ancestors did it." This, for Cato, being the ultimate encomium for anything at all.

Pompey pushed his way through to us, the soldiers parting before him by sheer habit.

"What is the meaning of this?" he demanded. "As if that absurd demonstration yesterday wasn't enough, now I have *two* packs of thugs elbowing each other in the Forum!"

"Two?" I said. Then, "Oh, I suppose Curio is here. Don't worry about these soldiers, Proconsul. They'll disperse as soon as the trial is over. Curio's lot you are going to have to contend with for a while, I fear. When I have time a little later I'll tell you all about Pisistratus."

"Pisistratus! The tyrant of Athens? Cut-Nose, is your son completely crazy?"

"We've been discussing that very possibility, Proconsul, but Cato is of the opinion that it's a passing phase. I myself am not so sure."

Pompey shrugged. "Well, being mad never stopped anyone from being elected praetor before this. But I'll not have a great show of force here in the Forum on the day before the election."

"We're Metelli," said Creticus, "not Claudians or Antonii or any other sort of congenital criminals. We'll do this the proper way and abide peacefully by the decision of the court."

"See you do. I'm going to go talk with Curio now, and see if I can get him to disperse his gang. Pisistratus, indeed!" He bustled off, and I could understand his anger. For a year his proudest boast had been that he had cleared Rome of the criminal-political gangs that had plagued us for generations. Now it looked as if his good work was being undone.

The bleachers were now almost full, my jury, each man wearing the narrow purple stripe and gold ring of his equestrian status, taking his place. They were a prosperous-looking lot, wealthy and usually self-made. Such men could be counted on to dislike an aristocrat like me. On the other hand, they had little love for the Clodian rabble. We were even there.

The Tribunes of the People were seating themselves, arranging their plain togas, which lacked the purple border despite their great power. Their tunics likewise lacked the senatorial stripe, although they could attend Senate meetings and interpose their veto there. They would enter the Senate as full members in the following year.

As the tribunes sat I identified them and almost reflexively rated each according to the political obsession of the day. From the left: Caelius, pro-Caesar; Vinicius, pro-Caesar; Vibius Pansa, pro-Caesar; Cornelius, pro-Caesar; Nonius, pro-Caesar; Minucius, anti-Caesar; Didius, anti-Caesar; Antistius, anti-Caesar; Valerius, anti-Caesar and, last of all on the right end of the bench, that unknown quantity, Publius Manilius.

When all were present, Manilius stood and gestured for silence. Gradually, the babble of the multitude was stilled.

"Citizens!" he began. "I, Tribune of the People, Publius Manilius Scrofa, declare these proceedings to be open. In the *contio* of the Plebeian Order, this matter was deemed worthy of trial before the *comitia tributa* and thus we shall proceed.

"The accused"—here he gestured in my direction—"is Decius Caecilius Metellus, a senator of Rome, charged with the murder of Marcus Fulvius, citizen of Rome, formerly resident in Baiae, at the time of his death dwelling in the Temple of Tellus district. Is the defense ready to present opening arguments?"

"We are!" Father shouted.

"Then ascend the podium and address the people of Rome."

We climbed the steps in stately fashion; a gaggle of Metelli, along with Cato and a number of prominent men, some of them ex-consuls, to attest to my character.

"Who speaks for you?" Manilius demanded.

Cato stepped forward. "I am Senator Marcus Porcius Cato, a friend of the accused, and I will prove his innocence of these base charges."

"Proceed," said Manilius. He pointed to the slave who stood by the old bronze water clock. The man pulled out its stopper and water began to drain into a large glass beaker that was graduated to reveal the passing minutes. Opening arguments would be over as soon as the beaker was full. A good Roman lawyer could time his argument to the syllable.

"First," Cato began, "I must protest this wretched, unconstitutional trial. The *contio* that called for it was informal, and there were no sacrifices. Auguries were not taken. The gods of the state were not called upon to witness, and so it is invalid. The *comitia tributa* has no power to try a capital case, and I assure everyone here that that is just what they will try to make of it!" Cato had an unpleasant voice, but he also had a masterful command of a sort of old-fashioned, almost sacerdotal Latin that was extremely impressive in events of this nature. He completely eschewed the florid, embroidered rhetoric practiced by Hortalus.

Then Cato launched into his oration. He spoke of the glory of my family, naming its many censors, consuls, and praetors, and of the battles won by Metellan generals. He spoke of my early career, of my service in the rebellion of Sertorius, in the suppression of the Catilinarian conspiracy, in the war in Gaul, most recently in my little campaign that very year against an outbreak of piracy near Cyprus.

He then launched into my political career, citing my many investigations against criminals and criminal activities, my quaestorship, during which I had infiltrated Catilina's ranks, my unprecedented double aedileship, when I had not only cleaned up the streets and sewers, but had vigorously prosecuted the crooked building contractors whose shoddy practices had cost so many citizens lives (nobody counted the dead slaves and foreigners). He cited the games I had celebrated, including the funeral games for Metellus Celer, at which I had presented a *munera* where an uncommon number of famous champions had come out of retirement to fight. Milo had been responsible for this, but I got the credit. There were murmurs of appreciation from the crowd. Everybody had loved those games.

When the beaker was full, Cato stopped and my character witnesses came forward. Some swore before all the gods that I was as virtuous a Roman as any since Numa Pompilius. All swore that I was incorruptible (actually, few people had considered me worth corrupting). All extolled the worthiness of my ancestors. Those who had been praetors told of important investigations I had undertaken for them. At one time I had been something of a professional *iudex*.

Then Cato resumed his oration. The water clock was reset for this phase, always the most enjoyable part of a trial: denunciation of the other side.

"Who," cried Cato, "was this Marcus Fulvius? He was a nobody from nowhere. He was a resident, not of Rome, but of Baiae, that sordid cesspool of every sort of luxury, vice, and perversion! Can there be any doubt that Marcus Fulvius was himself the very embodiment of all that is vile, disgusting, and un-Roman? Citizens! Did you all not, just yesterday, see that insolent fool's own sister, the most notorious whore in Rome, climb upon the Rostra—that monument of our ancient greatness—and put on the most unholy, scandalous, and lascivious display ever to offend the eyes of the public?" At this the audience cheered and whistled. "Has Rome seen so horrid a woman since Tullia ran over her own father with a chariot?"

Here Curio and his claque booed, hissed, shouted, and made rude gestures. Cato ignored them.

"The gods of Rome," he went on, working himself up to a foaming frenzy, "must be appalled! First, that we even allow this hideous family to reside among us, polluting the sacred precincts of Romulus. Second, that we should even consider a trial of this virtuous young Roman for the murder of one of them! Rather, the Senate should declare days of thanksgiving to the gods for the death of Marcus Fulvius. There should be holidays and rejoicing! We should deck the temples in festive array, people should feast their neighbors and give sacrifices in gratitude that Marcus Fulvius no longer offends the sight of gods and men!"

"Cato's in fine form today," muttered someone behind me.

"This is extreme even for him," Father said. "There's such a thing as going too far in a denunciation."

"It's traditional," said Scipio, with a shrug in his voice.

"Where is the evidence," Cato went on, "that Decius Caecilius

Metellus the Younger slew Marcus Fulvius, richly though that man deserved it? He spent almost the entirety of that night together with the most illustrious men in Rome, not only the great men of his family, but the distinguished consular Hortensius Hortalus and the estimable Appius Claudius!

"Can it be a matter for wonder that Marcus Fulvius ended up dead? A man like him can number his enemies as an astronomer enumerates the stars! The only cause for wonder is that he could step from his doorway even once without being set upon by the hordes of those he had mortally offended, each of them bent upon revenge and justice! How many aggrieved, cuckolded husbands must have thirsted for his blood? How many fathers of children debauched by Marcus Fulvius must have whetted their daggers in anticipation of that blessed consummation?"

He went on in this vein for some time, making Fulvius sound like a greater menace to Rome than Hannibal had ever been, while I was a savior to compare with Quintus Fabius Maximus Cunctator. It was, as Scipio had intimated, a conventional defense. It was just that Cato was better at the vituperative part than almost anybody. Only Cicero, on one of his best days, could match him.

He ended up with, "Let no tear be shed in Rome for the likes of Marcus Fulvius. Allow the name of this loathsome wretch to be forgotten by all honorable citizens. Let his ashes be entombed in Baiae, along with all the fornicators, whores, and catamites of that accursed city, whose entitlement to Roman citizenship was one of the great moral failings of Roman policy. Let us instead rejoice that we have, and will continue to have, the unstinting, patriotic services of Decius Caecilius Metellus the Younger, a soldier, a statesman, a seeker after justice, a smiter of the wicked and protector of the innocent, whose illustrious ancestors have adorned our city in glory for centuries. Romans, you must find him innocent, even of this crime that was no crime at all!" And with the last word the water clock was empty and the beaker was full.

223

It was a wonderful performance, and the applause was loud and lasted a long time. Then Manilius rose from his bench and the noise abated. The slave put in the plug, hoisted the beaker and poured the water back into the bronze cylinder of the clock. He set the beaker back under the spout and, at the tribune's nod, removed the plug again.

"Citizens," he began, in a voice that was not strident like Cato's but carried as far, "the illustrious Marcus Porcius Cato has provided us with splendid entertainment but little of substance. As to the constitutionality of this court, it is a favor to the esteemed Senator Metellus that we hold it at all. When the late Marcus Fulvius leveled his charges against the senator, the praetor Marcus Juventius Laterensis scheduled a trial in his court for the next day, in violation of the usual custom. And why was this? Because, as all know, it is election time. Any trial not held now will have to be carried over into next year, with a new set of magistrates in office. That would mean that the senator could not stand for praetor in tomorrow's election, and would he wish that?"

Voices throughout the crowd proclaimed that this would certainly not be the case. I tried to make out who was saying this, but couldn't discern much in the sea of faces. Probably Manilius's clients, I thought, whose duty it was to applaud and repeat their patron's most telling points. My own would do the same.

"As for the competence of the *comitia tributa* to try a capital case, that is debatable, but it is not at issue here. Roman justice does not call for the death penalty to be applied against a Roman citizen for the slaying of another, save in very special, narrow circumstances. Citizens," here his gestures, expression, and tone conveyed great sadness, "the sorry fact is that we have become so accustomed to murder that we are no longer shocked by it. A slaughter that once would have roused the public to fury is now greeted with shrugs and yawns. This, even when the victim is of senatorial status. And who has brought us to such a pass? Why, the senators themselves, who, from being the dispensers of justice, have become the perpetrators of internecine butchery!" Now his voice climbed in high emotion.

"I don't like the sound of this," Scipio said behind me. All the others agreed.

"Have we not all seen," Manilius went on, "how these supposed 'conscript fathers' have schemed and conspired against one another for power, prestige, and honor? One after another has trodden upon the bodies of the others to make himself 'first among equals,' only to be brought down in his turn. Cneaus Pompeius Magnus"—here he extended a finger toward Pompey—"has inveighed against the violent street gangs and taken action to drive them from Rome. But who was behind those gangs? Were they enriching themselves? Nonsense! Were they advancing the cause of the people? Laughable! No, they were each and every one in the employ of one or another of the little senatorial cliques, of vile, ambitious men who keep their own hands clean while ordering others to do the dirty work!"

The crowd vented an ugly grumble. This was looking bad. What made it worse was that everything he said was perfectly true.

"He's not talking like a prosecutor," Father said. "He's talking like a candidate!"

"What's the difference?" asked Creticus, setting off a nervous chuckle from the others.

"And now," Manilius went on, "absolutely no one is surprised that an obscure man, a man of great family but one who had not yet won distinction in Rome, was murdered. And why? Because he had shown the temerity to attack, openly and honestly, a member of one of the Senate's most powerful families! Did he attack this Metellus from behind, at night, with a dagger? No! He accused him openly of criminal malfeasance on Cyprus, took his accusation to a praetor, and then went to the Forum and sought out Metellus, repeating the charges in public, to his face. Are these the actions of a cowardly, dishonest, conniving wretch? Are these not, rather, the actions of a man devoted to the service of the state in the greatest Roman tradition?" This was received with an angry, frightening cheer. Gaul was sounding better by the minute.

"The esteemed senator Marcus Porcius Cato," he drove on relentlessly, giving an amazingly contemptuous twist to the word "esteemed," "has denounced the family of Marcus Fulvius as infamous. Upon what basis does he make this scurrilous charge? Residence at Baiae? Only Cato, that upright, righteous defender of Roman virtue, could find fault with that lovely resort city, where Cicero, Hortensius Hortalus, and Gnaeus Pompeius Magnus himself all own villas!" This time there was derisive laughter, which was at least better than the angry growl.

"You've locked your teeth into the wrong backside this time, Cato," said Creticus.

"He denounces this murdered man's grief-stricken sister as a scandalous woman. And why? Merely because, in her extremity of distress, she performed a womanly gesture of mourning hallowed by a thousand years or more of funerary custom, one immortalized in many poems written by those very ancestors Cato professes to admire. It fell from practice only because the women of his own class now consider themselves too dignified for such low-bred demonstrations. They think such things are beneath them!"

"She wasn't grieving for her brother!" Cato cried. "The bitch was pissed off that her boyfriend got his head bloodied!" But his shout went unheard in the roar that met Manilius's harangue.

"And who might be this Fulvius, and his sister Fulvia, whose family Cato defames? They are the grandchildren of the Gracchi! Their great-grandmother was the sanctified Cornelia, mother of the Gracchi! And *her* father was Scipio Africanus, greatest of Roman generals and savior of the Republic, humbler of Carthage, who defeated Hannibal at Zama! *This* is the lineage Cato compares disparagingly with that of Caecilius Metellus! And we all remember who robbed that greatest of generals of all his richly deserved honors, don't we?"

Probably, most of the crowd was a bit hazy about such distant history, but someone out there had been well primed.

"Cato the Censor!" bellowed a Stentorian voice.

"Exactly," Manilius cried, with a gesture of triumph. "Cato the Censor, great-great-grandfather of the man who so basely denigrates a man whose career was so promising, cut tragically short by murder!"

"He was my great-great-*great*-grandfather!" Cato cried to no avail. "And he was the finest, most patriotic Roman who ever lived!" Once again his voice was drowned by the roar of the crowd.

"It could be worse," I told him. "At least they're mad at you, not me."

"Patron!" The call came from below, and I looked down. It was young Burrus, looking concerned. "Do you want to make a run for it? We'll get you out safely."

"Might be the best idea," Father said. "Go join Caesar in Gaul, come back when this is all forgotten."

"No," I told young Burrus. "I'm not ready to panic yet. I have a few things to say to this political rat. But stay handy. I may want to panic later."

"How will you play this?" Scipio wanted to know.

"We'll start out the old way, then see what develops."

"This man," Manilius cried, pointing now at me, "unwilling, nay, afraid to face Marcus Fulvius in court, instead set upon him at night and murdered him! He had not the courage to step up to him decently and stab him. Instead, he and his slaves or confederates held Marcus Fulvius from behind and butchered him wretchedly with knives. We all saw that ravaged corpse, did we not? Marcus Fulvius was rent with a score of gashes, as if he were tortured to death rather than given a clean, soldierly thrust in the heart. This was not mere hatred, but the cruelest of malice!"

He was getting the crowd well whipped up. The jury stared at me with stony eyes. Of the tribunes on the bench, the anti-Caesarians glared at me, the pro-Caesarians watched expectantly to see what I would do.

"He's not a well-trained orator," Scipio said. "See, he's getting out of breath already. If you want to save your career, Decius, you'd better step in quick."

"A moment," I said. "I want to see what this is winding up to."

Manilius took a deep breath. "Decius Caecilius Metellus the Younger," he yelled, now getting hoarse, "resorted to murder rather than face charges of malfeasance, of despoiling Roman citizens while on Cyprus. Rather than face trial, he murdered his accuser! What greater proof do you need that he is guilty of all the charges Fulvius laid against him? Malfeasance *and* murder, Citizens! Is this a man you want sitting in judgment upon you in a curule chair? Does this man deserve to be praetor?"

The crowds shouts and gestures showed a dangerous edge forming. The pro-Metellans and Caesar's troops tried to shout them down, but it only added to the disorder. The time was past when we had enough support among the plebs to control the Forum.

"Well," I said, "time to do my bit. Watch yourselves. If I don't pull this off, they may storm the podium."

I strode forth, using my best forceful-but-with-anger-restrained stride. I was taller than Manilius and drew myself up to emphasize my stature. From the tribunal bench, Vibius Pansa winked at me and whispered, "Decius, show this puffed-up toad how a real Roman orator handles the likes of him."

"Publius Manilius Scrofa!" I yelled, as if he weren't just three steps before me. "You are a liar, a perjuror, and an unworthy servant of the people of Rome! Begone before you disgrace yourself and your sacrosanct office further!"

He was nonplussed. He hadn't expected this.

"Metellus, by what right do you speak? Cato is your advocate!"

I had two things in my favor: he had split the crowd's wrath between Cato and me, and I was still a popular man.

"I speak forth because I am a servant of the Senate and People of Rome and because I am a better man than you!" The crowd calmed down, expecting something even better than they had heard so far. Well, I intended to give it to them. I turned to face that great sea of citizenry.

"Romans! Have I, Decius Caecilius Metellus the Younger, not served the state indefatigably since I shaved off my first beard?"

My supporters led the cheer, and it was picked up, weakly at first. "Have I not, as Cato has said, prosecuted the wicked and protected the innocent?" More cheers. "And when I was aedile, *twice*, Citizens, did I not provide you with wonderful games?"

Now the crowd remembered why they liked me. The cheers were loud and heartfelt. Everyone had loved those shows.

"Who else," I said, "has ever brought that many famous champions out of retirement for your entertainment? Could any other man have provided you with that final combat in the funeral *munera* for Metellus Celer, when the great Draco and the equally illustrious Petraites, greatest champions of our time, contended for a full hour, brave and skillful as Homeric heroes? Petraites spent *six months* recovering from his wounds!"

Now the cheers were genuinely ecstatic. Some openly wept with enjoyment at the memory. These people *really* loved those spectacles, and at that moment I didn't begrudge a single denarius of the fortune I had spent on them.

"What are you babbling about, you buffoon?" Manilius cried. Somehow he had lost control of the situation.

I strode over to him, stood no more than a foot before him, and studied his face.

"What are you doing?"

"Speaking of wounds," I said, conversationally but loud enough for everyone to hear, "where are yours? I'm looking for scars. I don't see any. You see this?" I drew a finger along the ragged scar that decorates my face, "An Iberian spear made this. That was in the rebellion of Sertorius. I haven't been able to get a decent shave in all the years since."

Now I turned to face the crowd. Did they think Fulvia was the only one who could strip in public? Well, now they had a show coming. I flung off my toga, making it unfurl dramatically as it flew through the air. Hermes caught it adroitly. Then I tore my tunic open with a loud rip, letting it fall to drape around my hips.

"Citizens! This," here I pointed at an ugly puncture on my left shoulder, "was made by a German spear! And this," I displayed a foot-long gash along my ribs, "is the mark of a Gallic longsword! Here and here," two deep punctures on my right side, "arrows shot from a pirate ship off Cyprus! And this," I hauled up the skirt of my tunic, exposing a truly awesome scar that ran from my left hipbone all the way down to the knee, "is where I was run over by a British war chariot!" The air filled with gasps and murmurs of admiration. This was a real crowd pleaser. The night before, Julia had touched up my scars with cosmetics to make them show better.

I stood with feet planted wide and spread my arms, showing off my many lesser scars, most of them won in street brawls but a good many in battle. "I have been wounded in every part of my body, and all these wounds I have suffered on your behalf, the Roman people, the greatest people in the world!" Now the cheering was frantic. When it quieted a little I swung an arm and pointed to Manilius, making sure that everyone got a good look at the long scar inside my right upper arm. Clodius had given me that one with a dagger.

"What wounds, what hardships has this man endured in your service? I've heard that he served, briefly, with my friend Gen. Aulus Gabinius in Syria. That excellent general saw immediately what sort of man had been fobbed off on him and never saw fit to give to him any position of distinction. You can bet that Gabinius watched him closely, too! Sent him back home with no commendations, much less decorations for valor, just another time server, putting in enough months with the eagles to qualify him for office!"

I was swinging wild, putting together what little I knew of the man, but I was connecting solidly. His face went scarlet. So this was his weakness, eh?

"The honors fall upon you and your kind," he shouted, "because the great generals are all your *relatives!* So you served in Spain against

Sertorius? How did you come by your command of native troops, young as you were? I'll tell you. It was because your great-uncle was Metellus Pius, who had the command before Pompey took over! Have you served all over Gaul and Britain? It is only because you are married to Caesar's niece!"

"And now would you defame *Julia?*" I bellowed. The growl from the crowd wasn't pleasant to hear, but at least it wasn't directed at me. Sallustius had been right. The people *adored* the Julian women.

"I do no such thing!" He was losing track of his thoughts now. "You are trying to confuse the people with this absurd display and with your wild accusations. You think you can escape your guilt with this spectacle of breeding and glory."

I held up a hand for silence, and gradually the crowd quieted. It was time for a change of pace.

"Very well. Let's forget about families and scars, about services to the state and public spectacles, magnificent though they might be. Let us consider"—I paused dramatically—"evidence."

"Evidence?" he said, as if he had never heard the word. Maybe he hadn't.

"Yes, evidence. It refers to the tangible and perceptible signs that something has or has not taken place. All those things that do not in themselves constitute proof, but that, taken collectively, point to the truth."

"The concept is not unknown to me," he said, gathering up his dignity. But he was playing my game now. "Of what does this evidence of yours consist?"

I cast my gaze around. The crowd was respectfully silent now, intrigued by this unexpected turn. My family looked distressed, afraid that I would now trot out all the business of codes and conspiracies and make myself look like an idiot. I saw familiar faces watching me with varying degrees of anticipation. Pompey looked disgusted. Curio showed a cool amusement, but beneath that was something else: apprehension? A small crowd of high-born women watched from the steps of the Temple of Castor and Pollux, surrounded by their slaves to keep the rabble away. Among them I saw Octavia, watching with a fatalistic resignation. Fulvia was there, looking like she was enjoying herself. Julia smiled at me with sublime confidence. I smiled back, briefly.

"Evidence," I said, "can take the form of words spoken without thought, words that betray a man's hidden guilt. But in order for these words to constitute evidence, they must be heard by more than a single witness. Best of all is if they should be spoken in public."

"Very well," Manilius said, "what words were spoken and who heard them? Bring forth your witnesses, always taking into account, of course"—here he gestured broadly to the people—"that the rich and powerful can always bribe and suborn all the witnesses they need. Such evidence should be given no more credence than it deserves."

"Why," I said, "my witnesses are these citizens assembled in the Forum." Now it was my turn for the broad, sweeping gesture, taking them all in. "I think that all of these good citizens will agree that just a few moments ago, they heard you say that Marcus Fulvius was held from behind and foully butchered."

"Yes, so?"

"That he was slashed many times none can doubt. But how did you come to know that he was held from behind?"

"Why—it was obvious." Now he was badly rattled, unprepared for this.

"Not to me, it wasn't. Many distinguished men were on the steps of the basilica that day, not only members of my own family but the praetor Juventius, the consular Appius Claudius Pulcher, as well as many honest citizens of all classes. The terrible wounds on the body of Fulvius were apparent to all, but not such subtle details as the fact that he was restrained."

"It just makes sense!" he cried.

"Not without a certain amount of examination, an impossible task on those steps, in the dim light of early morning. In fact, I had the body taken to the Temple of Venus Libitina and there examined by the famous Asklepiodes. That learned man pointed out to me that Fulvius's wounds were all on the front of his torso, that he had been unable to turn or to bring his arms into play. Hence, he must have been restrained.

"When I speculated that he might have been bound, Asklepiodes informed me that, in that case, the marks of cords or shackles would have been plainly visible. They were not, hence Fulvius was *held*, from behind, by at least two powerful men while his assailants plunged their blades into his body. You are no Greek physician, Manilius. How did you know?"

There was dead silence throughout the Forum, and this was more ominous than the growling and shouting had been.

"But I had no cause to wish the death of Fulvius! Citizens, don't listen to this fool!"

"Oh, you barely knew the man. But then, you don't act for yourself, do you? Who told you to get rid of him? Might it have been the same person or persons who gave you that fine, rich villa in *Baiae?* One that is almost as fine as Cicero's or Pompey's?" A bit of an exaggeration, but not by much. I pointed up at the great building cloaking the hillside to the west. "The evidence is right there, Citizens! In the *Tabularium!* Last year, when he declared himself a candidate, he listed among his assets a splendid villa in Baiae that he did not own on the last census!"

The low rumble came again from the crowd. Even when I was inciting it, I was dismayed and frightened by how easily they could be swayed. One minute they thirsted for my blood, the next for his.

"He was bought! Tell us, Manilius! Who owns you? Who were your accomplices in the murder of Marcus Fulvius? Were they one and the same?" Now I looked around again. The Marcelli were nowhere to be seen, but they could be lurking in the shade of porticoes or hiding in covered litters. Curio had gone pale. Curio, who had told me that he and Manilius had worked closely together the previous year. Curio, who had somehow known that Fulvius had been murdered elsewhere and carried to the basilica steps.

"You barely knew the man. But there are men in the Senate, and prominent members of the Equestrian Order, who know otherwise. In the last year, Fulvius gave a number of dinners where radical politics were discussed. You were at *every one* of those gatherings, weren't you, Publius Manilius? Remember, this crowd is full of witnesses who know the truth, though they may be hesitant to speak up now. They also know that the policies you now espouse are at variance with those discussed in those meetings. You and Fulvius had a falling-out, didn't you? A deadly one."

Manilius drew himself up. "You may not accuse, nor lay violent hands upon, the person of a Tribune of the People!"

"Until sundown, Manilius," Cato shouted, pointing at the angle of the sun. "At sundown you and all the other tribunes lay down your powers and become ordinary citizens. How far can you get by sundown, Manilius?"

"I declare this procedure at an end!" Manilius cried. "All citizens are to disperse!" With the shreds remaining of his dignity, he descended the steps and began his long walk across the Forum. People drew back from him as if he carried some deadly contagion. It gave new meaning to the word "untouchable."

Cato strode to the edge of the podium and spoke to the soldiers. "A tribune loses his powers and his sacrosanctity if he passes the first milestone. Post men on all the roads out of the city and arrest him as soon as he passes the milestone."

"Bring him back here alive," I told them. "I want the names of his accomplices."

"What are the chances," Father asked, "that he'll even reach one of the gates?"

"Slim," I acknowledged. "Too many people need to clean up after themselves."

"Unfortunate," said Metellus Creticus. "It would be nice to get the Marcelli barred from the consulship."

"Yes," I said, "and now we'll have to keep an eye on Curio."

"Curio is Caesar's man," Scipio said. "Why would he be involved in this?"

Cato shook his head in disgust. "It's like casting your net for a whole school of fish and drawing back only one, and that one not the biggest of them."

"Sometimes," I said, "you just have to catch them one at a time."

ALL THAT WAS A LONG TIME AGO. OF course, the Marcelli held onto the consulship and, as everyone knows, Caesar became dictator and Octavia's brother, Octavius, became his heir; he is now our First Citizen. Ironically, Marcellus, the son of Caius Marcellus and Octavia, turned out to be the First Citizen's favorite nephew and would have been *his* heir had he not died tragically young. Fulvia eventually married Antonius, but then, so did Octavia, although she lost him to Cleopatra. When you consider how it all turned out, it's a little hard to understand what they were all fighting and clawing at one another for during those dying days of the Republic. But it all somehow seemed terribly important at the time.

THESE WERE THE EVENTS OF FIVE days in the year 703 of the City of Rome, the consulship of Servius Sulpicius Rufus and Marcus Claudius Marcellus.

GLOSSARY

(Definitions apply to the year 703 of the Republic.)

Arms Like everything else in Roman society, weapons were strictly regulated by class. The straight, double-edged sword and dagger of the legions were classed as "honorable."

The *gladius* was a short, broad, double-edged sword borne by Roman soldiers. It was designed primarily for stabbing. The *pugio* was also a dagger used by soldiers.

The *caestus* was a boxing glove, made of leather straps and reinforced by bands, plates, or spikes of bronze. The curved, single-edged sword or knife called a *sica* was "infamous." *Sicas* were used in the arena by Thracian gladiators and were carried by street thugs. One ancient writer says that its curved shape made it convenient to carry sheathed beneath the armpit, showing that gangsters and shoulder holsters go back a long way.

Carrying of arms within the *pomerium* (the ancient city boundary marked out by Romulus) was forbidden, but the law was ignored in troubled times. Slaves were forbidden to carry weapons within the City, but those used as bodyguards could carry staves or clubs. When street fighting or assassinations were common, even senators went heavily armed, and even Cicero wore armor beneath his toga from time to time.

Shields were not common except as gladiatorial equipment. The large shield *(scutum)* of the legions was unwieldy in narrow streets, but bodyguards might carry the small shield *(parma)* of the light-armed auxiliary troops. These came in handy when the opposition took to throwing rocks and roof tiles.

Balnea Roman bathhouses were public and were favored meeting places for all classes. Customs differed with time and locale. In some places there were separate bathhouses for men and women. Pompeii had a bathhouse with a dividing wall between men's and women's sides. At some times women used the baths in the mornings, men in the afternoon. At others, mixed bathing was permitted. The *balnea* of the republican era were far more modest than the tremendous structures of the later Empire, but some imposing facilities were built during the last years of the Republic.

Basilica A meeting place of merchants and for the administration of justice. Among them were the Basilica Aemilia (aka Basilica Fulvia and Basilica Julia), the Basilica Opimia, the Basilica Portia, and the Basilica Sempronia (the latter devoted solely for business purposes).

Campus Martius A field outside the old city wall, formerly the assembly area and drill field for the legions of old, named after its altar to Mars, now a prosperous suburb growing full of expensive businesses and fine houses.

Centuriate Assembly The Centuriate Assembly *(comitia centuriata)* was a voting unit made up of all male citizens in military service. It seemingly dealt with major policy decisions, but by the Roman historical period the votes were largely symbolic and almost always positive, usually taken when decisions had, not already only been made, but sometimes even acted upon. The body was divided into five different parts based on wealth; the result was that the highest level or two always won, and the lowest classes were not even called upon to vote.

Centuries Literally, "one hundred men." From greatest antiquity, Rome's citizens had been organized into centuries for military purposes. They assembled by their centuries for the yearly muster to be assigned to their legions. Since this was a convenient time to hold elections and vote upon important issues, they voted by centuries as well. Each man could cast a vote, but the century voted as a whole. By the late Republic, it was strictly a voting distinction. The legions had centuries as well, though they usually numbered sixty to eighty men.

Cerialia The annual festival in honor of the goddess Ceres, the Greek Demeter, who was imported to Rome in accordance with an interpretation of the Sybilline Books.

College of Augurs Augurs had the task of interpreting omens sent by the gods, usually thunder and lightening and the flights of birds. An augurate was for life, and new augurs were co-opted by the serving priests. The augurate was largely a political appointment and was a mark of great prestige. Augurs could call an end to official business by interpreting unfavorable omens, and this became a potent political tool. The *lituus*, a crook-topped staff, was a symbol of this sacred office.

Curia The meetinghouse of the Senate, located in the Forum, also applied to a meeting place in general. They included the Curia Hostilia, Curia Pompey, and Curia Julia. By tradition they were prominently located with position to the sky to observe omens.

Curule A curule office conferred magisterial dignity. Those holding it were privileged to sit in a curule chair—a folding camp chair that became a symbol of Roman officials sitting in judgment.

Duumvir A duumvirate was a board of two men. Many Italian towns were governed by *duumviri*. A *duumvir* was also a Roman admiral, probably dating from a time when the Roman navy was commanded by two senators.

Eagles The eagle was sacred to Jupiter, and from the time of Caius

239

Marius gilded eagles were the standards of the legions. Thus, a soldier served "with the eagles."

Extortion court   A court presided over by a praetor that dealt only in cases of extortion, blackmail, and protection rackets, a plague of the time.

Families and Names   Roman citizens usually had three names. The given name **(praenomen)** was individual, but there were only about eighteen of them: Marcus, Lucius, etc. Certain praenomens were used only in a single family: Appius was used only by the Claudians, Mamercus only by the Aemilians, and so forth. Only males had praenomens. Daughters were given the feminine form of the father's name: Aemilia for Aemilius, Julia for Julius, Valeria for Valerius, etc.

Next came the **nomen.** This was the name of the clan (gens). All members of a gens traced their descent from a common ancestor, whose name they bore: Julius, Furius, Licinius, Junius, Tullius, to name a few. Patrician names always ended in *ius*. Plebeian names often had different endings. The name of the clan collectively was always in the feminine form, e.g., Aemilii.

A subfamily of a gens is the **stirps**. Stirps is an anthropological term. It is similar to the Scottish clan system, where the family name "Ritchie" for instance, is a stirps of the Clan MacIntosh. The **cognomen** gave the name of the stirps, i.e., Caius Julius Caesar. Caius of the stirps Caesar of gens Julia.

The name of the family branch **(cognomen)** was frequently anatomical: Naso (nose), Ahenobarbus (bronzebeard), Sulla (splotchy), Niger (dark), Rufus (red), Caesar (curly), and many others. Some families did not use cognomens. Mark Antony was just Marcus Antonius, no cognomen.

Other names were **honorifics** conferred by the Senate for outstanding service or virtue: Germanicus (conqueror of the Germans), Africanus (conqueror of the Africans), Pius (extraordinary filial piety).

Freed slaves became citizens and took the family name of their master. Thus the vast majority of Romans named, for instance, Cornelius would not be patricians of that name, but the descendants of that family's freed slaves. There was no stigma attached to slave ancestry.

Adoption was frequent among noble families. An adopted son took the name of his adoptive father and added the genetive form of his former nomen. Thus when Caius Julius Caesar adopted his great-nephew Caius Octavius, the latter became Caius Julius Caesar Octavianus.

All these names were used for formal purposes such as official documents and monuments. In practice, nearly every Roman went by a nickname, usually descriptive and rarely complimentary. Usually it was the Latin equivalent of Gimpy, Humpy, Lefty, Squint-eye, Big Ears, Baldy, or something of the sort. Romans were merciless when it came to physical peculiarities.

Fasces A bundle of rods bound around with an ax projecting from the middle. They symbolized a Roman magistrate's power of corporal and capital punishment and were carried by the lictors who accompanied the curule magistrates, the *Flamen Dialis,* and the proconsuls and propraetors who governed provinces.

First Citizen In Latin: *Princeps.* Originally the most prestigious senator, permitted to speak first on all important issues and set the order of debate. Augustus, the first emperor, usurped the title in perpetuity. Decius detests him so much that he will not use either his name (by the time of the writing it was Caius Julius Caesar Octavianus) or the honorific Augustus, voted by the toadying Senate. Instead he will refer to him only as the First Citizen. *Princeps* is the origin of the modern word "prince."

Flamines (*See priesthoods.*)

Floralia Festival of the goddess Flora.

Forum An open meeting and market area. The premier forum was the Forum Romanum, located on the low ground surrounded by the Capitoline, Palatine, and Caelian Hills. It was surrounded by the most important temples and public buildings. Roman citizens spent much of their day there. The courts met outdoors in the Forum when the weather was good. When it was paved and devoted solely to public business, the Forum Romanum's market functions were transferred to the Forum Boarium, the Cattle Market near the Circus Maximus. Small shops and stalls remained along the northern and southern peripheries, however.

Freedman   A manumitted slave. Formal emancipation conferred full rights of citizenship except for the right to hold office. Informal emancipation conferred freedom without voting rights. In the second or at least third generation, a freedman's descendants became full citizens.

Games *Ludus,* **pl.** *Ludi*   Public religious festivals put on by the state. There were a number of long-established *ludi,* the earliest being the Roman Games *(ludi Romani)* in honor of Jupiter Optimus Maximus and held in September. The *ludi Megalenses* were held in April, as were the *ludi Cereri* in honor of Ceres, the grain goddess and the *ludi Floriae* in honor of Flora, the goddess of flowers. The *ludi Apollinares* were celebrated in July. In October were celebrated the *ludi Capitolini,* and the final games of the year were the Plebeian Games *(ludi Plebeii)* in November. Games usually ran for several days except for the Capitoline games, which ran for a single day. Games featured theatrical performances, processions, sacrifices, public banquets, and chariot races. They did not feature gladiatorial combats. The gladiator games, called *munera,* were put on by individuals as funeral rites.

Imperium   The ancient power of kings to summon and lead armies, to order and forbid, and to inflict corporal and capital punishment. Under the Republic, the imperium was divided among the consuls and praetors, but they were subject to appeal and intervention by the tribunes in their civil decisions and were answerable for their acts after leaving office. Only a dictator had unlimited imperium.

Insula   Literally, "island." A detached house or block of flats let out to poor families. Fire was their deadliest enemy.

Iudex   An investigating official appointed by a praetor.

Iugerum, pl. iugera   An *iugerum* was a Roman area measurement equivalent to about 5/8 of an acre, where an acre is a square of four sides of 208.71 feet or 63.61 meters, thus an *iugarum* was 130.44 feet or 39.75 meters per side of a square. It traditionally was the amount of land that a yoke of oxen could plow in a day. A plebeian family could subsist on the annual income from 7 to 10 *iugera*. Publius Manilius Scrofa's estate of 200 *iugera* would be about 125 acres or nearly 5 miles square.

Janitor   A slave doorkeeper, so called for Janus, god of gateways. In some houses they were chained to the door.

Legion   They formed the fighting force of the Roman army. Through its soldiers, the Empire was able to control vast stretches of territory and people. They were known for their discipline, training, ability, and military prowess.

Lictor   Bodyguards, usually freedmen, who accompanied magistrates and the *Flamen Dialis,* bearing the fasces. They summoned assemblies, attended public sacrifices, and carried out sentences of punishment.

Lupanar   A brothel.

Lustrum   A ceremony of purification performed every five years by the census.

Master of Horse (*Magister Equitum*)   When the Senate named a dictator, the dictator immediately named a Master of Horse, who was his second in command, charged with carrying out his decrees. Essentially, the enforcer and hatchetman. Marc Antony was Caesar's Magister Equitum.

Military Terms   The Roman legionary system was quite unlike any military organization in existence today. The regimental system used by all modern armies date from the Wars of Religion of the sixteenth century. These began with companies under captains that grouped into regiments under colonels, then regiments grouped into divisions under generals, and by the Napoleonic wars they had acquired higher organizations such as corps, army groups, and so forth, with an orderly chain of command from the marshal down through the varying degrees of generals, colonels, majors, captains, sergeants, corporals, and finally the privates in the ranks.

The Roman legions had nothing resembling such an organization. At the time of the SPQR novels the strength of a legion was theoretically 6,000 men, but the usual strength was around 4,800. These were divided into sixty centuries. Originally, a century had included one hundred men, but during that time there were about eighty. Each century was commanded by a centurion, making sixty centurions to the legion. Six centuries made a cohort. Each centurion had a *optio* as his second in command. The centurionate was not a single rank, but a complex of hierarchy and seniority, many details of which are obscure. We know that there were first-rank and second-rank centurions. The senior centurion of the legion was *primus pilus*, the "first spear." He was centurion of the first century of the first cohort and outranked all others. Centurions were promoted from the ranks for ability and they were the nearest thing a legion had to permanent officers. All others were elected or appointed politicians.

Legionaries were Roman citizens. They fought as heavy infantry fully armored and armed with the heavy javelin (*pilum*), the short Spanish sword (*gladius Hispaniensis*), and the straight, double-edged dagger (*pugio*). They carried a very large shield (*scutum*) that at that time was usually oval and curved to fit around the body. Besides holding the center of the battle line, legionaries were engineers and operated the siege weapons: catapults, team-operated crossbows, and so forth.

Attached to each legion were usually an equal number of *auxilia*, noncitizen troops often supplied by allies. These were lightly armed troops, skirmishers, archers, slingers, and other missile troops, and cavalry. The legion had a small citizen cavalry force but depended upon the *auxilia* for the bulk of the cavalry. Through long service an auxiliary could earn citizen status, which was hereditary and his sons could serve in the legions. *Auxilia* received lower pay and had lower status, but they were essential when operating in broken terrain or heavy forest, where the legions could not be used to advantage. In battle they often held the flanks and usually, with the cavalry, were charged with pursuing a broken and fleeing enemy, preventing them from reforming or counterattacking.

There were other formations within a legion, some of them obscure. One was the *antesignani*, "those who fight before the standards." Already nearly obsolete, they were apparently an elite strike force, though how it was manned and used is uncertain. Apparently exceptional bravery was required for assignment to the *antesignani*.

There were awards for valor. Greatest of these were the crowns. The Civic Crown (*corona civica*) was awarded for saving the life of a fellow citizen in battle. The Wall Crown (*corona muralis*) was awarded to the first man atop an enemy wall or battlement. The Grass Crown (*corona graminea*) was awarded by the centurions to a general who had won a great victory. It was braided from grass growing on the battlefield. There was great competition among officers for the crowns, because they made election to higher office a near certainty. The citizens loved them. For the rankers there were bracelets awarded for valor. Among Roman men only soldiers wore bracelets, and these only as decorations for bravery. Torques, twisted Gallic neck-rings in miniature form, were also awarded in pairs, slung over the neck on a scarf. Centurions might be awarded *phalerae*: seven or nine massive silver discs worn on a harness atop the armor. Apparently these were for exceptional service rather than a single feat.

In Decius's time the legions were still formed as a unit, served for a number of years, then discharged collectively. Even when on many years' service, they were ceremonially disbanded, then reformed every year, with the soldier's oath renewed each time. This archaic practice was extremely troublesome, and when a few years later Augustus reformed the military system, legions became permanent institutions, their strength kept up by continuous enlistment of new soldiers as old ones retired or died. Many of the Augustan legions remained in service continuously for centuries.

The commander of a legion might be a **consul** or **praetor,** but more often he was a **proconsul** or **propraetor** who, having served his year in Rome, went out to govern a province. Within his province he was commander of its legions. He might appoint a legate (*legatus*) as his assistant. The legate was subject to approval by the Senate. He might choose a more experienced military man to handle the army work while the promagistrate concentrated upon civil affairs, but a successful war was important to a political career, while enriching the commander. For an extraordinary command, such as Caesar's in Gaul, or Pompey's against the pirates, the promagistrate might be permitted a number of legates.

Under the commander were Tribunes of the Soldiers, usually young men embarking upon their political careers. Their duties were entirely at the discretion of the commander. Caesar usually told his tribunes to sit back, keep their mouths shut, and watch the experienced men work. But a military tribune might be given a responsible position, even command of a legion. The young Cassius Longinus as tribune prosecuted a successful war in Syria after his commander was dead.

Munera   Special games, not part of the official calendar, at which gladiators were exhibited. They were originally funeral games and were always dedicated to the dead.

Offices   The political system of the Roman Republic was completely different from any today. The terms we have borrowed from the Romans have very different meanings in the modern context. "Senators" were not elected and did not represent a particular district. "Dictator" was a temporary office conferred by the Senate in times of emergency. "Republic" simply meant a governmental system that was not a hereditary monarchy. By the time of the SPQR series the power of former Roman kings was shared among a number of citizen assemblies.

Tribunes of the People were representatives of the plebeians with power to introduce laws and to veto actions of the Senate. Only plebeians could hold the office, which carried no imperium. **Tribunes of the Soldiers** were elected from among the young men of senatorial or equestrian rank to be assistants to generals. Usually it was the first step of a man's political career.

A Roman embarked upon a public career followed the "**cursus**

honorum," i.e., the "path of honor." After doing staff work for officials, he began climbing the ladder of office. These were taken in order as follows:

The lowest elective office was **quaestor:** bookkeeper and paymaster for the Treasury, the Grain Office, and the provincial governors. These men did the scut work of the Empire. After the quaestorship he was eligible for the **Senate,** a nonelective office, which had to be ratified by the censors; if none were in office, he had to be ratified by the next censors to be elected.

Next were the **aediles.** Roughly speaking, these were city managers, responsible for the upkeep of public buildings, streets, sewers, markets, brothels, etc. There were two types: the **plebeian aediles** and the **curule aediles.** The curule aediles could sit in judgment on civil cases involving markets and currency, while the plebeian aediles could only levy fines. Otherwise their duties were the same. The state only provided a tiny stipend for improvements, and the rest was the aediles' problem. If he put on (and paid for) splendid games, he was sure of election to higher office.

Third was **praetor,** an office with real power. Praetors were judges, but they could command armies, and after a year in office they could go out to govern provinces, where real wealth could be won, earned, or stolen. In the late Republic, there were eight praetors. Senior was the *praetor urbanus,* who heard civil cases between citizens of Rome. The *praetor peregrinus* (praetor of the foreigners) heard cases involving foreigners. The others presided over criminal courts. After leaving office, the ex-praetors became **propraetors** and went on to govern propraetorian provinces with full imperium.

The highest office was **consul,** supreme office of power during the Roman Republic. Two were elected each year. Consuls called meetings of the Senate and presided there. The office carried full imperium and they could lead armies. On the expiration of the year in office, the ex-consuls were usually assigned the best provinces to rule as **proconsul**. As proconsul, he had the same insignia and the same number of lictors. His power was absolute within his province. The most important commands always went to proconsuls.

Censors were elected every five years. It was the capstone to a political career, but it did not carry imperium and there was no foreign command afterward. Censors conducted the census, purged the Senate of unworthy members, doled out the public contracts, confirmed new senators in office, and conducted the *lustrum*, a ritual of purification. They could forbid certain religious practices or luxuries deemed bad for public morals or generally "un-Roman." There were two censors, and each could overrule the other. They were usually elected from among the ex-consuls.

Under the Sullan Constitution, the quaestorship was the minimum requirement for membership in the Senate. The majority of senators had held that office and never held another. Membership in the Senate was for life, unless expelled by the censors.

No Roman official could be prosecuted while in office, but he could be after he stepped down. Malfeasance in office was one of the most common court charges.

The most extraordinary office was **dictator.** In times of emergency, the Senate could instruct the consuls to appoint a dictator, who could wield absolute power for six months, after which he had to step down from office. Unlike all other officials, a dictator was unaccountable: He could not be prosecuted for his acts in office. The last true dictator was appointed in the third century B.C. The dictatorships of Sulla and Julius Caesar were unconstitutional.

October Horse   An annual race and sacrifice.

Optimates   Supporters of a continued senatorial dominance, *optimates* were an aristocratic party in Republican Rome.

Orders   The Roman hierarchy was divided into a number of orders (*ordines*). At the top was the Senatorial Order (*Ordo Senatus*) made up of the senators. Originally the Senate had been a part of the Equestrian Order, but the dictator Sulla made them a separate order.

Next came the Equestrian Order (*Ordo Equestris*). This was a property qualification. Men above a certain property rating, determined every five years by the censors, belonged to the Equestrian Order, so named because in ancient times, at the annual hosting, these wealthier men brought horses and served in the cavalry. By the time of the SPQR novels they had lost all military nature. The equestrians *(equites)* were the wealthiest class, the bankers and businessmen, and after the Sullan reforms they supplied the jurymen. If an *eques* won election to the quaestorship he entered the Senatorial Order. Collectively, they wielded immense power. They often financed the political careers of senators and their business dealings abroad often shaped Roman foreign policy.

Last came the Plebeian Order (*Ordo Plebis*). Pretty much everybody else, and not really an order in the sense of the other two, since plebeians might be equestrians or senators. Nevertheless, as the mass of the citizenry they were regarded as virtually a separate power and they elected the Tribunes of the People, who were in many ways the most powerful politicians of this time.

Slaves and foreigners had no status and did not belong to an order.

Patrician The noble class of Rome.

Pontificial College The pontifexes were a college of priests not of a specific god (see Priesthoods) but whose task was to advise the Senate on matters of religion. The chief of the college was the *Pontifex Maximus,* who ruled on all matters of religious practice and had charge of the calendar. Julius Caesar was elected *Pontifex Maximus* and Augustus made it an office held permanently by the emperors. The title is currently held by the pope.

Popular Assemblies These consist of the following three **comitias,** which were legal assemblies of the people, an amalgamation of both the patricians and the plebeians: *comitia centuriata,* which was originally the centuries of the citizen soldiers of Rome who voted as a century bloc, i.e., one vote per century. Later, in Decius's time, this comitia was dominated by a handful of great families. The *comitia centuriata* elected the higher magistrates such as the consuls, praetors, and other magistrates with imperium. It was presided over by a consul and was the body that declared war, passed some (but not all) laws, and served as a supreme court in capital punishment cases. The ***comitia curiata*** was the original legislative body of Rome, but by the time of this book it held only the ceremonial function of investing the higher magistrates with imperium after their election or of conferring the rite of inauguration upon certain priests such as the flamines and the *rex sacrorum*. There were two bodies that comprised the ***comitia tributa***. The first, the *comitia tributa* proper, was an assembly of the entire people (by tribes) that elected (one vote per tribe) lower magistrates such as aedile, curule, quaestor, etc. and was presided over by a praetor. The second and more important, ***consilium plebis***, was an assembly only of the plebeians of the *comitia tributa* that elected tribunes and plebeian aediles. It also was a law-making body passing statutes by plebiscite. It could not rule on capital punishment cases.

Another assembly called a ***contio***, which contained both patricians and plebeians, functioned somewhat like a recommending committee that discussed a pending matter and decided whether or not it should be put forth before the entire comitia. The actions by the *contio* held by Tribune of the People Publius Manilius are illegal.

Populares   The party of the common people.

Priesthoods   In Rome, the priesthoods were offices of state. There were two major classes: pontifexes and flamines.

Pontifexes were members of the highest priestly college of Rome. They had superintendence over all sacred observances, state and private, and over the calendar. The head of their college was the ***Pontifex Maximus***, a title held to this day by the pope.

The **flamines** were the high priests of the state gods: the *Flamen Martialis* for Mars, the *Flamen Quirinalis* for the deified Romulus, and, highest of all, the *Flamen Dialis*, high priest of Jupiter.

The Flamen Dialis celebrated the Ides of each month and could not take part in politics, although he could attend meetings of the Senate, attended by a single lictor. Each had charge of the daily sacrifices, wore distinctive headgear, and was surrounded by many ritual taboos.

Another very ancient priesthood was the ***Rex Sacrorum.*** "King of Sacrifices." This priest had to be a patrician and had to observe even more taboos than the Flamen Dialis. This position was so onerous that it became difficult to find a patrician willing to take it.

Technically, pontifexes and flamines did not take part in public business except to solemnize oaths and treaties, give the god's stamp of approval to declarations of war, etc. But since they were all senators anyway, the ban had little meaning. Julius Caesar was *Pontifex Maximus* while he was out conquering Gaul, even though the *Pontifex Maximus* wasn't supposed to look upon human blood.

Princeps (First Citizen) This was an especially distinguished senator chosen by the censors. His name was first called on the roll of the Senate, and he was first to speak on any issue. Later the title was usurped by Augustus and is the origin of the word "prince."

Ram Latin rostrum, pl. rostra. Most naval ships (at least those designed to do battle) had a large battering ram attached to its prow. These allowed the ship to "ram" another and sink it without resorting to hand-to-hand combat. The rams on pirate ships were small, designed for display only, since the pirates mostly raided shore villages and their ships had to beach and escape quickly, a difficult task with a large ram sticking out in front.

Decius has had new, fearsome-looking rams added to the pirate ships he captured while he was on Cyprus, both to honor the people and his own family's glory.

Rite of Bona Dea Bona Dea, "the Good Goddess" was honored in Rome with a special service presided over by the wife of the *Pontifex Maximus,* during which no male could enter the house. All the participants were highborn married women. Clodius violated the rite when Caesar's wife presided. *(See SPQR III: The Sacrilege.)*

Rostra (sing. rostrum) A monument in the Forum commemorating the sea battle of Antium in 338 B.C., decorated with the rams, rostra, of enemy ships. Its base was used as an orator's platform.

SPQR Senatus Populusque Romanus The Senate and People of

Rome. The formula embodied the sovereignty of Rome. It was used on official correspondence, documents, and public works.

State Archives   These were located in a sprawling building, the *Tabularium* on the lower slope of the Capitoline Hill. They contained centuries' worth of public documents. Private documents, such as wills, were kept in various temples.

The **Treasury** was kept in a crypt beneath the **Temple of Saturn,** also the repository for military standards. Money was coined in the **Temple of Juno Moneta**. The **Temple of Ceres,** goddess of the harvest, housed the offices of the aediles. Treaties and wills were kept in the **Temple of Vesta,** site of the sacred fire tended by the Vestal Virgins and dedicated to the goddess of the hearth. War was declared in the **Temple of Bellona,** Roman goddess of war. Minor temples housed lesser civic functions.

Tarpeian Rock   A cliff beneath the Capitol from which traitors were hurled. It was named for the Roman maiden Tarpeia who, according to legend, betrayed the Capitol to the Sabines.

Toga   The outer robe of the Roman citizen. It was white for the upper class, darker for the poor and for people in mourning. The *toga candidus* was a specially whitened (with chalk) toga worn when standing for office. The *toga praetexta* bordered with a purple stripe, was worn by curule magistrates, by state priests when performming their functions, and by boys prior to manhood. The *toga trabea,* a striped robe, was worn by augurs and some orders of the priesthood. The *toga picta,* purple and embroidered with golden stars, was worn by a general when celebrating a triumph, also by a magistrate when giving public games.

Trans-Tiber   A newer district on the left or western bank of the Tiber. It lay beyond the old city walls.

Triclinium   A dining room.

Triumph   A ceremony in which a victorious general was rendered semidivine honors for a day. It began with a magnificent procession displaying the loot and captives of the campaign and culminated with a banquet for the Senate in the Temple of Jupiter, special protector of Rome.

Ultimate Decree of the Senate (*Senatus Consultum Ultimum*) A decree that overrode all other legislation, taken only in times of emergency. Usually it meant that the Senate was naming a dictator, but it might involve other extralegal activity, as when the consul Cicero ordered the arrest and execution of senators to crush the Catilinarian conspiracy.

Vestal Virgins   Virgin priestesses, chaste like the goddess Vesta, six of them served for thirty years, any violation of the vow of chastity was punished by burial alive. Vesta's shrine was the most sacred object of Roman religion.

Credible words are not eloquent;
Eloquent words are not credible.

The wise are not erudite;
The erudite are not wise.

The adept are not all-around;
The all-around are not adept.

The sages do not accumulate things.
Yet the more they have done for others,
The more they have gained themselves;
The more they have given to others,
The more they have gotten themselves.

Thus, the way of *tian* is to benefit without harming;
The way of the sages is to do without contending.

—from the *Dao de jing*